orth Y

ONE
DAMN
THING
AFTER
ANOTHER

ONE DAMN THING AFTER ANOTHER

Dan Latus

ROBERT HALE

First published in 2017 by
Robert Hale, an imprint of
The Crowood Press Ltd,
Ramsbury, Marlborough
Wiltshire SN8 2HR

www. crowood.com

www.halebooks.com

British Library Cataloguing-in-Publication Data
A catalogue record for this book is available from the
British Library.

ISBN 978 0 7198 2251 3

Typeset by Catherine Williams, Knebworth

Printed and bound in Great Britain by
TJ International, Padstow, Cornwall

Dedication

For Sandra, with love.

Chapter One

It was a quiet, peaceful place. Or so I had been assured. A small boutique hotel in an unfashionable quarter of the city, a couple of miles from the usual Prague tourist spots. Perhaps it was quiet and peaceful normally. But when I stepped outside onto the pavement, and the ornate timber door closed automatically behind me, things looked very different.

A Range Rover with darkened windows was parked immediately across the pavement, a rear door open, ready for someone to step inside. A Toyota Land Cruiser, also with darkened windows, was parked close behind, and there was another one in front.

The man who probably should have been holding the door open lay prone on the pavement, bleeding heavily, his chauffeur's cap by his side. The man who I assumed had been about to step inside the Range Rover was being badly beaten by three other men, who looked as if they didn't know when to stop.

There were no screams or cries for help. There was no shouting in either triumph or despair. Nothing like that. Just a lot of grim, determined grunts and thuds, as the three doing the attacking slammed into their victim savagely and relentlessly.

The victim had his back to the vehicle. He was sagging, pretty well spent. But he wouldn't go down, and he was still flailing wildly and hopelessly at his assailants.

It was a good time to turn around and step back inside the elegant tranquillity of the boutique hotel. Instead, I did a stupid thing – not for the first time, some would say.

Instinct shouldered reason aside. This couldn't be allowed to go on. I yelled at the men in front of me to stop, grabbed one by the shoulder and pulled him back. Then I stepped forward into the middle of it and lunged sideways, knocking another of them out of the way with my shoulder.

The third man turned and swung a fist that thudded heavily into my chest, knocking me back. I kicked out and hit his lower leg hard, as an arm wrapped round my throat from behind. I was hauled backwards but managed to stamp on somebody's instep with my heel hard enough for the arm to drop from my throat.

I spun round, my back to the Range Rover. The guy who had been about to collapse to the ground was straightening up now I'd relieved him of some of the weight and pressure. Together, side by side, we fought back. A fist crashed into the side of my head, and another into my chest, but my blood was up and I registered little pain. I kicked and punched my weight automatically, without any thought whatsoever.

Suddenly there was blood everywhere. It was on my hands and in my eyes. The guy beside me let out a loud grunt and sagged. Then I saw the man in front of him was using a knife, and about to thrust with it again.

I reached out, grabbed the knife arm with both hands and put my whole body weight into throwing it over and back. Bone snapped as the arm broke free of the elbow joint. Somebody screamed. The knife dropped loose and disappeared from sight.

Then a bright overhead light came on, a security floodlight. It was followed by lots of yelling and shouting, and suddenly there was breathing space. People stopped hitting me, and the bodies in front of us thinned out until there was nobody left for me to hit back at.

I doubled over, breathing hard, but ready for more of the same if it started up again. It didn't. Nobody came back. The pavement between me and the door of the hotel had cleared.

Engines roared into life. The Range Rover shook as something slammed into it heavily. Tyres squealed. Both Land Cruisers were departing in a hurry.

It was over. I was heaving for breath and felt like vomiting, but somehow I straightened up. I glanced sideways. The man beside me gasped something I could barely hear, and couldn't understand anyway. Then the effort of trying to speak became too much for him. He just pushed his head into my shoulder, a gesture of thanks, and slowly straightened up himself.

While I stayed where I was, and continued struggling to get my breath back, he staggered forward a couple of paces and leant down to attend to the man on the ground. I could see he was in no state to manage alone. So I joined him and tried to help.

The chauffeur was conscious, but a long way from having his wits about him. We sat him up, with his back against the door of the vehicle. He was still leaking blood from the head wound, but by then uniformed staff were streaming out of the hotel and I eased back to let them take over.

Remarkably, the man who I had fought alongside was recovering fast. He shook my hand and thanked me in what sounded, surprisingly, like Russian. I nodded and gave him a brief appreciative smile. Then I did my best to melt away out of sight.

I sought the sanctuary of my ornate baronial-style room inside the boutique hotel, where I laid down on the bed to recover, and to wonder why such things happened to me. Other people can go on holiday and nothing out of the ordinary ever happens. Not me, though. Oh, no! If not this, then something else. It's inevitable. Just one damn thing after another!

Chapter Two

AFTER A WHILE, THE blood thundering in my ears quietened down and my pulse rate dropped to a survivable level. I opened my eyes and stared at the ceiling, or what I could see of it in the early evening gloom.

Dim light from the sodium street lights outside the hotel allowed me to pick out men on horseback hunting a stag through rocky country without trees or discernible cover. I found myself wishing the stag luck. A tram squealed to a halt not far from the window of my room and a procession of vehicles dutifully stopped behind it, their engines throbbing as they waited more or less patiently for the tram to move off again.

Someone knocked on the door of my room. I waited, listening. Nothing was said. The knocking, a heavy, confident sound, was repeated. I grimaced. Clearly, I was wanted.

'Yes?' I called reluctantly, sitting up on the bed.

'Mr Doy? May I speak with you, please?'

'Who is it?'

'The hotel management, Mr Doy.'

I supposed I'd better answer the door. Once I did that, though, I might be invited to start looking for another hotel. The management wouldn't be very keen on guests who partook in mayhem on their doorstep. Good thing I was leaving soon.

On the other hand, I thought, hesitating, my visitor might be nothing at all to do with the hotel management. So I stood well to one side and flung the door open wide suddenly with outstretched arm, hoping I didn't have to fight whoever was on the other side.

I didn't. The man standing there was familiar to me. Tall, slim, fit looking, and stern-faced, he was often behind the reception desk. I had spoken to him once or twice in the short time I'd been here.

'Yes?'

'Mr Doy, I am sorry to disturb you.'

'That's all right,' I said with a polite smile.

'Mr Podolsky sends his best regards, and says that he wishes to see you.'

'Who does?'

'Mr Podolsky, the owner of the hotel. He would like to see you.'

'So it's a summons, is it? What for? Fighting in the street?'

He didn't smile. Not even a hint of it.

'Please,' he said, politely but insistently.

So it looked as if I really would be required to vacate the premises. They didn't want my sort staying in their smart hotel.

10

'Do you know what it's about?' I asked again.

'I do not have that information. Please,' he repeated, making it sound even more like an instruction than a request.

'When?'

'Now, please. If you will come this way, I will take you.'

I gestured at myself, my clothes torn, dirty and bloody from the recent exercise. 'Let me change first.'

'That will not be necessary, Mr Doy.'

So I gave in and followed him along the corridor and up a flight of stairs. Then we passed through a door that was heavily security locked – which I thought interesting – and along another corridor or two.

By then, I realized, we must have passed beyond the apparent limit of the hotel and now were inside the building next door. Clearly, the owner's hold on the terraced street was greater than appeared from outside. That wasn't too surprising. All those ancient Prague streets were a mystery to me. What lay beyond the shadowed front doors was an unknown world so far as I was concerned.

My guide stopped, tapped on a door and opened it. 'Mr Doy to see you, sir,' he announced, for all the world like an old-style butler announcing the arrival of an important guest. He ushered me into the room, and I came face to face with Leon Podolsky – again. He wasn't particularly tall, and he wasn't especially broad, but he was a big man in all sorts of ways, and a strong one. In the brief moments we had fought together side by side, I hadn't really appreciated that, but I should have guessed it from the way he had stayed on his feet and kept on fighting when he was heavily outnumbered and being badly beaten.

But when I looked at him now, naked from the waist up, massive bruising spreading fast across his torso, with dressings and sutures from knife wounds that luckily didn't seem to have done serious damage, it was his welcoming smile that dominated the room. He was a tough guy. No doubt about it. And his powers of durability and recovery were truly remarkable.

'Mr Doy! Welcome. I am Leon Podolsky,' he said in good, if

heavily accented, English. 'So we have found you? Please let me thank you, for coming here now and for the help you gave me this afternoon.'

He stepped away from the man in a white medical coat who was attending to his wounds and came towards me, one hand outstretched. I took it and he clasped mine firmly for a moment. No big performance. No iron grip to demonstrate his mental or physical strength. Just a straightforward handshake. He rose even higher in my estimation.

'I stepped outside the hotel at the wrong moment,' I said with a rueful smile, 'and there you were. Then I interfered when you were doing fine on your own.'

'No, no! Absolutely not. It was exactly the right time to arrive. I am forever in your debt. If you had come even earlier,' he added, 'it might have saved my chauffeur from a fractured skull.'

I grimaced. 'How is he?'

Podolsky shrugged. 'Maybe he will live. I hope so. But I don't know yet.'

He didn't seem overly concerned. It was not uncaring indifference on his part. I had seen how his first thought when the fracas ended had been for the injured man. It was more as if he was accustomed to violence and serious injury, and had learned to take them in his stride. That thought should have led me to walk away right then.

'What was it about?' I asked. 'Do you know?'

'Not yet.'

He stood still to allow the medical man to adjust some of his dressings and then added, 'What was it about? That is a very good question, Mr Doy. We will find out sooner or later. And then I will let you know, too, my friend.'

I wasn't sure I wanted to know, but already I quite liked the guy. He was intriguing, and full of life. He seemed pretty decent as well, although it was odd that a pretty decent hotel owner should have been attacked on his own front doorstep.

By then, though, I was sure he was Russian, which explained a lot. Phrases like "organized crime" leapt to mind automatically.

Not that I was yet ready to assume anything untoward about Podolsky himself. It was more the world in which he lived that was suspect.

But I was curious, a trait that has always been hard to deny, even though it has got me into a lot of trouble over the years. I admit it. Really, I did want to know what had been going on out there. It hadn't been a simple street mugging. It hadn't been an attempted assassination, either. Assassins would simply have shot him, probably in a hail of bullets from a sub-machine gun. It looked more like an attempted abduction to me. I guessed someone had wanted him picked up, either as a hostage or for ransom money – perhaps both.

'Before we go any further,' he said, 'I would like my personal doctor to deal with your injuries.'

'I'm all right, thanks,' I said, shaking my head.

'Please,' he added, gesturing to the man in the white coat who had been attending to him.

'I'm fine. There's no need for that.'

'No, you are not fine,' he said sternly. 'I can see with my own eyes some of the damage. You are possibly even worse than me.'

I doubted that. But I smiled, and his laughter filled the room.

After that, I was shepherded into an adjacent room that seemed to serve as a clinic. Somehow my clothes disappeared off my back, and I found myself swaddled in a luxurious bathrobe and stretched out on a bed.

'Hey!' I protested weakly as I saw my apparel leaving the room.

'Don't worry, my friend,' the doctor said with a chuckle. 'They will be back, cleaned and repaired by housekeeping, before I have finished with you.'

I must have been weary. Probably the street battle had taken more out of me than I had first thought, when the adrenaline was still flushing around my system. At any rate, I gave in and allowed myself to be inspected by the doctor, and then pampered with cooling lotions and a massage by a young woman I had not even seen enter the room. Happily, there was no significant damage. But there were plenty of bruises, cuts and grazes to be worked on.

'So what do you think, Doc?' I asked the man in the white coat when he returned to peer at me.

'About what?'

'Me!'

'You have mild concussion, but nothing life threatening. Just get some rest and you'll be good as new.'

'That's nice to know.'

Later, rested, refreshed and dressed again in clothes that really had been cleaned and repaired, I was shown into yet another room. There, I found Leon Podolsky waiting for me once more. Now he was fully dressed, too, and eager for me to join him for dinner.

'It is not much,' he said apologetically, 'but at short notice the chef has done his best.'

I was staggered by the amount of food on the table. For the two of us? It was ridiculous. MacDonald's would have suited me.

'Mr Podolsky, there is no need ...'

'Nonsense! You must allow me to begin to repay you – for your courage, and for your instinctive commitment to helping someone in need. And it's Leon – please!'

I shook my head, quite unable to respond to his flowery, but apparently sincere, tribute. Then I stayed for dinner. Of course I did. My curiosity had got the better of me once again. Besides, he had a way with him that attracted me.

Chapter Three

MY HOST HAD SOME difficulty cutting the meat on his plate. This was not because his knife was blunt. It was more, much more, because his fingers looked as if they had been stamped on by an African elephant – or because he had been punching something very hard, with all his weight behind the blows. Someone, some-where, would have a face to match.

Still, we ate. The food was terrific. Some sort of steak, cooked in red wine. Excellent. The wine wasn't bad, either. He said it had come from a famous vineyard in Georgia, a place where many people lived to be well over a hundred years old. He said other interesting things, too, lots of them. Even in the state he was in, he was a convivial host.

Something that puzzled me slightly was why so much time had elapsed before I had been sought and then offered such lavish hospitality. It's human instinct to thank someone right there and then, if you are going to do it at all. Offer them a cup of tea or a drink. Show concern over any bodily damage done to them. Apologize, explain – or whatever. Podolsky had not done that. He had let an hour or two go by before giving me a summons. I was soon to learn why.

'You are an interesting man, Mr Doy,' he announced with a sly smile, waving his fork at me in a friendly way.

'Not everybody thinks so, but thank you. It's Frank, by the way.'

'Frank? Good.' He nodded and went on to say, 'You do interest-ing things, Frank.'

'Do I?'

'Your work, I mean – for example.'

Ah! So he'd had me checked out. Hence the delay. What a cau-tious street victim he was! Or a capable chess player, perhaps. Competent businessman, even.

'So you know what I do for a living?'

He nodded. 'You're a security expert, right?'

'And a private investigator. Jack-of-all-sorts, really.'

'I understand.'

He pushed his plate aside and studied me for a moment, wearing a serious face now underneath the bruises. 'What I would like to know, Frank, is who you are working for right now.'

'No-one,' I said with a shrug. 'I'm here on holiday.'

'Perhaps,' he said with a knowing smile.

15

'No, really.'

He poured more wine for us both. I decided I was finished with my plate, too, if we were going to get serious. I pushed it aside. Then I raised my glass and met his eye.

'To victory?' I suggested.

'To victory!' he responded with great enthusiasm and a bellow of laughter.

I wondered how much he knew about me. How well had he used the time he'd had?

'You can fight,' he said abruptly. 'Where did you learn that skill?'

'I've always had it,' I told him. 'And much practice over the years has made me better at it. How about you?'

'Special forces,' he said with a shrug. 'That was my first career.'

'Russian special forces? *Spetsnaz*?'

He nodded. Then he grinned and added, 'You and me. We did well together!'

I smiled, even though it hurt my face to do so, and happily agreed.

'The question now, Englishman,' he continued, 'is whether we can extend our relationship. You say you are working for nobody at the moment. Very well. I accept that. You are here only by accident.'

I nodded. 'That's right.'

'I can offer you work – if you want it?'

My interest was piqued, I have to admit. The offer came out of nowhere, but I was interested enough to want to hear more from him.

'Let's talk,' I suggested.

He was an honest businessman, he said. Of course he was. What else could he be? Lots of honest businessmen fight for their lives on city pavements. It happens all the time. Every day. Especially if they are Russian businessmen.

'I own this hotel, for example,' he said with a modest shrug. 'You like it here?'

'I do, actually. It's very comfortable.'

'Also, I have other businesses – many other businesses.'

'In this country?'

'In this country,' he agreed with a judicious nod. 'And also in other countries.'

'Russia?'

'I am Russian,' he said with a shrug. 'So, yes, I have business projects in Russia. But my interests are global.'

Oligarchic even, I wondered a little sceptically. It was going to be fun to see where this conversation led. Already I quite fancied doing some investigating in Barbados or Thailand, the Maldives perhaps – or even Cyprus. Lots of Russians in Cyprus these days, owning villas with high security fences around them, shopping for fur coats in Limassol, paying local politicians to look the other way.

Not really my scene, though. Perhaps I should call a halt now, I thought, and say goodbye. I seriously doubted if Podolsky and I could make a match.

'I have interests in your country, too, Frank.'

'The UK?'

He nodded. 'One project there at the moment might appeal to you.'

I doubted that, but it seemed polite to hear him out.

'I have bought a house in Northumberland. Do you know that area?'

'Yes, I do. But I live further south, in North Yorkshire.'

'I know that. I have had you checked out.'

'Really? That was rather presumptuous of you.'

It was also no more than I had expected.

He laughed and wagged a finger at me. 'Frank, please! Do not play games with me. We are both old enough, and experienced enough, to know that no-one makes an offer to another man without knowing something about him first. Agreed?'

I smiled and conceded the point. As I said, he had a way with him. Bright guy. Fun. Good company. And interestingly enigmatic. I liked him. He intrigued me.

'It is rather a big house,' he continued, 'and rather a ruin. Oh, it has a roof, and the walls are still standing, but many years of neglect by owners who could not afford the upkeep of such a house anymore have taken their toll. Sadly, some of your aristocracy have gone the same way as ours.'

Not literally, I thought. We didn't shoot ours and drop them down a well. Actually, I felt like pointing out, there were plenty of the Russian variety still around, although for understandable reasons they tend to live in places like Paris rather than anywhere in Russia.

'So you are renovating a house?'

'Precisely. And I would like you to oversee security while that work is ongoing. Possibly afterwards, too. That is my offer. I will pay you well.'

Night watchman, it sounded like. Not my cup of tea.

'You don't need somebody like me, Leon. Surely the contractor will arrange security? Besides, I would get bored. Thank you for the offer, but ...'

'Frank, you will not be bored. I can promise you that. If you are lucky, you might even survive the experience.'

He broke off into raucous laughter.

I might survive, might I? Some joke.

'What security is needed there? Northumberland isn't exactly the Wild West, you know,' I pointed out.

'No, but I come from the Wild East. We Russians have much trouble when we build our businesses, and then we have even more trouble keeping them.'

The Wild East, eh? The Moscow business world used to be called that years ago, in Yeltsin's time. I wondered how much it had changed.

'So what's the problem with restoring an old house?'

'Good question.' Podolsky frowned and admitted, 'I don't know yet. Why don't we go there, so I can show you the project? Then you can say yes or no, no strings attached.'

I turned it over in my mind. I was curious. I admit it. Besides, where was the harm? What did I have to lose?

'When?'

'Now.'

'Now?'

'Right now. My plane is waiting at Havel – the blessed Havel! – Airport. They used to call it Prague Airport, you know. Now it is Václav Havel Airport Prague, by order of the Czech Government.'

'I know that,' I said, feeling a little dazed by the speed with which things were developing. 'But I have a return ticket with ...'

'I know. For this evening, I believe. But I won't charge you,' he said with a chuckle. 'Besides, there is more leg room in my plane. Surely that must count for something?'

I grinned and folded my objections and reservations. The offer of extra leg room was hard to turn down.

Chapter Four

I WAS BACK IN my room, collecting my gear together, and thinking it looked like it might start to snow soon, when any feelings of peace and a sense of returning normality were shattered. I heard the rumble and vibration of a powerful engine outside on the street. Then, extraordinarily, there was the unmistakable sound of a burst of automatic gunfire, followed by the sound of sheets of window glass splintering and crashing to the pavement.

I hurtled across the room and flattened myself against the wall adjacent to the window. When the gunfire paused, I risked a glance outside. There wasn't much to see. Just a big pickup truck on massive tyres, and a man holding a machine pistol standing in the back of it.

The man gestured to people I couldn't see, who appeared to be under my window and close to the hotel entrance. Then two more men stepped into view, and all three began firing in a concentrated way at what had to be the front door. There were no windows on the ground floor for them to attack.

The door seemed to be a harder nut to crack than they had

anticipated. The ancient timber facing the street would soon have disintegrated but I guessed there must be thick sheet steel behind it. Ordinary bullets wouldn't penetrate that. Semtex would have been a better option.

As if coming to the same conclusion, the gunmen gave up on the door and started spraying the upper windows of the hotel again. I flattened myself on the floor, arms wrapped around my head, just in time. Shards of glass blasted across the room and tinkled as they fell all around me. Then the door to my room burst open and I feared the worst.

'Mr Doy!' a voice called between fusillades.

I looked up and saw the main man from reception, who I now knew was called Charles, beckoning to me. 'This way, Mr Doy!'

I did a fast shuffle across the room and through the door, grabbing my bag as I went. Charles slammed the door shut behind me.

'Are you hurt?' he asked anxiously, picking bits of glass from my jacket.

I just shook my head. I didn't bother asking him what was going on. It didn't seem the right moment for that, and I didn't suppose he knew any more than I did anyway.

He grimaced and touched my elbow, a gesture of sympathy, and set off quickly along the corridor. I followed. Once again, I was taken through a maze of corridors and staircases, doors and rooms, until at last we went down, down, down, and emerged into a courtyard at what I assumed was the far end of the street.

Leon Podolsky was waiting there, holding open the rear door of a big Lexus saloon, ignoring the bitter cold and the snowflakes that were drifting around his head. He ushered me inside, climbed in himself and slammed the door shut. The driver got us moving immediately.

Two men opened heavy doors that filled the entrance to an archway under a building. We crept forward, under the arch. The doors closed behind us. Another man opened a second pair of doors, looked outside and then waved us through. We emerged onto a cobbled street, turned left and accelerated smoothly away, twisting and turning through narrow lanes and alleys until we hit a main road that seemed to be heading out of town.

Podolsky turned around, grinned at me and said, 'Lively, eh?'

I didn't feel like grinning back. I just grimaced and nodded. Then I glanced out of the side window and caught sight of a road sign that included the airport in its menu of destinations. I was pleased to see it. It was time I got out of this city, time I went home.

'Another thing I like about you, Frank,' Podolsky confided, 'is that you don't ask stupid questions when people are too busy to answer them. It's a rare quality.'

'Believe me,' I said bitterly, 'I feel like asking them. What the hell was all that about, back there?'

'Who knows?' he said with a shrug.

Who, indeed, if not him?

I was surprised the Russian special forces had ever let him leave their ranks. Panic and fear didn't seem to afflict him in the way they do ordinary mortals. I even wondered if he was perhaps enjoying all the action, having missed out on epic battles like Stalingrad and Kursk, not to mention the more recent shenanigans in Crimea.

'Well, try this,' I said with some irritation. 'Anybody hurt?'

'Maybe.' He shrugged again. 'Charles will let me know.'

Good old Charles! The guy from reception, who seemed to have been left to hold the fort.

'They were coming for you, I take it?'

He nodded. 'I think so.'

Two attempts on him in one day? Unbelievable. This was serious stuff.

'I always think,' I confided, beginning to relax a little, 'that a stout front door is a sound investment.'

'Yes?'

'That's what I tell all my clients. You have obviously taken good advice yourself from someone in the business.'

He laughed, shook his head and said, 'Fools! They didn't have enough firepower to get through that door. Nowhere near enough.'

My thought, exactly. I was having serious second thoughts

about even considering the possibility of working for Leon Podolsky. In fact, I knew I didn't want to do it. Whatever game he was involved in was too big for me. He needed the French Foreign Legion – the whole of it! – or a Ghurka battalion, not just one man, to protect his house in Northumberland, if this was anything to go by. I decided to tell him before we got any further.

'Leon, I've changed my mind. I appreciate your offer but the job you outlined is not one for me to consider. Thanks for the offer of the flight, too, but I'll leave you at the airport and make my own way home.'

'Too hot for you, eh?' he said, sounding disappointed.

'Something like that.'

He sighed. 'I can't say I blame you, Frank. It's a pity, though. We would have done well together.'

Doing what, exactly, I wondered?

'There's just one thing,' he added. 'You've missed your flight now. So you might as well come to Newcastle with me. Otherwise, you may have to wait a few days for the next flight.'

I glanced at my watch with surprise and realized he was right. I cursed silently. What to do now?

'No strings,' Leon said. 'I owe you, not the other way around. So please accept my offer of a flight back to Newcastle. Then feel free to take off to wherever you wish to go.'

'Thanks,' I said. 'That probably is best.'

It would be three days before there was another direct flight to Newcastle. I didn't want to wait that long. I didn't want the hassle of finding another way to get home, either. So I decided to travel with Leon, and then try to forget what had happened back here on the last day of my short break holiday.

'It's a nice city, Prague,' he said next, as if nothing untoward had happened.

'Until today,' I said, 'I thought so, too.'

He laughed.

I turned to look out of the side window. The snow that had started as we were leaving the hotel was getting heavier now. All in all, it seemed a good time to be going home.

Chapter Five

THE WHITE STUFF STARTED coming down faster and thicker. Suddenly we seemed to be inside a cloud, with great masses of snow swirling around and cascading over us. It was impossible to see more than a few yards ahead. The car slowed to a crawl in first gear. Podolsky leant forward to have an urgent word with the driver, who then pulled into the side of the road and stopped. We sat waiting, anxiously, with the engine running.

Podolsky's phone went off. He took it out, glanced at the screen and answered it. He listened for a few moments and then, sounding exasperated, started snapping out instructions. It seemed to do him no good. Nor did raising his voice.

He shut the phone down, grimaced and said something to the driver, who nodded and gave a brief reply before getting us moving again. We turned around in a side street and headed back the way we had come, driving through a thick curtain of snow. The conditions were increasingly slippery. A couple of times the driver lost control in skids that turned us broadside on. It was sheer luck that prevented us slamming into the vehicles parked along the edges of the street.

I said nothing, but I looked at Podolsky expectantly. He shrugged and said, 'They've closed the airport.'

'Because of the snow?'

He nodded. 'They say it's not safe, and they're not going to let planes take off any time soon.'

Great, I thought. Now what?

Leon's smile returned. 'But don't worry, Frank! We'll just have to postpone our departure until tomorrow. Nothing is spoiling.'

I wondered about that. I really did. From now until tomorrow, a hell of a lot of stuff could happen in his life – and mine, as well, if I stayed with him.

'So what now? Back to the hotel?'

He shook his head. 'They will be too busy cleaning up and

repairing the damage. And maybe the police will be there.'

'So?'

'I am not ready for all that. There is somewhere else we can go, over in Vinohrady.'

I debated getting out at the nearest tram stop or taxi rank and making my own way back into the city centre but I decided not to. For one thing, the way the snow was coming down it looked as if it would soon be a lot more than the airport that was at a standstill.

The driver dropped us off in a street in a part of town I had not previously visited. It was an elegant street, with six-storey apartment buildings of old stone on each side that occupied entire blocks. The buildings were all painted in the traditional mustard colour that seemed to be so popular in this country, and the paintwork looked fresh. Newly planted small trees, without leaves at this time of year, were dotted along the pavements at regular intervals. It was a street with money, I decided, and one that had been recently refurbished.

I shivered and ducked my head against the wind-driven snow as I followed Leon towards a doorway. Although there was no name or sign over the entrance, once I was inside I saw the place seemed to be some sort of medical clinic. As soon as we passed through the double doors, we entered another world, one with bright lights and ultra modern styling. Podolsky called a cheerful greeting to a white-coated woman at the reception desk and led me down a long corridor. We passed a couple of men and another woman, all dressed in white medical garb.

'What is this place?' I asked. 'A medical centre?'

'Yes. A private medical centre.'

'Another of your businesses?'

He nodded and stopped outside a lift, where he keyed in a code and pressed buttons. The doors slid open. We stepped inside and were whisked away silently at speed.

When the doors reopened, we stepped out of the lift straight into the living space of one of those modern, opulent-lifestyle apartments. Marble floors, expensive looking rugs, subdued lighting, and rich furnishings. One wall of the huge room we entered was glass, quite simply an enormously wide floor-to-ceiling window that gave a wonderful view of the falling snow.

'I will show you to your room, Frank,' Leon announced. 'Then you must excuse me for a little while. There are things I must do. But make yourself at home. If you want anything you can't see, just pick up the phone. It will be answered instantly.'

'Thank you,' I said, intrigued, if not altogether happy. 'You will be back soon?'

'Of course.'

He laughed and led the way down a short corridor. The room he showed me into was almost as opulent as the living room we had just left. I dumped my bag on the floor and turned towards him.

'Better than waiting in the departures lounge at the airport, eh?' he said, chuckling.

Without waiting for an answer, he turned and departed. I shrugged and glanced around before sinking onto the inviting bed. The truth was that I was too tired to care very much about the posh surroundings, and I hurt in various places more than I had noticed until now. The adrenaline was long gone from my system, and the aches and pains from the fight were catching up on me.

I couldn't believe Leon hurt less than me, and I have to say I admired his fortitude and durability. Whatever he had gone off to do must be very important, I thought, before I closed my eyes and dozed off.

I woke up feeling a bit better, and glanced at my watch. Just after eleven. I shook my head and got to my feet. What the hell was I doing here? I should have been well on the way home by now.

I wandered back to the main room, and stared with astonishment through the big window. The snow hadn't stopped. It was coming down heavily still, and already the world had been transformed. The walls across the street were cloaked in white, while down below the street itself was deep in cotton wool. The parked vehicles that lined the sides of the roadway were no more than suggestive humps and bulges.

I watched a taxi creeping along until it could go no further and stalled in the middle of the road. After a few moments, the driver climbed out, slammed the door and walked off, abandoning his vehicle. He had my sympathy. I suspected nothing was going to be moving far or fast in this city for some time.

That thought made me wonder when, or if, I would see Leon again. I grimaced. I shouldn't be here. It was a mistake. I would have been better off bedding down at the airport. But how could I have got there?

I shrugged and decided to take a look around the apartment. Fancy furniture and artwork on the walls were all very well, but I was getting hungry. A cup of coffee would be welcome, too.

It was a big bachelor pad, I soon decided. Certainly not a home. Plenty of expensive sound equipment, home cinema stuff and artwork, but nothing to suggest anyone lived here on a continuing basis. There were a few suits and coats in a wardrobe in the master bedroom. There was even women's clothing in one wardrobe, some of it brand new, still in wrappers. I smiled and wondered if Leon had a wife or a partner. If he did, she didn't live here.

I found a galley kitchen with well-stocked cupboards and fridge, and realized I wasn't going to starve for a long time. First, though, I needed coffee. I put some water in a jug kettle and switched it on. The thing was hi-tech and high-powered. I watched with amusement as it emitted a changing range of colours as water heating proceeded. The water was bubbling long before I found a jar of instant coffee.

Perhaps because of the noise the kettle made, I didn't become aware that I was no longer alone until too late. The voice was a woman's. The words she spoke were unintelligible to me, but their meaning was quite clear. I froze for a moment, and then slowly raised my hands above my head and turned around to face the gun the woman was holding.

She was quite small and slim, and athletic looking. The

expression on her face was grim as she barked a question or instruction at me. The gun she held in both hands didn't waver. She was serious, and she meant business.

I grimaced and tried to convey my lack of understanding. Another crisp demand followed.

I shrugged now and smiled, to try to reduce the tension. 'I don't understand,' I said as calmly as I could manage.

That seemed to disconcert her for a moment. Then she stared even harder, as if she suspected me of lying.

'I don't understand,' I repeated. 'I don't speak Russian.'

'*Český?*' she demanded.

I shook my head. 'British.'

'*Britský?*'

I nodded.

She mulled that over, but while she did so the gun didn't move.

'I am a guest here,' I said gently.

She understood that. Maybe she didn't believe me, but at least she understood. 'Where is passport?' she demanded.

'In my coat pocket, in the big room. On the sofa, I think.'

'Show me.'

She stood well clear as I moved carefully towards the doorway. Then she followed me along the corridor and across the lounge to where my jacket lay on the sofa.

'Stop!' she snapped.

I stood still and watched as she scooped up the jacket and began to search the pockets with one hand, the other keeping firm hold of the pointing gun.

'The top pocket,' I advised her, patting the left side of my chest.

She found the passport and my airline ticket. She opened the passport and studied it, comparing the photograph with what she could see standing in front of her.

'So. You are Franklin Doy,' she said eventually.

'Frank,' I said, trying to make it friendlier.

The gun didn't move an inch. It was still trained on me.

She dropped the passport and ticket onto the sofa and demanded, 'What are you doing here?'

'I came here with Mr Podolsky. He asked me to make myself at home, and to wait for him.'

'How do you know Mr Podolsky?'

'I was a guest in his hotel. I met him there.'

'And he brought you here?' she said scornfully. 'To his private residence?'

'Yes, he did,' I said with a shrug.

'I will ask him,' she responded. 'Sit down in that chair.'

She pointed with her free hand, the gun in her other hand remaining focussed on me. I sat down. She wanted me unable to move quickly while she used her phone. I could almost admire her systematic caution, but that damned gun was still bothering me a lot.

She fiddled with her phone but something was wrong. I watched, and waited. She tried several times before she gave up.

'He is not answering,' she said, putting the phone away.

All I could do was shrug once more.

'I have much to do,' she said then. 'It will be best if I just shoot you now.'

Chapter Six

I GOT LUCKY. She didn't do it.

'Phone the hotel,' I said quickly, when I saw her hesitating over whether to pull the trigger. 'Speak to Charles in reception. Ask him about me.'

'You know Charles?' she asked, looking puzzled.

'Tall, short fair hair, dark suit,' I said, desperately trying to recall anything else about him. 'Oh, yes! He's very serious. No laughing.'

She looked at me as if I wasn't right in the head. I shrugged and held my breath, and assessed my chances of getting away with it if I just rushed her. Not good, I decided.

'That is Charles,' she said eventually. She stared at me a moment longer and then reached for her phone again.

I listened as she launched into a series of interrogatory remarks to whoever answered. None of them made any sense to me. I assumed the language was Russian, but it could have been any one of a dozen east European languages, for all I knew.

I knew I was safe when her gun arm was lowered at last. I began to relax. For the first time in many minutes I was not looking down a barrel.

'So,' she said, 'Charles knows you, and he says you left with Leon.'

I nodded.

'So where is Leon now?'

'I wish I knew. He left me here, saying he would be back shortly. That was ...' I squinted at my watch, and added, '... quite a while ago.'

That worried her. It did me, too.

'So who are you?' I dared to ask.

'That is no concern of yours.'

'I think it is,' I said with a forced smile. 'I would like to know the identity of the person who was going to shoot me – and who may still do so.'

She shook her head impatiently. 'What were you doing when I arrived?'

'Making a cup of coffee, and thinking about getting something to eat.'

'Get on with it,' she said dismissively. 'I have calls to make.'

So I had a lot more to think about now. Who was she? Someone close to Leon, obviously. His mistress, girlfriend? I had no idea. All I knew was that she was here in his apartment, she knew Charles and ... well, she was a tough lady. That added up to quite enough for me.

She was worried about Leon, too. That gave me some concern. Where the hell was he? What had been so important that he'd had to dump me and scoot out into a blizzard? For that matter, how had he been able to travel anywhere at all this evening?

And what about this place? What was it?

I had plenty of questions, but no answers.

At least I had coffee now, though, and poking through the contents of the fridge, I found cheese and ham to make a sandwich to go with it. For a few minutes, I occupied myself sensibly in the kitchen. All the while I could hear the woman on the phone in the lounge.

I couldn't understand exactly what she was saying, but I had a good idea. She was phoning around the people in her contacts book to try to find where Leon was. That she kept it up suggested he was proving hard to find, and that something unusual had happened. I wondered if Leon was in trouble. Did his absence have anything to do with the attack on his hotel that afternoon? It seemed entirely possible, likely even. One way or another, things didn't look good for him.

With my sandwich in one hand and a second cup of coffee in the other, I wandered back into the lounge and over to the window. The snow was easing off now, but down on the ground it was deeper than ever. By the look of things on the street, the sky must just about have emptied. One or two cars, in addition to the taxi I had seen earlier, had tried to force their way through but now they were all stranded and abandoned, with the snow halfway up their doors.

There were no pedestrians in sight. I wondered if Leon had found somewhere warm and dry. It wasn't a night to be out and about, whatever your business, and however urgent it was. Meanwhile, the woman behind me continued hunting him by phone. It seemed pointless. Either his phone was switched off or he didn't want to answer. It was as simple as that.

Except it wasn't.

A vehicle came powering along the street, disturbing the serenity of the scene. It was a truck with a big blade up front that was sending waves of snow cascading into the air. I smiled at the unexpectedness of it. A snowplough. Quick off the mark, too. Somebody in this street must have political clout.

The truck stopped in the middle of the road down below. I

watched as several figures emerged from it, bristling with energy and purpose. They headed towards the entrance to our building.

Strange. That didn't seem right. I frowned and turned to the woman behind me. 'Hey! Something's going on down here.'

She looked up. I waved her over urgently. She came across the room to join me, and I pointed down below. She looked, and swore. At least, that's what it sounded like.

Then she pocketed her phone and dashed for the door.

I watched her go, and wondered if I should leave too. But she was gone before I could ask her.

By then, I felt as if I had had enough of Podolsky hospitality. This wasn't what I had thought I was letting myself in for when I accepted a lift to the airport. I might not be able to get there myself for the moment but surely I could find somewhere more sensible to stay until I could?

I collected my travel bag, took a last look around the most luxurious accommodation I had ever experienced, and headed for the lift without any regrets at all.

The lift was already in motion. I could hear it rising behind the stainless steel doors. Any moment now the doors would spring open. I frowned. Who would be coming out of it? Suddenly I was concerned about that, very concerned. There was so much trouble around Leon Podolsky. I didn't want to be collateral damage.

I glanced around, looking for an entrance to a stairwell. There didn't seem to be one. No emergency exit? Not good, Leon. What if there was a fire in the lift shaft?

The lift pinged, the doors about to open. I stepped into an alcove alongside and stood behind a huge crystal and stainless steel ornament, or sculpture. Whatever it was, it concealed me quite well, which was all I wanted until I knew who was in the lift.

I heard the doors open. Two men, dressed in black, moved out into the room. They were holding guns in outstretched arms and were moving cautiously, covering each other as they advanced. I grimaced and held my breath, and kept very, very still.

I didn't think much of my chances of persuading them not

to shoot if they saw me. My guess was that they were intent on completing the business they had started back at the hotel that afternoon. It was Leon they were after, but I would probably do if they couldn't find him.

They moved quickly and silently across the room and into the corridor leading to the bedrooms. I couldn't see them not spotting me when they returned. So it was now or never. I edged out of the alcove.

The lift doors had been locked in the open position. I stepped inside, pressed the button that released the lock and another button that got the doors closed and the lift moving. The control panel had only two destinations: where I'd just come from, and where I was going next. There were no intermediate stops.

Within seconds the doors opened again, revealing the corridor Leon had led me along a few hours earlier. I locked the lift in position to prevent the two men in the apartment following me soon. Then I set off down the corridor, which was brightly lit still but ominously quiet. The people I had seen working here had probably all gone home hours ago, but I couldn't believe the place was empty. Surely there must be somebody still here?

I was right. Leon's staff hadn't all gone home. As I neared the end of the corridor, I spotted the woman in a white coat last seen in reception. She was lying spread-eagled on the floor, a pool of blood from her leaking across the white marble. She wasn't moving.

I grimaced and stopped to consider my options. There weren't many, and none of them were good. How long had I got before the two guys upstairs used their phones to bring someone in from outside to unlock the lift doors? How many men were waiting outside, between me and freedom?

Then something else came into the equation. Someone nearby let fly with a subdued burst of automatic gunfire. That got my pulse racing and my head shrinking into my collar.

But I couldn't just stand there, out in the open. And I had to know what was going on. A quick glance around the corner into the reception area told me some of it. There was a second unmoving body on the floor, this one clad in black. It had fallen in an untidy heap.

A man similarly dressed was behind an overturned desk, wielding what looked like an Uzi sub-machine gun fitted with a suppressor. Whoever he was firing at in short bursts was on the far side of the room, behind a pillar in the entrance porch and invisible to me. Stalemate – for the moment.

Things changed. With a great boom, someone outside the building began pounding the front door with what sounded like a sledgehammer. Then I saw movement in the porch, caught a quick glimpse and realized it was the woman who had wanted to shoot me. She had got this far, but now she was trapped.

Her situation wasn't good. The front door wouldn't hold for long with the hammering it was taking, and when it caved in she would be in full view of whoever was outside wielding the sledge-hammer. Then there was the gunman trying to shoot her, and the two more gunmen somewhere behind me. Things didn't look good for either of us.

Pragmatism came to the fore. I focused on the lesser of the two threats to me personally. The woman and I were not exactly best mates but at least she hadn't shot me. Also, she seemed to be on the same side as Leon, whereas the guys in black clearly were not. It was a quick and ready calculation but I came down on her side. By helping her, perhaps I could help myself.

Another mighty crash against the front door, this one accom-panied by the sound of something splintering, spurred me on to do something. There was no time for more thought. Either I acted now or not at all.

I steeled myself and raced the few strides across the reception hall. The guy sheltering behind the desk heard me coming but he was too late to stop me. His head turned but by then my boot was swinging. I caught him in the head with a good one. He collapsed, face down, his gun spilling across the floor.

I straightened up, and looked towards the porch. The woman had seen what had happened and was coming out of cover.

'Quick! We must go!' she called, breaking into a run.

I agreed – but where to?

She hit some wall panelling on the far side of the room with the heel of her hand, and a concealed door slid open. Then she turned and beckoned impatiently. I hesitated for a moment, but another splintering crash told me the front door had just about given way.

I ran to join her.

Chapter Seven

SHE SLAMMED THE DOOR shut after us, turned and ushered me down a spiral wrought-iron staircase that was illuminated by emergency-standard lighting. I went down fast, my feet clattering on the latticed metal steps. At the bottom, in a little vestibule, there were three rusty metal doors, each set in a different wall.

'Which one?'

She pushed past and opened one of them. Then she stepped sideways into the darkness and pulled down a heavy lever. Suddenly we had light. Weak light, but good enough to see where we were going.

I followed her through the doorway and paused to stare ahead, thinking, ah! I might have known. We were in a tunnel, an ancient looking, stone-walled escape tunnel. A chain of dim lights set in the wall stretched out ahead of us as far as I could see.

The woman set off at a fast walking pace, verging on jogging. I struggled to keep up with her.

'Where are we going?' I demanded.

'We must hurry,' she snapped over her shoulder, as if that was answer enough.

I considered stopping in my tracks until I got answers to at least some of my questions – such as who she was, and what the hell was going on. Common sense prevailed. She knew where we were, and where we were going. I didn't. For the moment, at least,

I needed her a lot more than she needed me. She was leading us both away from a sudden, violent death. There wasn't any doubt about that, none at all.

We cracked on. There were no sounds of pursuit, which was something to be grateful for but hardly surprising. The concealed exit back in the reception area would be no more obvious to the men in black than it had been to me.

The tunnel was a long one. It ran straight for a hundred yards, perhaps more, and then curved gently for the same distance again. But we still hadn't finished with it. We walked on for another few minutes. Then, without us having reached an end to the tunnel, the woman stopped and began climbing a narrow flight of stone steps. I followed.

The steps led up to a cast-iron manhole cover. The woman braced herself and began to push up with both arms. It was a struggle. I moved up alongside her and joined in. Together, we raised the cover an inch or two. She eased off and took a quick look around. Satisfied, she began to push again. We lifted the cover higher and moved it aside.

I let her climb out first. When I followed, I found we were in some sort of small shop with an earthy, herbal smell about it. The shop was in darkness, but a dim light shining through a window revealed that it was located in one of the ancient interior malls that are so common in the historic centre of Prague. There seemed to be nobody about, either inside or outside the shop, and I assumed the blizzard had sent everyone home early. The entire mall was now closed and locked up for the night, or for the duration of the storm.

I helped the woman replace the manhole cover. Then I sat down wearily on a sack of something soft and said, 'You must tell me who you are, and what's going on.'

'There is no time,' she snapped once again. 'We must hurry.'

I shook my head. 'Who are you? And what is your connection to Leon? I'm going no further until I know that.'

She shut up then and studied me for a moment, as if assessing how far I could be trusted. 'You helped me, back there,' she said at last. 'So I thank you.'

'You're welcome.' I shrugged. 'OK, you needn't tell me what's going on yet, but I do want to know who you are.'

'I am Lenka, Leon's sister.'

'Ah!'

Somehow it didn't surprise me. She seemed every bit as tough as he was.

'Also ex-Russian special forces?' I queried.

It was her turn to shrug, but I believed I'd got it right.

'OK, Lenka. My name is Frank, Frank Doy. I am – or I was – a British tourist on a short break holiday in Prague.'

'Perhaps,' she said, just like her brother had said earlier.

'So who were we fighting back there?'

'You don't need to know that,' she told me, reverting to type.

'OK. Try this. Where's Leon? What's happened to him?'

That got to her and ruffled her composure. 'I don't know,' she said bleakly.

I believed her, and felt even more worried for Leon.

'So where are we going now?'

She didn't even bother trying to answer that one. Instead, she moved to the shop door and began to unlock it. When the door was open, she looked back over her shoulder and motioned to me to follow her.

At that point, I could have stayed where I was, and let her go on alone. Probably I should have done. But I didn't. Of course I didn't. Curiosity again. It always gets the better of me.

Lenka led the way out of the mall and into the street, out into a different world. We set off, trudging through knee-deep snow, ducking our heads against the bitter cold. A rising wind was driving the snow that was still falling into our faces, and lifting more of it from the ground in clouds.

I had no idea where we were but guessed that the tunnel had taken us half a mile away from the clinic and Leon's luxury apartment. That didn't really mean much to me. I still didn't know where I was. The name of the area, Vinohrady, didn't mean much to me, either. So I just concentrated on keeping up with Lenka, who seemed to know exactly where she was and where she was going even if she wasn't prepared to tell me.

We reached the end of the first street and turned into another one. Halfway along that, Lenka led the way up a short flight of steps and into one of the old apartment blocks that filled all these streets. She used a key to get us through the external door, and then we pushed through a second set of doors into a spacious and rather grand entrance hall. The walls were clad in dark wood panelling, the ceiling furnished with ornate plasterwork in the traditional, Baroque style, and the floor tiled in an intricate ceramic mosaic. Very upmarket at one time; now a bit shabby, and in need of restoration.

There was no-one in sight. Lenka paused, watchful, listening. I waited. Seemingly, she heard nothing to concern her. She straightened up and nodded at me. 'Come!' she said.

Then she was off again, this time heading for the staircase that was an alternative to the wire-cage lift. I approved of her choice. I hate those old lifts. You feel as helpless as a cornered rat in those things.

We climbed six short flights of stone steps, and on the third floor turned into a corridor. Lenka walked swiftly along until she reached a certain door. There, she stopped, looked around and then pressed the buzzer sharply twice.

We waited.

The door began to open. Lenka gave a little cry and pushed her way forward. I followed. Then I just stopped, astonished, and stared. I couldn't believe it.

Chapter Eight

'YOU SHOULDN'T BE HERE, Frank,' Leon said, when he had disentangled himself from Lenka's embrace.

I shrugged and tried to act casual. 'So where should I be?'

'Where I left you. You were safe there.'

I shook my head. 'Tell him, Lenka.'

She started off in a torrent of Russian, telling him the story. By then, we had all three of us moved further inside. It was a flat, an ordinary, traditional sort of flat with old-fashioned décor and furniture. To my mind, it was something of a museum, full of bits of Bohemian history. Crystal glasses and earthenware jugs. Watercolours of forest and stream, mill and ruined castle, lines of cattle plodding their weary way somewhere, home probably.

The main living room was admittedly comfortable enough, with its tired furniture and its big, old-fashioned radiators that threw out heat like small power stations, but it was nothing like Leon's bachelor pad. No wonder he thought he had left me in the right place.

We were all still standing, Leon listening intently to Lenka's tale of woe. I looked around, and began to notice all sorts of little homely touches that had been applied to the room. There were vases of dried flowers and gaily coloured, embroidered cushion covers. A big tapestry occupied most of one wall. It featured a wooden church with an onion dome, surrounded by fields of spring flowers bathed in sunshine. Family photographs – they looked like – had their place on a bureau.

Already the flat was looking better to my eye. Someone had taken a lot of trouble over it, and given it much loving thought and care. Unlike Leon's contemporary bachelor pad, it was very definitely somebody's home.

Lenka finished her account. Leon gave her a kiss on the cheek and turned to me. 'I am very sorry, Frank. It seems that my troubles have fallen on you for a third time today.'

I gave him a rueful smile and shrugged it off. 'These things happen, Leon.'

'Not in your world, surely? Only in mine.'

'Perhaps.'

'Please sit down, Frank. You deserve a rest after all that.'

I sat down on a sofa and Leon dropped into a big, old chair, while Lenka rounded up a tray with three glasses and a bottle with a colourful label. I wasn't sure alcohol was what I needed right then, but what could I do? I drank a toast with them, although I wasn't sure to whom or what it was dedicated. Then Leon started to explain things. He said he owed me that, which I thought was true. So I listened.

'This flat belongs to my sister,' he began.

I looked at Lenka, surprised she had not told me.

'No, no!' Leon said quickly. 'Not this one. My other sister. Our other sister,' he corrected himself. 'She is called Olga. I have two sisters.'

That was more like it. I couldn't imagine Lenka living somewhere like this. It wasn't her style at all. Lenka would have been better off in the place where she had found me, or out in the woods perhaps. Somewhere bracing, rather than homely.

'Olga is not here?' I asked, trying to coax a little more from him.

Leon sighed and had several exchanges with Lenka before replying to me.

'She is not here,' he agreed. 'I came to see her, but she was not here. So I have been waiting. Now,' he added with a frown, 'we do not know where she is, and we are both worried about her.'

'Was she a target, like you?'

'Perhaps. It is possible.'

The conversation wasn't going very fast. My impatience was growing.

'However, thank you for helping Lenka, Frank. I gather she would not be still with us without your valuable assistance. So today you have saved us both. I thank you. We both thank you.'

I couldn't help wondering if Olga needed saving, too. The day wasn't over yet.

'What's going on, Leon?'

'It is complicated.'

Lenka cut in then with what seemed to be a very incisive piece of advice. Leon smiled and said, 'My sister says don't tell you anything – for your own good. Perhaps she is right.'

He turned back to her and said, 'Lenka, you must have realized by now how capable and formidable this man is? From what you say, if he had not intervened this evening, you would not be here. You would be dead. I could say the same thing for myself, earlier today. We are in his debt. He deserves to be told something.'

'Perhaps,' Lenka admitted reluctantly, in English, 'but not everything, Leon. We know nothing about him.'

'Well, I may not know everything about him, it is true, but I know enough to have offered him work. He declined, of course, but I am still hopeful,' he added with a cheerful smile.

'Work? Doing what?'

'Providing security for the house in England.'

'Oh, that!' she said, making clear where that stood in her list of priorities.

'Lenka, my dear. One day we might all be glad that we have such a house.'

'Does Martha know about this?'

'Not yet, no.'

I wondered if that was another sister. A wife even?

Lenka shook her head and sighed, and then decided to make us all tea in Olga's samovar.

'About Olga,' I said to Leon. 'What do you think has happened?'

'Maybe she has been abducted,' he said with a shrug, 'and maybe she has a new boyfriend. I don't know. The snow, perhaps?'

'But you expected to find her here?'

'Yes, I did. It is her home.'

I looked around the room thoughtfully and said, 'Your sister seems to live differently to you.'

He nodded. 'She does. She has her own way. I respect her for that. Lenka does too, but less so, I think.'

'This flat is very ... homely,' I suggested.

'Homely?' He looked puzzled for a moment, and then said, 'Like a home, yes?'

I nodded.

'It is true. Olga is a person who likes where she lives to be a home, a traditional home she has made herself, not something very modern that was designed by an architect.'

He chuckled and added, 'Olga is still a socialist, I fear! Or is she a conservative? I don't know.'

I didn't know, either. But it did seem remarkable that the three of them were siblings, and so close still. They weren't much alike. Perhaps it was Leon's wealth that kept them together.

'What do you intend doing about her?' I asked him.

'For now, we will wait. Sooner or later we will hear something, either from Olga herself or from somebody who knows about her.'

Fair enough. I couldn't see any alternative to waiting. Leon was a sensible man – in some respects.

'I am sorry, Frank, that your travel plans have been so disrupted. Without the snow, you would have been home by now. As it is, you must stay here with us. This is not the height of luxury, I know, but it would be difficult for you to find anywhere else tonight. Even if you could find somewhere, of course, we couldn't take you. We must wait for Olga.'

I just nodded in agreement. He was being sensible again, and so would I have to be. For the time being, we were stuck with each other. So we each took a cup of the very strong, black tea Lenka had made, and then we waited. It seemed to have been a long evening already, and a very long day. I couldn't help wondering what more there was still to come. It seemed to be just one damn thing after another.

Chapter Nine

THE BREAKTHROUGH CAME JUST before one in the morning. Leon got a phone call. When he took it, Lenka hung on his every word. So did I, even though I couldn't understand any of them. But you could tell something significant had happened.

There were flurries of two-way exchanges before Leon switched

41

off. He looked round at us and got to his feet. 'We know where she is,' he said calmly.

I guessed what that meant. 'She's been abducted?'

He nodded. 'Yes. But one of my men has located where she is being held. Now we will go to free her.'

He turned to Lenka and began to rattle out instructions. She nodded and got to her feet. They both began checking weapons that appeared from beneath clothing. These were people, I realized then, who probably never travelled light.

'Are you going far?' I asked.

'Not far, no. They are still in the city, but by tomorrow they might not be. The snow has held them back.'

In English, Lenka said, 'Where did they get her?'

'Roman said from the street, when she was coming home.'

'Not from here?' I asked.

Leon shook his head. 'They don't seem to know about this flat. In fact, they probably don't know much about Olga at all. They must have gone for her because they couldn't reach me.'

So the abduction had been improvised. Nonetheless effective for it, of course, but it did seem to mean the flat was safe ground for now. So I could stay here – if I wanted to.

'I'll come with you,' I said.

'No!' Lenka snapped.

Leon looked from her to me, and back again. 'No?'

'He will be useless,' she insisted. 'A burden.'

'I think not,' Leon said softly. 'I have seen him fight. So have you, you told me. Frank, we will be honoured to have you with us.'

I must be mad, of course. There was absolutely no need at all for me to volunteer for this. It wasn't my fight.

Lenka muttered to herself and disappeared into the bathroom.

'Don't worry about her,' Leon said. 'She is nervous. That is all. And impatient. She wants to do everything herself, but really she knows she can't.'

I just nodded. Maybe I was going on a split decision, but I was still going. As to why I was going, I couldn't really have told you. It just seemed a better thing to do than to sit there alone in the flat while the others were facing great danger. Besides, I had some sort of bond with Leon already. I liked the guy, as I've said, and I wanted to help him.

'Where are we?' I asked, looking around as we left the building.

'Vinohrady,' Leon said.

'Still? And where are we going?'

'Žižkov.'

'I know it.'

'You do not,' Lenka said scornfully.

'Red Prague,' I responded. 'Isn't that what they used to call it?'

'And what did you see there? Anything?'

'A big man on a big horse. And a T34 tank.'

Leon chuckled. 'You see?' he said. 'Frank really does know it.'

Lenka shut up.

'Lenka,' I said, anxious to close the gap between us, 'whatever you think, I really am on your side.'

'Perhaps,' she said non-committally, but as we crossed a patch of light I was nearly sure she smiled.

The man on a horse I had referred to was a Czech national monument. It was located at the Army Museum in Žižkov, and related to some semi-mythic figure in Czech history. Just as well, really. The Czech army hadn't exactly covered itself in glory in recent centuries.

The T34 at the entrance to the museum, on the other hand, was a reminder that the Red Army had been here, not just a bunch of local communists. Such things are dear still to Russians, and they famously hadn't liked it at all, back in the death throws of the Soviet Union, when David Černy painted another T34, on another plinth in Prague, a bold pink. That became a "diplomatic incident".

The snow had almost stopped falling at last but there was plenty of it on the ground. Walking was difficult. Trudging was a better description of what we were doing through the knee-high snow. Žižkov wasn't far, but if we were to walk all the way there, I thought it might take us the rest of the night.

Fortunately, we only walked to the end of the street. A big vehicle on balloon tyres was waiting patiently there for us, clouds of exhaust fumes puffing contentedly into the night.

'Gregor is here,' Leon said with satisfaction.

Whoever he was, Gregor had done very well to get here. I had seen no other vehicles moving on these streets. The Czechs would be used to moving quantities of snow quickly, and no doubt work was under way somewhere, but probably only on main roads. We climbed into the truck's big cab and basked in the heat while Gregor gave Leon a briefing.

'It's not far,' Leon said, turning back to me. 'We will drive as close as we can, and then go on foot. They have Olga in an old department store that now is not used.'

I nodded. A department store? I hoped Leon could narrow down the search area a bit. 'How many men are with her? Does Gregor have any idea?'

'He says six, maximum. Maybe only four right now.'

And we were three plus me. I wondered if we had enough manpower.

'If we brought in more men,' Leon said, reading my mind, 'there would be delay. Better like this.'

I nodded. He was probably right.

Leon's phone vibrated in his pocket. He took it out and glanced at the screen. Then he switched off and instructed Gregor to get us moving.

'Bobrik,' Leon said then, to no-one in particular. 'He will want to begin the negotiations.'

'He's the guy behind all this?' I asked.

Leon nodded. 'Do you have a gun?' he asked.

I shook my head.

'Do you want one?'

I was inclined to say no, but in that case what was the point in me being there? It seemed more than possible that there would be a firefight.

'What are you offering?' I asked.

'What are you used to?'

He seemed to take it for granted that I was no stranger to fire-arms in my walk of life, which was only partially true. Usually, I avoid carrying a gun. Usually, I avoided running into guns, as well. But I knew that would be difficult this time, if the previous afternoon's events were an indicator of what was likely to happen.

'I use a Glock pistol, a Glock 19, when I need it.'

Leon pulled open a hatch set in the floor of the vehicle and rooted around until he found what he wanted. He handed me a Glock 19 and some ammunition. I checked the gun, loaded it and put it away.

After we had been travelling for about fifteen minutes, Gregor pulled into the side of the road and turned to speak to Leon. I gathered we were as close as he felt it sensible to go. We piled out and began to trudge through the snow again. Not far this time, though. Gregor led us into the cover of an open-sided shopping arcade and began to point out the geography ahead.

As luck would have it, two men came out of the doorway Gregor was indicating. They climbed into another truck on big tyres and drove away.

'Now there are certainly only four left,' Leon said with satisfaction.

The unspoken consensus seemed to be that things were looking up.

Chapter Ten

IT WASN'T MUCH OF a lock on the front door but Gregor didn't waste time doing anything clever with it. He produced a tyre lever, inserted it and cracked the lock. We were inside within seconds. After that, very dim occasional lights showed us the way through the shadowy interior.

The store might well have been disused, as Leon had said, but it was still full of stuff. Whoever had called it a day on trading had not got around yet to clearing the contents. We skirted sofas and filing cabinets, rounded mountains of cartons and mattresses, and kept on heading towards the area at the back of the ground floor where voices could be heard. As agreed, I stayed behind the others. This was their fight, not mine, but they needed someone to watch their backs.

There were four men playing cards in an old store room, smoking cigarettes and drinking from bottles of beer while they played. We could see them through little windows set in the interior wall.

The room was one of half a dozen in a row on the far side of the store. Leon used sign language to send Lenka one way and Gregor the other, while he kept the door to the main room covered – and I kept them all covered. They were looking for Olga. They wanted to know exactly where she was before they made their move.

I watched and saw Lenka try a door that wouldn't open. All the others had opened easily. I saw her look through a window covered with metal mesh, and then turn to give Leon a thumbs-up sign. She had found Olga.

Gregor and Lenka returned to Leon's side. A brief whispered conversation followed. Then Leon led the way into the main room. It was a tense few moments. I waited anxiously for an eruption of gunfire.

It didn't happen. Instead, there were raised voices – a bit of shouting and yelling – and then silence. I hung back and waited.

It was as well I did. Gregor had got his arithmetic wrong. There was a fifth man.

I watched him sauntering along to the store room, and I closed up behind him. As he reached the entrance, I stuck the Glock in his back and urged him forward. He was quick-witted, and rational. He sized up the situation fast, made no protest and headed through the doorway.

Leon relieved him of a gun, which he added to the pile he had collected from the others. Then he had him join the rest of the gang at the table. A brief interrogation began, which I couldn't follow in any detail. Basically, Leon asked questions, and one or other of them responded. It was tense, but entirely reasonable. Nobody had gone berserk and the guns had been made safe. We'd had it easy.

I didn't know what Leon had in mind now, or how this thing would end, but it was going well so far. We had found the missing sister. We had captured all the men who had abducted her, except the two who were leaving as we arrived. Game over, so far as I was concerned. Leon didn't really need anything more. Maybe some information, but that was all.

That was the way I was thinking. As I said, I didn't really know how it would end, but end it suddenly and inexplicably did.

Leon glanced at Lenka and Gregor, and nodded.

Then all three of them began shooting. There wasn't much noise. They were using suppressors. And it was all over in a second or two, with five dead men slumped over the table. I watched, paralyzed by shock, as Lenka and Gregor walked quickly around the table, firing a head shot into each corpse to make sure.

'Let's get Olga and go,' Leon snapped to the others, before turning to me.

I couldn't believe what I'd just witnessed. It took a few moments for my brain to process what my eyes had seen. But then the message got through.

I stared hard at Leon, aghast at the sudden and unexpected violence. 'Jesus Christ, Leon!' I croaked. 'What the hell have you done?'

'It was necessary,' he said, stooping to start collecting the empty shells.

This wasn't what I'd signed on for. Incredulity and horror gave way to anger.

'Necessary? What the hell's wrong with you, man? You can't do stuff like this!'

'Let's go,' Leon said evenly.

He looked me in the eye, a look without emotion. Lenka and Gregor had moved alongside him. I was suddenly aware that I had to be careful here. One more corpse could easily be arranged.

Lenka spat something at me scornfully. I stared hard at her, knowing what she meant but not prepared to back down.

'In my country,' I said carefully, 'we think badly of people who shoot unarmed prisoners. And we believe in the law.'

'This is not your country, Frank,' Leon said calmly.

'It's not yours, either!'

Lenka added something contemptuous.

'My sister thinks we should shoot you, as well,' Leon said, grinning now.

'I gather that.'

'Give me your gun,' Lenka demanded.

'Fuck off!' I said. 'I'm keeping this as long as you have a gun.'

Leon laughed and turned away.

Gregor kicked down the door of the room where Olga was being held. She was on her feet, ready to leave, and the others wasted no time getting her out of there. Then Leon led us all out of the room, and out of the store.

I went with them because realistically there was nothing else I could do. Leon and Lenka were both right. This was not my country any more than it was theirs. I was a fool ever to have got involved with them. But I was also aware of how vulnerable I was.

While Gregor went off to get the vehicle, the rest of us shivered and sheltered from the renewed snow in the entrance to another building a little further down the street.

'This is Frank, an Englishman,' Leon told Olga. 'He has been helping us.'

I had been aware of the curious glances coming from her. Now I turned to look at her and nodded. She smiled back and reached for my hand. For a moment, she held it in hers.

'Thank you, Frank,' she said in English, in a halting, kindly voice. 'Thank you all so much,' she added, turning to the others. 'I knew you would come for me.'

It wasn't much, but it sounded like the voice of humanity.

Starting to feel conspicuous, we moved on rather than wait for Gregor to return with the vehicle. Lenka was back-marker. I helped Leon shepherd Olga through the snow. She wasn't strong on her feet. I didn't know if that was just her or because of her ordeal, but either way we had to hold her up and keep her moving. It wasn't easy in the deep snow.

Thankfully, Gregor arrived with the vehicle a few minutes later. It was a relief to get inside and feel how well the heater was doing its job. Lenka took charge of her sister then, while Leon rode shotgun and Gregor drove. I was a spare part. I didn't mind. There was a lot to think about, especially from the last hour.

I had begun to feel I was well out of my depth. Frankly, I didn't know what to do, or to think. What had happened back there in the old department store was just plain wrong. I was in no doubt about that. I shuddered to think what my old mate Bill Peart, a DI with the Cleveland police back home, would think – either of what had just happened, or of my involvement in the first place.

That said, I could also understand Lenka's contempt for me. I had been found wanting. My concern now was that she and her brother might come to feel that keeping a witness like me alive was not in their best interests. So staying alive was actually a more pressing issue for me just then than wringing my hands over the killing of five violent men who had declared war on Leon and abducted his innocent sister.

I watched Olga during our journey, and sensed again how different she was to her brother and sister. There was a calm and poise, a goodness even, about her that radiated throughout the vehicle. She was quiet, unobtrusive; yet she was also the centre of attention. She seemed to mean a great deal to the others, which helped to explain some of the ruthless single-mindedness with which they had gone after her abductors.

Our journey lasted the best part of an hour, and it took us into another part of the city that I didn't recognize at all. We were well off the usual tourist routes, and into a district of large, detached villas set in their own grounds. I knew we had crossed the river, the Vltava, that runs through the middle of the city, and climbed a hill, but after that I had lost my bearings. We were somewhere out west, possibly Střešovice, I thought, trying to recall the map I'd left behind.

It was something of a miracle that we could move at all on a night like that, but Gregor kept us going, manoeuvring around the countless stranded vehicles, floundering at times as the whereabouts of the road beneath the snow became a mystery. Occasionally we caught sight of people struggling along on foot, but we saw no other moving vehicles.

Finally, we left the line of the road to pass through a stone gateway and head along a short drive towards a big, old house that sat in quiet dignity beneath its blanket of snow, awaiting the return of its master. Gregor drove around the back and brought the vehicle to a shuddering halt. We were there at last, wherever it was.

We clambered out, sinking into snow that was knee-high on me, and headed for a big door that was helpfully illuminated as if in welcome. As soon as I passed through the entrance I realized this must be Leon's home. The apartment he had taken me to earlier was something else, his bachelor pad, perhaps, or accommodation for business visitors. But this house felt different.

Old and comfortable, warm and quiet, I sensed that it was not a place where casual guests or new acquaintances would ordinarily be taken. Perhaps I had moved up a notch or two in his estimation, despite my feeble objections to what had happened in the old department store.

As we entered the house, domestic help arrived to look after Olga. She consented happily to be taken away from us by the two women who came to fuss over her. She needed a bath and a rest, she said with a weary smile. It was understandable.

But apart from fatigue, she showed no signs of having been injured physically or damaged mentally by her ordeal. Nor did she seem concerned by the fate of her captors. To me, all that suggested a certain psychological resilience, despite her apparent surface fragility. It was a trait that seemed to run in the family.

Before she left us, Olga made a pretty little speech, first in Russian and then, for my benefit, in English.

'I wish to thank you all, everyone who took part this evening. It was wonderful when I realized that people had arrived to help me. You, Leon, my dear brother, and you, Lenka, my beloved sister, I thank you both so much.'

Leon smiled, visibly touched. 'I hope you never doubted that we could come for you, Olga. I am only sorry that it was necessary.'

'And you, Mr Frank,' Olga added, turning to me with a charming smile, 'you who I have never seen before in my life, I thank you, too, from the bottom of my heart.'

'Thank you, Olga,' I said, feeling a bit of a fraud. 'But I did very little. If anything, I impeded the others.'

Even without looking, I knew that Lenka would be nodding her head at that. But Leon objected to my modesty and sang my praises, further embarrassing me.

'I needed help,' Olga said in conclusion, 'and you came – all of you. So thank you again. Now I will take a bath, and then sleep, I think. It has been a long night.'

Then she was gone. It was as if we had been visited by royalty. The light in the room dimmed when Olga left us.

Chapter Eleven

'ANY NEWS FROM THE airport?' I asked Leon.

He shook his head. 'Nothing good. It is still closed.'

'When it reopens, I'll make my own way there. I must get back home.'

'My offer is still good, Frank.'

'Thank you, Leon, but I won't be accepting it. This ... this life. It's not for me.'

'You disapprove of what happened tonight?'

'I do. I told you that at the time.'

He sighed. 'It was either that or let them go, Frank. And if I'd let them go, they would have been back at our throats in a couple of hours.'

'You could have turned them in to the police.'

He just shrugged. He didn't have to tell me how absurd that suggestion was. What would the Czech police have made of one lot of Russians attacking another lot? How likely was it that they would have launched an investigation rather than simply deport the whole damned lot of them? Even if they had investigated, how far would they have got?

In practical terms, Leon had done what was in his own best interests, and his family's best interests. I was just out of my depth here, tired, battered, bruised, and in danger of losing my moral compass. I needed to go home.

'Get some sleep, Frank,' Leon advised. 'We all need to do that. In the morning, we will see what can be done to get you out of Prague.'

'It's morning now,' I said, yawning.

'You're right,' he said with some surprise, glancing at his watch. 'Come! I'll show you to your room.'

Shamefully, perhaps, I got my head down in a wonderfully comfortable bed and went to sleep without any difficulty. When I awoke several hours later it was fully light, light but grey. The snow had stopped altogether, but looking out of the window I could see we really didn't need any more. The bare-limbed trees in the grounds looked quite beautiful set so starkly against the deep virgin snow. I almost expected to see a sleigh pulled by reindeer come flying through the scatter of birch and the more distant fir trees.

My room was en-suite. So I took a shower and then re-dressed in the same old clothes. My possessions were minimal now, as I had lost my travel bag somewhere along the way in my mad retreat with Lenka. So I contented myself with emptying my pockets and then putting the few things I still possessed back in again. There wasn't much. Just the Glock Leon had given me, my passport and wallet, and a few odds and ends. It didn't matter. I had all that I really needed.

Then I went to see if anyone else was up and about. I found Olga alone in a dining room, finishing her breakfast. She looked up at me with a welcoming smile.

'Good morning, Mr Frank!'

I smiled back, surprised and pleased to see her. 'How are you feeling this morning, Olga?'

'I am very well, thank you. I hope you are, too?'

I nodded and assured her that I was, observing the conventional civilities. 'Is Leon around?'

'Not at the moment. Please help yourself to some breakfast.'

She waved a hand to point me towards a nearby table, where almost anything a reasonable person might fancy for breakfast was laid out waiting. I took a glass of orange juice and helped myself to scrambled eggs and toast. Then I added a couple of rashers of bacon. By the time I had taken a seat at the table, a pleasant young woman had appeared to ask if I would like coffee or tea. It was five star service in the House of Leon. A life of luxury, marred only by the things that went on around the edges.

'Leon has gone to talk to the police about yesterday's attack on the hotel,' Olga confided.

But not about his sister's abduction, or the bodies in a disused department store, I assumed.

'You've heard about that already?' I asked, curious.

'Oh, yes.'

She couldn't have had very much sleep, I was thinking. Nor could Leon. As for Lenka.... Well, who knew? She was the one I hadn't seen after our arrival here. Perhaps she had mounted an all-night patrol outside the house.

'When Leon returns, we are all to go to England,' Olga added, beaming with evident pleasure at the thought.

I smiled back. Perhaps she didn't care for snow, and would be glad to get out of it. Perhaps she had seen more than enough of it in Russia. Or perhaps she just wanted to go somewhere safer.

'I am so pleased,' she added, 'that you are coming with us, Frank. I will be able to practise my English on you.'

'Your English is perfect, Olga,' I assured her. 'You don't need to practise any more.'

'No, no! It is not true. You seek to flatter me, Frank. That will not work.'

53

I smiled again. I couldn't help it. She was a lovely little thing, so innocent and happy seeming, despite what had happened to her the day before. Yet, endearingly fragile though she appeared, she also had to be tough. She had come through her ordeal in good spirits, and seemingly untroubled by it.

But I felt I ought to tell her how things stood with me. I didn't want any misunderstanding.

'I don't know what Leon has told you, Olga, but I won't be travelling with you. As soon as the airport reopens, I'll be leaving you and making my own way back to England. I have a ticket, you see.'

Her face fell. 'Oh, how disappointing! I am so sorry to hear that, Frank. I believed you were coming with us.'

I shook my head. 'No. I must go home.'

Looking puzzled now, she said, 'But in that case, surely you must come with us? Prague airport will be closed for another day or so, but we are leaving this morning. Are you sure you won't come with us?'

It was my turn to be puzzled. 'What do you mean? How can you leave this morning if the airport is still closed?'

She smiled. 'Ah! Leon didn't tell you? We will travel to another airport, one that is open, and fly from there. It is agreed.'

'Another airport? Where?'

She mentioned a town I had never heard of, and said it was more than a hundred kilometres away.

'How will you get there?' I asked, still puzzled. 'The roads must be ...'

'Not by road,' she said, shaking her head. 'We will travel by helicopter. It will come here for us.'

That was another surprise.

'Does Leon have such a thing, a helicopter?'

'Yes, of course he does.'

Of course he did. He had everything. By then, I was wondering if I had decided to make my own way too hastily.

'You should change your mind, and come with us, Frank,' Olga said earnestly. 'It will be no fun here – especially with only Lenka

54

for company!' she added with a surprising grin. 'My sister is so very serious.'

It was a persuasive point. I hadn't thought of that. It might even be dangerous to stay here, knowing Lenka as I did.

Olga laid one hand on top of mine and pressed. 'Come with us, Frank,' she pleaded.

What else could I do?

Chapter Twelve

WHEN LEON RETURNED NOT long afterwards, he looked a bit tired but he still managed a grin.

'Everything all right?' I asked.

He shrugged. 'The police are investigating at the hotel, which means that it is closed until further notice. But at least repairs are underway. Charles will see to things there.'

Useful guy, Charles, I couldn't help thinking once again.

'He is the manager?'

'Amongst other things, yes.'

I didn't bother speculating about what else Charles might be responsible for.

'Was the hotel the only thing the police were interested in?'

Leon nodded, not rising to the bait. Events overnight were obviously in the private category, not for officialdom to be concerned about.

'So are we leaving soon?' I asked.

'Soon, yes.' He glanced at his watch and frowned. 'Today already?' he murmured.

'For quite some time, actually.'

He grinned again. Then he frowned and sighed. 'My business rival wants a meeting.'

'Your business rival? Is that the same guy who sandblasted your hotel with machine guns and had your sister abducted?'

'Bobrik, yes. He wants to negotiate.'

'What about?'

Leon shrugged, as if to say he hadn't a clue.

'What are you going to do?'

'I don't know. Maybe I should meet him. I'm not sure. Would you negotiate, Frank?'

Surprisingly, perhaps, it seemed like a serious question. He meant it. Would I negotiate? Given the circumstances?

'Well, it might save more bloodshed,' I suggested diplomatically.

'That is not always a good thing, Frank. Sometimes ...'

'Always it is,' I said firmly.

'You have this experience?'

'I do,' I said, prepared to exaggerate like hell if necessary.

In this case, though, I had no idea who the opposition was, or what they wanted from Leon. The situation was a complete mystery to me. So there was no way in the world my opinion was worth a hill of beans, as some might say. I should keep out of it. My only real interest was in getting back to Newcastle, and then home to Risky Point on the Cleveland coast, as quickly as possible.

'He wants to meet,' Leon repeated with a yawn.

'So you said. Where?'

'Kotor.'

'Where's that?'

'Montenegro.'

I wondered if I had heard correctly. 'Montenegro?'

'It used to be part of Yugoslavia, in Tito's day, and for a short time afterwards when Milosovic was running things.'

'And waging war.'

Leon nodded.

'I know about Yugoslavia,' I said, thinking suddenly and inappropriately of gaily coloured postage stamps in the album I had had as a boy. 'Montenegro used to have a king, I believe. But that was a long time ago.'

'A very long time ago,' Leon agreed. 'But it's still there.'

Montenegro, he meant, not the king.

'Why does Bobrik want to meet there?'

'Neutral ground,' Leon said with another of his shrugs. 'Also we both have yachts there.'

Of course they did. Oligarchs both, presumably, as well as deadly rivals. So they had to have yachts, and maybe Montenegro was as good a place as any for people like them to moor their yachts.

Neutral, slavonic ground, too, I was thinking. And, like Serbia, akin to Russia culturally. Perhaps they both felt at home there.

'Will you go?'

'I don't know.' Then he looked me in the eye and added, 'If I do go, will you come with me, Frank?'

After I had stopped laughing, I told him no – just in case he hadn't got the message.

'That's a pity,' he said sadly.

'Leon, what good could I possibly be?'

'You're an experienced man,' he said. 'Calm, rational – and a good fighter if it comes to that.'

I laughed again, but I was more incredulous than amused.

'Montenegro's quite warm at this time of year still,' he added, 'even if it does rain a lot.'

'Forget it,' I said shortly.

He dropped the idea then. At least, I thought he did. He turned to Olga, who had been listening with rapt attention, and spoke to her in Russian. She nodded. Then he went off to do something else.

'The helicopter will be here soon,' Olga told me.

'That's good.'

I walked over to the window and stood there moodily, watching a small squall deposit a little more snow in the garden. As if there wasn't enough already. Then I wondered if it ever snowed in Montenegro. Despite Leon's airy comment about the weather there, I rather thought it would do. There were mountains in Montenegro, I was nearly sure, and mountains meant snow. Wasn't it one of those regions of the old Yugoslavia with a skiing industry?

'The helicopter is coming,' Olga called, rousing me from my

absorption in things that didn't really matter, or concern me, very much.

It was good news. I turned, smiling gratefully at her. Escape from the mad Podolsky world suddenly looked like being possible.

The helicopter landed in the garden, on what was presumably lawn underneath the snow. By then, I had accepted Leon's repeated offers of a lift. Not the least of my reasons was that I had satisfied myself that Prague Airport really was out of action. When I rang them, a recorded announcement in umpteen languages said all flights had been cancelled until further notice. That was enough for me to swallow my reservations and agree to travel to Newcastle with Leon and Olga.

The chopper took off without any fuss once we were aboard, raising a fresh snow storm that obliterated the view of the house – and of Lenka. Big sister was staying put, apparently, which was a relief to me. I had had enough of her disdain, bordering on contempt, and I could tell that she still wanted to shoot me. There would have been plenty of opportunities for her if she'd come with us, I suspected. I couldn't always be on guard.

Leon had seemed to appreciate my standing by his side outside the hotel but when it came to being tough, I wasn't in the same league as his sister. I'd never met such a battle-hardened woman as Lenka.

The chopper whisked us away across the city and in a few minutes, we were out over open countryside and farmland. Leon had told me that it would be a twenty minute flight. I was surprised the authorities at the airport we were heading for had been able to keep their runway open. Leon said it was because it was a small airport favoured by the military, who liked to be able to depart for anywhere in the world at a moment's notice. Useful to know, something like that.

'And you keep a plane there?' I asked.

'No. I charter one from there occasionally, like now. My own plane I keep at Prague Airport.'

'What about a pilot? Does he come with the charter?'

Leon nodded towards one of the two men who had come aboard

with us without being introduced, the one that wasn't piloting the chopper. 'Pyotr is my pilot,' he said. 'He will fly us to Newcastle.'

Leon was certainly well organized. It was quite a set-up he had. I wondered if the Czech Republic was his main business base, and his country of residence now. I guessed it was. That made me wonder if he was *persona non grata* back in Russia. I wouldn't have been surprised. There were plenty like him dotted around the globe, usually people who had fallen foul of the current ruling elite.

We landed, transferred from helicopter to private jet and were air-bound again in a matter of minutes, with a minimum of fuss and a lot of unseen help. I sensed Leon was a known and valued customer. No doubt he was paying hefty retainers every month for the service he received.

The plane was comfortable and afforded me lots of leg room, as Leon had promised. Olga chose to sit next to me, which I welcomed. She was a pleasant companion, and a breath of normalcy in a dangerous world. Surprisingly, she also seemed to be interested in me. She was keen to ask about my life in England, which made me wonder what Leon had told her about me. Next to nothing, probably. The truth was too complicated, and the telling of it would have taken more time than he had had to play with since last night.

So I told her a little, and tried to make my life in England sound as normal and uneventful as possible. I didn't dare tell her the truth. She might have moved to another seat. As it was, she even wanted to know about the weather. She must have read up on the subjects that interest the English.

From the way Leon got his head down and drifted off to sleep almost immediately, I guessed he had not gone to bed at all overnight. While I had been snatching a few hours in a comfortable, warm bed, he had been talking to the police about the attacks on his hotel, arranging for repairs to be made and no doubt dealing with a great many other matters that occupy oligarchs on a daily, and a nightly, basis.

What I didn't think – not for one moment – was that the killing of Olga's abductors had kept him awake. He didn't seem to be that kind of man.

But Olga and I were both rested, relatively speaking, and she was interested in conversation with me.

'My brother tells me you are a private investigator, Frank.'

'Sometimes,' I admitted. 'Also a security consultant.'

'Really? How interesting. But you came to Prague on holiday, Leon says.'

'I did. Just for a short break. Although Leon was reluctant to accept that.'

She laughed. 'My brother must always be vigilant. Sometimes, perhaps, I think he overdoes it. Not everyone is a potential enemy, I tell him.'

'Thank goodness for that, Olga! He needs an adviser like you.'

'It is the world in which we live,' she said philosophically. 'But Prague is an attractive city, I think. Don't you?'

'I did – until yesterday afternoon.'

She shivered. 'Oh, yes. How terrible the events at the hotel must have been.'

'Not as bad as what you experienced.'

'Perhaps not. But I am so sorry you have become involved in this terrible situation. Please don't judge my family on what has happened to us this past day or two.'

I didn't reply to that. It was hard to believe that the past twenty-four hours had been so exceptional for this family. Leon and Lenka, at least, seemed well used to this sort of life, and well equipped for it.

Not Olga, of course. She was very different.

'What about you, Olga? How do you spend your time? Are you involved in the family business, too?'

'In a way,' she admitted, 'but not like Leon and Lenka. Computers are my life. I am an IT specialist.'

That rather floored me. I had taken her for someone with an artistic leaning, an aspiring artist even, perhaps.

'But now,' she said, 'I am looking forward to seeing our new house. Will you come with us to Northumberland, Frank?'

I shook my head. 'I don't think so, Olga. I have a lot to do when I get home.'

'Oh?' She sounded disappointed. 'But you are our friend! Leon has told me. You must come to see our new English house. Please, Frank!'

I was touched, not to say moved, but my answer was still no.

'I will be all alone, except for Martha,' she said miserably.

'Who's that?'

'Oh, you know,' she said with a sigh.

But I didn't. Martha? Lenka had mentioned the name, but that was all I knew.

'You will have Leon with you.'

Olga shook her head. 'He cannot stay. He has much to do back in Prague. The hotel, for instance. It must be repaired.'

I knew she was right. Leon would have plenty to do back there. There was no question about that. He had a business empire to defend and protect, and to keep functioning.

Right on cue, Leon woke up and entered the conversation as if he had missed nothing.

'Come and see our house, Frank. I know you don't want the job I offered you, but come and see it anyway. We would be very pleased if you would.'

That was Leon in best friend mode. He was hard to disappoint. Olga was even harder. They worked on me, and by the time we landed in Newcastle, I had agreed to give their new house the once-over. Why not? I thought. What was wrong with that?

Quite a lot, as it happened. Will I never learn?

Chapter Thirteen

THE CHESTERS HAD ONCE been a grand house, a wonderful palace of a house. About two hundred years ago, maybe. Perhaps longer. When I first saw it, I thought it was a total ruin.

61

One of Leon's men had collected us at the airport in a Range Rover and driven us north into lonely Northumberland. Leon assured me that I would be brought back to Newcastle just as soon as I desired. As we headed out into wet, misty countryside, under a lowering dark cloud, I was tempted to say, 'Hey! Don't bother. Let me out now.'

The main reason I didn't was that I wouldn't have wanted to disappoint the luminous Olga, who was so excited it was like sitting next to a child on Christmas morning.

'How lovely it all is!' she exclaimed, as in the gathering gloom we sped down green lanes overhung by wildly dancing trees, not another vehicle in sight.

While Olga shivered with delight, I just thought miserably that I could be halfway home by now, instead of racing down these god-forsaken roads. Early afternoon, and already the light was fading fast. The world was covered in cloud, and the new clouds coming from the west were even blacker.

'It will snow, I think,' Olga declared excitedly, peering out to the west.

I shook my head. 'It's too warm for that. Just more rain.'

'Rain is good,' she said confidently, the very model of positive thinking.

Then we reached The Chesters. I stared aghast as the driver edged us carefully between collapsing stone gate posts and began the run up a gravel drive that had long since been invaded by shrubs and trees, as well as grass and ferns. I focused on the building ahead of us. What had happened to the roof, I wondered? And was there glass left in any window at all?

Olga saw it differently. 'It's so beautiful,' she breathed. 'Oh, Leon! How wonderful. Martha will love it, too.'

That name again. Who the hell was Martha? Not knowing was starting to drive me crazy.

Leon was non-committal when it came to his opinion about the house. He was staring ahead at it just as hard as I was.

Something occurred to me for the first time. 'Have you been here before?' I asked Olga, guessing what her answer would be.

'Never,' she said, shaking her head.

'Leon?' I called to her uncharacteristically quiet brother up front. 'Have you been before?'

He, too, shook his head.

Dear God, I thought with a wince, astonished. 'How long have you owned this property, Leon?'

'A couple of months,' he replied, without turning around.

'Seven weeks and three days,' Olga said definitively. 'And I have been looking forward so much to seeing it for the first time.'

I gave up then and leant back in my seat. All I could think was what the hell is any of us doing here. Seriously.

The Range Rover came to a stop on a patch of overgrown gravel at the front of the ruined house.

'Do you want the job, Frank?' Leon asked with a grin before he opened his door.

I chuckled, without feeling at all amused. 'We've been through that before, Leon.'

'Do you want it?' he repeated doggedly. 'And will you stay here with Olga, or do you want to come back to Newcastle with me?'

'You're not staying? You've come all this way, but...'

'I have to get back to Prague. There's a lot for me to do there.'

'Please stay, Frank,' Olga said quietly.

I looked at her and then back at Leon. I could feel her willing me to give the answer she wanted. It was unnerving, and the situation no longer seemed so straightforward.

'What is the job?' I asked after a moment. 'Remind me, Leon.'

We entered what was said to be the living accommodation, and while Olga set out to explore it, Leon quietly explained his ridiculous and all-embracing proposal to me. I was staggered.

'First, I want you to fly to Montenegro with me, and protect my back, while I have discussions with Bobrik.'

'Me?' I said faintly. 'Why me?'

'Because I trust you, Frank. And you're a capable man. I'd like you on my side. Then,' he continued, 'I would like you to come back here and protect Olga, while she settles in and the renovation work on the house is organized. I'm talking just a few weeks, five or six maybe. Then I will have my problems sorted, and you will be able to go your own way.

'No, hear me out!' he said, as I tried to tell him what I thought of the proposal. 'If you do all that for me, Frank, you can name your own price – seriously. And I will pay upfront. What do you say?'

That last bit shut me up. Name my own price. Payment upfront. I knew it was a genuine offer, and it made me think again. Name my own price? I could do that. All I needed was a pencil and the back of an envelope. Perhaps not even that.

'I charge by the day,' I said slowly, thinking hard. 'My daily rate is £1,000, and this would be a 24/7 commitment. Six weeks max, you say? That would be a lot of money.'

'Forty-two thousand pounds sterling,' Leon said, while I was still doing the arithmetic. 'I'll make it up to fifty. Plus expenses. What do you think?'

A sum like that didn't seem to trouble Leon. Probably it didn't mean as much to him as it did to me. I felt like doubling my daily rate, but I guessed even that wouldn't put him off. For some reason I didn't really understand, he wanted me on board.

The other thing I thought was that this was big league, a lot bigger than the usual stuff I did.

'What do you say, Frank?'

Could I handle it? Well, there was only one way to find out.

'OK, Leon,' I said with a sigh. 'Let's do it.'

We shook hands. Then we went to see where Olga had got to.

One wing of the house was habitable. In it, there were half a dozen bedrooms plus several living rooms, a couple of bathrooms and a huge kitchen. That seemed to me to be more than enough for anything but an absolutely enormous family. Not for Olga and Leon, though. They obviously had thoughts about restoring, or rebuilding, the whole place. Good luck to them. They had their work cut out.

Olga and one of the Russians there already, who seemed to be some sort of architectural adviser, were soon deep in conversation about their plans. Leon interrupted them only to tell Olga that we were leaving, but that I would be returning in a couple of days to help out. She seemed pleased about that. She gave me a flowery little speech of thanks, and us both kisses on the cheek. Then we left.

It was quite dark by then. I had a sense of big stone walls, but not much else about the house. That would have to wait until I returned and saw it in daylight at my leisure. Another of Leon's men on the spot drove. Leon sat in the back with me. It seemed a good time to try to straighten out a few things.

'It would be helpful if you told me something of what's going on, Leon. What are we heading into?'

'It is complicated,' Leon said, 'but you are right. Some things you need to know.'

Then he went silent, as if he didn't know where to start. We sped along lonely roads, the powerful engine purring and the headlights showing us trees dancing in the squalls of wind and rain. My patience grew thin.

'Do you really have things to do in Prague?' I asked. 'Or do we go straight to Montenegro?'

'We go to Montenegro, to the town called Kotor.'

'And there?'

'We will stay on my yacht while I make arrangements for us to meet Bobrik.'

It was a start. Now I had to grasp the end of the tangle and gently tug and tease a bit more information out of him.

'What's the problem between you two? Bobrik obviously wants something you have, or can do. What is it?'

Leon pulled his thoughts together, and with a sigh, made an effort.

'You must understand all this goes back a long way, Frank. It started in Russia many years ago.'

'Now there's a surprise.'

'Isn't it?' he agreed with a chuckle.

'Yvgeny Bobrik and I were both in the army. We were col-leagues. I wouldn't say friends, but we fought together, and kept each other out of trouble on the battlefield.'

'Battlefield? Where would that have been?'

'The North Caucasus,' he said with a shrug. 'Chechnya and Dagestan mostly. Sometimes in the borderlands in the Far East and Siberia, where there are always struggles with Afghans and the Chinese. Places like that. There was no shortage of battlefields. Russia is a big, big country, with plenty of hostile neighbours.'

'Battlefields overseas, too?'

'Sometimes.'

He declined to elaborate. I could guess some of it, but Serbia and Kosovo weren't the only places that had been visited by Russian special forces in the past decade or two.

'When we left the army, we left as business partners. We had some projects running already, and we expanded fast. There were opportunities. Lots of industrial sectors were run down and badly in need of investment. People who could bring in investment could often buy whole industries very cheaply.

'It wasn't like it had been in the very early nineties, when Yeltsin was around, but there was no shortage of opportunities for ambitious young businessmen.'

'Like you?'

'Like me, and like Bobrik, yes. We did well.'

The driver broke in then. He called something over his shoulder. I gathered a message had come in on the car phone. Leon leant forward to discuss it and to pass on instructions.

I wondered what the joint business had been. Presumably not hotels. Presumably something for which service in the army, in special forces even, gave you a good launch platform.

I winced. I didn't like the direction my thoughts were taking. Illicit trade in weapons was one obvious possibility. I really hoped it wasn't that.

'Trouble?' I asked, when Leon leant back again.

He shrugged. 'Perhaps. I don't know.'

'The bodies?'

'No. Gregor will have disposed of them.'

No risk of them being discovered then. Nothing to tie anything like that to Leon. No reason even for anyone not involved to suspect anything at all had happened in that disused department store.

'Presumably Bobrik knows what went down?'

Leon nodded. 'He knows. It's why he wants to meet.'

We were headed for a damage limitation conversation, then. Not a bad thing. Far better than a shoot-out. I'm all in favour of talk-talk when it's possible.

That made me wonder if it was why Leon had wanted me on board. Perhaps his own men were better at war-war. My own inclinations must have been very obvious when we rescued Olga. Lenka certainly hadn't been in any doubt.

I waited for Leon to continue with his tale and tell me why, and how, he and Bobrik had fallen out. It didn't happen. He was no longer in the mood for reminiscing. We were close to the airport now. There were things to be done there. Phone calls to be made. I tried to relax. There would be time later to hear more of the story. I intended to make sure of that.

Chapter Fourteen

THERE WAS THICK CLOUD over the airport. We saw nothing of the Montenegrin landscape until we were down to the last few hundred feet.

'Disappointing,' I said. 'This is the Med, isn't it?'

'The Adriatic,' Leon said. 'They get a lot of rain this time of year. Come in the summer if you want it hot and dry.'

'I'll try to remember that,' I said with a grin. 'But perhaps you won't need me in the summer?'

He grimaced. 'Who knows?'

Fortunately, Leon's pilot was too good to be worried by low cloud. We landed with scarcely a bump and swept effortlessly along the runway before turning into a taxi lane, and, eventually, a berth. Leon was on the phone long before we came to a stop.

The co-pilot, or whatever he was, got up and came back to us. 'They're here,' he announced.

Leon nodded. 'Thank you, Yuri. Let's go.'

By then the door was open, steps were in place and I could see a Range Rover with darkened windows waiting for us. Somebody had been efficient.

Two men who looked both vigilant and capable waited for us at the bottom of the steps. Security, or bodyguards, obviously. Leon spoke to one of them and shook his hand, and then led the way to the vehicle. Within half a minute we were moving. Both of the guards came with us.

'Where did you say it was we were going?' I asked Leon.

'Kotor. Originally a Roman town, then something else, then Venetian, Serbian, French – and even British for a time – before we slavs took it back.'

'A cosmopolitan history, then.'

He smiled and leant forward to speak in Russian to one of the men who had come with us.

'No problems,' he said to me, when he sat back up again. 'Andrei says all is quiet. We should be there in twenty minutes, despite the cloud and the rain.'

We were. And a hair-raising drive it had been, on a narrow road over jagged mountains in dense cloud. There was little to be seen most of the way. Mid-afternoon here, I decided, was no different to England at this time of year. The oligarchs would be well advised to move their yachts.

Then we crested a ridge, and suddenly we were dropping down out of the cloud. I leant forward to study the view. It was worth the effort.

We were coming down from a high ridge. Below was an immense fjord, with steep-sided mountains rising from sea level on each side. Somehow, down at waterside, a town had been built to service a port. The big cruise ships I could see lined up against the stone jetties were ultra modern, but the town was not. The castle and huge town walls, together with a cathedral-like church, indicated medieval origins, even if the Romans had been here first.

I was impressed. No wonder the place had changed hands so often. Kotor must always have been seen as a great prize for warring states and pirate raiders.

'And this is where you keep your yacht?'

'This is where it is right now,' Leon said. 'It spent the summer here, with all the others.'

I got it. Kotor was where the oligarchs had gathered this year. A conclave of oligarchs. Who knew where they would head for the deep winter?

'With you on it?' I asked.

'Occasionally.' He shook his head and added, 'I don't really like the sea.'

'Or boats?'

'Or boats,' he agreed. Then he grinned and added, 'But I do need to keep an eye on everybody!'

The trials of the oligarchs, I was thinking. What a life!

Leon's yacht was called *Samarkand*. I don't suppose it was particularly big, for one of its kind, but it certainly impressed me. It didn't have its own submarine or its own anti-ballistic missile system, like some I've read about, but it did have its own helicopter, and a lot more besides. It seemed too big to be called a yacht, but you could say that about a lot of vessels that come into the category these days.

The Range Rover came to a stop nearby on the quayside. My hand went to the door lever. Leon's hand closed on my arm. 'Wait,' he said. 'Wait a moment.'

The bodyguards got out first. They moved around the vehicle and checked things out. Two or three more men came from the yacht. Together, they formed a huddle.

'OK,' Leon said. 'Let's go.'

We got out and joined the crowd, which then began to move over to the yacht. Leon was in the middle, like the President of the United States, the hired help gathered around him and supposedly prepared to stop the bullets. It was sensible of Leon to be taking precautions, but I couldn't help also thinking it was a hell of a way to live.

Once on board, we went straight below deck to a beautifully furnished wardroom – I believe it would be called – where Leon went into conference with his skipper and a couple of advisers. I felt like a spare part, which was what I was really. I was out of my depth here. Why Leon had thought it would be useful to have me along I couldn't imagine.

But perhaps I would find out soon enough.

The initial meeting didn't take long. As the group began to disperse, Leon spoke to me.

'With all this racing around, there hasn't been time for you to replace the clothes and other things you lost in Prague, Frank. You can do that now, if you like. Would you like to go ashore with Yuri to do some shopping, or do you trust him to bring you something suitable?'

'If I'm going to be wearing 'em, I want to choose 'em,' I said with a wry smile.

Leon nodded. 'OK. Yuri will take you.'

Yuri spoke English, a kind of English, which was a relief.

'When we get to the town,' he said, 'you follow me. OK? But don't come with me. Follow me. OK?'

'You mean you don't want it to look like I'm with you?'

He smiled, nodded and said, 'Is very bad here. Enemies everywhere. Better for you to be alone.'

I shrugged. 'OK, Yuri. You're the expert.'

But I wondered why Leon had agreed to meet Bobrik here, if it was as bad as that. Pride, perhaps? Defiance? Refusal to be intimidated?

Still, these were serious, experienced people, and well used to threat and violence. They knew what they were talking about. So I had no hesitation in accepting Yuri's advice.

I followed him across the quayside and over a timber bridge that spanned the moat in front of the town wall, and I followed him through the massive stone archway into the town proper. My first impression was that it was indeed an historic town, one of great interest and beauty. The massive defensive walls, fifty feet high and more, suggested it had long been a town of great riches, too.

I followed Yuri along a narrow street between tall limestone walls belonging to ancient buildings five, six and even more storeys high. We walked on limestone that had been polished into marble by the passage of untold numbers of feet. Small craft shops and coffee bars lined our way at first. Well-dressed people in expensive, fashionable clothes threaded between us. These were not the peasants and serfs of a medieval mountain kingdom; these were people from the rich men's yachts and the cruise liners waiting along the quayside and in the berths set aside for them.

But perhaps the locals, too, belonged to that world now. Money, big money, was here in evidence all around us, and I didn't like it. I felt exposed and vulnerable, not least because of my association with Leon. This wasn't my world. But I had signed on for the voyage. So I had to see it through.

Yuri lifted an arm and dropped it again. Some sort of signal. I stopped and turned to gaze at Russian eggs in the window of a souvenir shop for tourists. Yuri turned and came back in my direction. He reached me, passed me and kept on walking. Twenty paces further on he turned into a shop doorway. I waited a minute or so, and then turned and headed for the same shop.

As I neared the doorway, two men came directly at me, fast. In the couple of seconds before they reached me, I saw them and understood their intent. I saw the knife blade flash and instinctively I braced myself. The gun in my pocket was of no use. I couldn't reach it in time. I just had to avoid the knife.

As the blade was thrust at me, I lurched aside and grabbed the arm behind it. I forced it up and backwards. The man was off-balance now and I rammed him into the wall. He jabbed me hard in the ribs with his free hand. I smashed the knife hand against the wall and tore it down against the rough stone.

The man kept hold of the knife and kicked out. Low down, an iron bolt stuck out from the wall. I smashed the back of his hand hard against it. He yelped. I did it again. This time, the bolt went right through his hand. Blood spurted. While he was distracted, I slammed his head against the wall. That did it. He finally slumped to the ground.

But it had all taken time, too much time, and there were two of them. I spun round desperately, looking for the second man, knowing I was too late. There was no time, no time!

He was almost on me when I heard the crack-crack of pistol shots. Someone screamed. I turned. Someone else shouted. The crowd parted. Then Yuri was between us, and falling, dropped by a bullet from the gun the man was holding.

I hurled myself sideways as the gun turned in my direction. The wall stopped me. I jerked frantically in the opposite direction.

Then the man seemed to stumble as I heard another crack-crack. He, too, went down, the gun falling from his lifeless fingers.

A space had suddenly cleared in front of me. I straightened up, desperate to get out of the way – but which way?

I heard another scream from somewhere nearby. Then a face I recognized appeared in front of me: Lenka.

Lenka?

There was no time to be surprised. With flashing eyes and a ferocious expression, she pushed me towards the entrance to the shop. I resisted, trying to stoop to see how Yuri was.

'He is gone,' Lenka snapped. She hurled herself against me. 'Move, Frank! Move!'

We fell through the shop doorway and barged into the cavernous interior, as I struggled to get to grips with what had happened.

My shocked brain registered racks of clothes everywhere, some even hanging from the ceiling. Plenty of clothes here, where Yuri had brought me, but clothes were the last thing on my mind now. Lenka pushed past and ran in front of me. She seemed to know where she was going. I raced after her.

Towards the back of the shop, an elderly man dressed formally in a black suit and white shirt and tie opened a door and bowed as we passed him. We ran through the gap and hit a wrought-iron staircase. Lenka led the way up it fast, our feet clattering on the metal, the sound echoing in the confined space of the stairwell.

On an upper floor, we ran along a tiled passageway that was half open to the elements, one side protected only by a low wall and by pillars every few yards that supported stone arches.

We fled along interior corridors, and up and down staircases. Lenka never looked back once. But I was breathing heavily and struggling to keep up. I was afraid of losing her.

Then we plunged downwards, and, finally, we hit the street again. It was a busy street in late afternoon sunlight, where people passing by were unaware of what had happened just a short distance away. Our frantic hustle stopped instantly. We straightened up. Lenka looked at me questioningly. I nodded. She turned. Together now, we walked away steadily, heading I had no idea where.

Chapter Fifteen

I DIDN'T BOTHER ASKING her why or how she was here. I was just grateful she was.

'Thanks,' I said when I'd got my breath back. 'I've never been more pleased to see you.'

She almost smiled at that. 'Always,' she said, 'we watch over our people when they are on a mission.'

'Without telling them?'

'It is necessary.' She shrugged. 'It is how we have always done things.'

I knew it probably was, too. Russian clandestine operators never had operated totally alone in the field. That was not the Russian way. Whether in the old Soviet days it had been protective cover or a need to keep an eye on people in case they tried to defect was a moot point. I was just glad Leon had retained the practice, even if all I had been doing at the time was shopping.

'I'm very sorry about Yuri, Lenka. He lost his life trying to save mine.'

She grimaced. 'Nowhere is safe. Yuri knew that. We are used to it.'

Some life they led, I couldn't help thinking once again. You had to wonder if the wealth and the exciting foreign travel opportunities made up for it. Or were they in it simply because they were competitors, and were hooked on the exhilaration of playing the game?

'Where now, Lenka? Back to the boat?'

She nodded. 'I think so. This town is not safe for us.'

But was the boat safe? By then, I was beginning to wonder.

Leon listened with a grave face as Lenka told him her version of the story. I felt for him. Yuri had clearly been a well-liked and trusted employee and colleague, and perhaps a friend, too.

He turned to me and said casually, 'So you didn't get any new clothes, Frank?'

'Not one,' I replied. 'And I'm not interested in doing any more shopping, either. I'm happy with what I'm wearing, I've decided.'

He nodded without much interest and looked past me. He was understandably distracted.

'I'm sorry about Yuri, Leon. He got hit because of me, but there was nothing I could do to stop it. I'm just lucky Lenka arrived when she did.'

'Yes,' he said with a sigh. 'That's how it sometimes goes.'

So that was that. Whatever arrangements were made about Yuri, I knew nothing about them. I didn't want to know, either. This was not my world, I thought yet again. The sooner we were done and out of here the better, so far as I was concerned.

I said, 'Leon, it's not safe here – for any of us. I think you should consider pulling out, while you still can.'

'I must attend the meeting.'

'Leon, they called the meeting, but they are still trying to kill us! They did kill Yuri. This is not a genuine truce. It's not even a cease-fire.'

'Even so,' he said equably, 'I must meet Bobrik. Perhaps we can settle it, if we meet.'

His mind was made up. I could see it was useless to argue.

'OK. Well, count me in,' I said with some reluctance. 'I'm still with you, for what that's worth.'

He smiled and slapped me on the back. 'Thank you, Frank!'

The venue for the meeting was supposedly neutral ground, a terrace restaurant overlooking the harbour. Frankly, I didn't like it even before I saw it. Open-air meetings are notoriously hard to secure. Besides, I didn't believe anywhere in or near this town could reasonably be regarded as neutral, let alone safe, for Leon – or for me. Not now. Yuri had known what it was like here, and had tipped me off, but he still hadn't been able to stave off disaster.

The arrangements agreed for the meeting were sensible, so long as both sides stuck to the rules. But would they? I couldn't be sure, but I suspected not.

Leon and Bobrik were each allowed to have one other person with them. They would meet at a table in the centre of the terrace, amidst the diners who were there for a normal evening out.

I assumed it would be me accompanying Leon, but he shook his head when I asked him. Now Lenka was here, and exposed, he said, he would take her with him. The main reasons were that she was family and she spoke Russian.

I accepted that. Lenka would be more use to him in negotiations. As well as the reasons Leon had given, she knew what was going on. I still didn't. She had also proved she didn't mind shooting people, and could do it without hesitation. That was another way in which she would be more use than me.

Guns and other weapons were not to be taken to the table. Leon said the four of them would be searched on their way into the restaurant to make sure of that.

'Who by?' I asked. 'Who will do the searching?'

'Each by a person from the other side,' Leon said. 'I will tell Bobrik he must bring a woman to search Lenka.'

A wise precaution, I couldn't help thinking, given Lenka's

mercurial temperament.

Otherwise, they probably wouldn't even get inside the restaurant, never mind hold a meeting.

'What about me? Where do you want me?'

He said he wanted me on the terrace, enjoying a meal, well before the meeting was due to start. My role would be to be on the lookout for foul play. Bobrik couldn't be trusted.

'They don't know you,' he added.

Maybe, maybe not. I certainly hoped not. But someone had spotted me that afternoon. Perhaps they had assumed I was just Yuri's sidekick, rather than a player.

'I'll stand out like a sore thumb, won't I – a solitary male diner?'

'Don't worry,' he said with a twinkle in his eye. 'You will have a companion for the evening, a woman.'

'Really? Sounds too good to be true.'

'You will like her, I think.'

I wasn't too sure about that. Some unknown woman? Who would she be – the mysterious Martha, perhaps? A prostitute, hired for the evening? Whoever it was, the arrangement didn't sound very good to me.

'Leon, I'm not sure that's a great idea.'

'Trust me, Frank. I know what I'm doing. And I want you there to use your skills and sensitivity to make sure nothing bad happens. Bobrik knows my people. He doesn't know you.'

So, basically, that was the reason he'd wanted me along. I was from outside the circle. It made sense, and I couldn't say I blamed him. Even so, I wasn't sure about the arrangement. In fact, I still wasn't sure about the whole damn thing.

'I should be armed,' I said.

'Of course,' he agreed. 'There would be little point in you being there otherwise.'

Any of Bobrik's men who just happened to be around the terrace in mufti would also be armed, of course. It wouldn't be plain sailing, or shooting.

Something else on my mind was what I could possibly talk

about over dinner to a woman I didn't know, and had never even met, in such testing circumstances. That was a worry, too.

Leon and I slipped away from the boat in the dusk of early evening. Others went before and after us, left and in most cases returned, to create a sense of movement to confuse anyone who might be watching. We timed our own departure to coincide with a flood of tourists from one of the big cruise liners in the harbour. It would have been a challenge for anyone watching to spot us.

Once inside the town walls, we walked briskly, threading our way through some very narrow lanes and alleys. Leon seemed to know the place well. No doubt he had spent some time in this town. Even so, I was surprised by how confident he was. After the shooting of Yuri, I saw dangerous shadows everywhere. Dangerous looking people, too. But Leon was like an old-fashioned cavalry officer, eager to confront danger head on, and in the open.

He paused in a quiet street and glanced around. There was no-one else in sight. We stood in silence for a moment, waiting and listening. Someone, somewhere, whistled, a soft single note that echoed briefly between the walls.

Leon touched my arm. 'My man, Petr,' he said. 'We have not been followed.'

Then he turned to a recessed doorway in deep shadow. We passed through and began to climb stone steps.

On the third floor, he used a key to go through a heavy door that led to another corridor, and possibly another building. He strode briskly along. I followed, thinking this reminded me of his hotel in Prague. I had no doubt now that we had entered another of Leon's many properties.

He tapped softly on a door at the end of the corridor and then used a key to open it, calling a quiet greeting as we entered the apartment. Once inside, the door locked again behind us, he led the way into a living room.

There, he paused, chuckled at me and said, 'Meet your lady for the evening, Frank.'

It took me a few moments to recognize her. Then I stared with astonishment at the figure that had risen from a chair to greet us.

'Hello, Frank,' she said with an amused smile.

Chapter Sixteen

'OLGA! HOW DID YOU get...?'

'Lenka brought me,' she said with a smile. 'She thought I might be useful.'

'But we left you in England.'

'The Podolsky family has more than one little plane, Frank.'

She was laughing at me now. It was a huge joke. To me, it was a huge deception. The whole lot of them were at it, the entire family. I was more than a little pissed off.

I turned to Leon. 'Is this a good idea?'

'Olga being your companion?' Leon said, smiling. 'Yes, I think so.'

'Do you disapprove, Frank?' Olga asked archly.

I slumped into a chair and stared from one to the other of them, wondering what to say, and what to do. 'This is a very serious and dangerous situation, Leon. Yuri has been killed already. You and Lenka will be at serious risk tonight. Now Olga, too, and she is not ...'

I stopped. I had been going to say she was not a suitable person to thrust into the firing line. But I couldn't bring myself to do it, not in front of her.

'They know you, Olga,' I pointed out. 'If you are with me on that terrace, we won't last two minutes.'

She shook her head. 'Bobrik doesn't know me, and the people who abducted me are no longer with us, as you know.'

That, at least, was true. She didn't seem troubled by the thought either. Tough lady, despite appearances.

'Frank,' Leon said, 'you didn't recognize Olga at first. I watched your face. So her disguise works well.'

That was true, too. Her hair colour was dark brown now, instead of straw blonde. She was dressed smartly in fashionable city clothes, instead of the retro hippy-style stuff I'd seen her wearing previously. She wore high heels, too, instead of winter boots. The difference all that made was huge. So maybe Bobrik and his thugs wouldn't spot her after all. Maybe.

'We haven't much time,' I said wearily, with a glance at my watch. 'Get your stuff together, Olga. Let's move.'

It was early when we arrived. Six thirty. The restaurant was almost empty. On the outside terrace, where the meeting was to be held at 7.30, only two of the dozen tables were occupied. At one of them, half a dozen American tourists were enjoying themselves noisily, making the most of their holiday in such an historic place. Two couples who might have been locals, but were probably also visitors, were at the other table. They looked as if the evening chill was getting to them, despite the umbrella overhead and the nearby presence of big patio heaters.

The Maitre d' who had greeted us was leading the way out onto the terrace but I stopped him. 'It's a little cool this evening,' I pointed out. 'My wife would prefer to be inside, I think.'

'Certainly, sir.' He spun round and asked, 'Which table do you prefer? At this time of the evening you can choose.'

I chose a table with a view of the terrace through a big window. It was just one over from the aisle accessing the terrace. Olga seemed puzzled. I smiled confidently, inviting her to trust me.

She had probably expected to be close to the table marked "Reserved", out there on the terrace, close to where the action would be. Tactically, though, that would have been a poor choice. Here, where the Maitre d' was seating us, was a much better position.

However the meeting went, the participants would not engage in a shooting match. I was confident of that. For one thing, none of them would be armed. So I didn't need to be that close to them. Because of the weather, the big umbrellas and the difficult light,

I ruled out a sniper up on the cliffs above the restaurant. Any danger would probably come from back here, where we were going to sit. Any attackers would need to come past us and go through the door onto the terrace. They would then have me behind them, ready to intervene.

Well, that was the idea, the plan.

'You think it is better here?' Olga asked anxiously after the Maitre d' had departed to find us a wine waiter.

'I do,' I said firmly. 'Anybody going to intrude on the meeting would need to come past us. I'm here to stop that.'

She looked doubtful for a moment. Then her face cleared and she smiled. 'You have done this before, I think.'

'Well, not exactly this, but ...'

'So you know what you are doing,' she said with satisfaction.

'I like to think so. This is the kind of stuff I do for a living. Security, protection and so on.' I shrugged and added, 'Amongst other things.'

'It is why my brother trusts you. I trust you, too.'

'I'm pleased to hear it,' I said, grinning.

We ordered a bottle of a Montenegrin red from the wine waiter, and a salad starter and grilled fish with a name unknown to me. Two or three couples wandered in to take tables, in one case on the terrace itself. None of them looked like a threat. We stayed calm, if not exactly relaxed, and waited.

The waiter returned with a bottle. He poured a little. I approved it. Then he filled both our glasses with the red, and two more with water. The civilized preliminaries observed. I toasted Olga, and we smiled happily at one another, the way couples out on the town for the evening generally do.

'But I won't be drinking the wine,' I said quietly. 'Not tonight.'

Olga nodded. She knew what I meant. I needed to stay sharp.

'So what's a nice girl like you doing in a dump like this?' I asked.

She had the grace to laugh and pretend it was funny. I was grateful for her effort. We couldn't afford to look like anything other than happy visitors.

'I used to like it here,' she confided. 'Then things changed.'

'This feud with your brother's ex-buddy?'

She nodded.

'What's it about? Do you know?'

'Greed, I think. And power. Things have not been good for several years.'

So it seemed. Whatever the origins of the trouble, the effects had been dramatic. Still, I didn't want to go any further into that now. History was for another occasion. That kind of history, at least.

'This town must have an interesting story to tell?' I suggested. 'It seems to be a very historic place.'

'Oh, yes. It is.'

She told me the same story I'd heard from Leon. That was OK. We couldn't just sit in silence. Besides, Kotor really was a place with a lot to talk about.

'The French had it for a while,' she said. 'Then... Oh, here they come, Frank!'

'Who?'

'The French were not here too long, though,' she continued with remarkable self-control, one eye on me and the other looking over my shoulder. 'Then I believe the English captured it from the French.'

'Who's coming?'

'Leon and Lenka. Only them.'

I nodded. So Leon was here first. Not a good move. I hoped they wouldn't go straight out to the terrace. I didn't want him and Lenka sitting out there alone, big juicy targets for a sniper on the rock wall behind the restaurant despite the poor light.

But Leon knew that.

'They have paused,' Olga said. 'They are waiting.'

'For Bobrik,' I said quietly. 'Leon will want the four of them to go to the table together.'

Olga stared pensively at me. 'This really is dangerous, isn't it?'

I shrugged. 'We'll see. Maybe not. Maybe they will settle their differences.'

81

'I think not.'

Well, there was nothing I could do about that. We would just have to sit here and wait. And hope. Maybe the killings that had taken place so far would turn out to have been enough.

'The others have arrived now,' Olga said calmly. 'Tell me about your life in England, Frank. I would like to know.'

We had to talk about something. So I began to tell her about my home at Risky Point on the Cleveland coast. As the four participants in the meeting approached, I told her about how I made my living from security work and private investigations. She appeared fascinated but I couldn't believe she heard a single thing I said.

'Now,' she said, her smile broadening deceptively into happy laughter.

I nodded but didn't look up as the four of them came past and stepped through the doorway and out onto the terrace, ushered by the Maitre d' and a waiter. Clearly, they were known, and favoured guests. Some of them, at least. But for how much longer?

'Anybody else?' I asked.

She shook her head. 'Are you the only person who lives at Risky Point?'

'Not quite. I have a neighbour.'

As I watched Leon and company get settled at their table, I told her about Jimmy Mack, a semi-retired fisherman who lives in the other cottage at Risky Point. Once, before coastal erosion took its toll, there was a small village there. Now there are just the two cottages left, and Jimmy and I are the only inhabitants.

'It would be wonderful to live close to the sea again,' Olga mused.

'The sea there isn't like it is here,' I said with a chuckle. 'It's cold and rough most of the time, even in summer. You need warm clothing most of the year when you're on the beach at Risky Point.'

'Even so,' she said with a sigh.

Discussions out on the terrace had begun. They were not going well, though. The four of them were too animated, seemed too argumentative. I winced inwardly. My guess was that they wouldn't even bother ordering a meal.

'Who is the guy with Bobrik?' I asked. 'Do you know?'

Olga shook her head.

'You said *again*?' I queried, picking up on what she'd said a minute ago. 'Did you once live close to the sea?'

'Oh, yes! Our family did. We grew up in Odessa.'

'Nice.'

'You have been there?'

I shook my head.

'It is lovely there, and also very historic.' She paused. 'Frank, two more men have entered the restaurant. They are coming this way.'

That didn't sound good. I steeled myself.

Chapter Seventeen

As THEY SWEPT PAST I could see they meant business, but they weren't interested in us. They were heading for the terrace.

I stood up fast and closed in behind them in the doorway. The guns were out by then, theirs and mine. Beyond, out on the terrace, I saw that the meeting was over already. Leon and Lenka were both on their feet and turning away from the table. Bobrik had summoned his men. It was not a time to mess about.

I swept my foot around the leg of the guy immediately in front of me. He lost his balance and fell forward, instinctively clutching at the lead guy as he went down, and unbalancing him. I jumped heavily on the hand holding the gun and felt it break beneath my boot.

Then I reached out, grabbed the lead guy by the collar of his jacket and jammed the Glock into his back. 'Drop the gun!'

It was really too late to be issuing a warning, even if he understood what I'd said. He was swinging round at me, his gun searching for the target, and he wasn't going to stop now. I pulled the trigger and shot him. He staggered away a couple of paces and brought his gun up again, aiming at me. I shot him a second time and took the gun from him. Then he went down for good.

'Frank!' Olga screamed.

I spun round. The man with the crushed gun hand was back on his feet, the gun held in his other hand. He was slow, uncertain, unfamiliar with left-handedness. I pointed the Glock at him, willing him to be sensible. He stared at me a moment and then lowered his gun.

I pointed again, ordering him to drop the gun. Reluctantly, he did so. Then I told him to get down on the floor. He did that, too, probably bringing his career with Bobrik to an end. As Leon and Lenka came past, Lenka picked up his gun and kicked him in the face for good measure. She didn't bother with the other one. He was dead.

A woman somewhere in the restaurant screamed. It broke the paralysis that had descended on everyone. Crockery crashed to the floor. Chairs scraped. Men shouted.

'Let's go!' Leon called, pressing his arm behind my back to hurry me up, and grabbing Olga by the arm.

I glanced back at Bobrik and colleague, who had got to their feet but were not coming after us. Then I turned and followed the others.

We encountered no opposition on our way out. But we did find the man Leon had delegated to do the body search on his behalf. He was in a heap near the entrance, shot, and dead. Leon checked him quickly and then urged us onwards again. We hit the street a second or two later.

But it wasn't over yet, not by a long way. To my surprise, we didn't head for the quayside and the yacht. We turned in the opposite direction.

'Leon?' I managed.

'It's not safe,' he shouted. 'This way!'

Almost as soon as the words were out of his mouth, a huge explosion ripped through the night sky. I ducked automatically and then paused momentarily to look back.

'Frank!' Leon called.

I guessed what it must be.

'*Samarkand*?'

Leon nodded grimly. Then all four of us were running hard away from the harbour, the sound of our racing feet echoing back to us from the medieval walls lining the narrow streets.

I assumed we would make for the apartment where Leon and I had met Olga. We didn't. After a couple of minutes, we turned a corner and stopped running. Then we walked quickly on, threading our way through the ancient streets and alleys until we came to another gate in the town wall. On the far side a Range Rover was waiting, its engine quietly murmuring. It might have been the same vehicle, and the same driver, that had brought us to Kotor, but I couldn't be sure.

We got inside and Leon rapped out instructions to the driver, who nodded and got us moving immediately. I wondered what would happen now. I had no idea, and for the moment I didn't care, either. I just wanted to get the hell out of Kotor.

'You did well, Frank,' Leon said. 'Thank you once again.'

I grimaced, thinking I wasn't so sure about that. Shooting people wasn't my usual style.

'I nearly left it too late,' I said. 'It all happened so fast at the end. What was going on?'

'I refused to give Bobrik what he wanted. So he said that was the end of the discussion, and we would be dead before we got out of the building.'

Nice guy, Bobrik.

'And he also told you what would happen to the yacht?'

Leon grimaced. 'I guessed that part. It is how he is. Now you must excuse me, Frank. I have phone calls to make. There is much for me to do.'

'OK. But first tell me where we're going.'

'The airport. We will leave immediately.'

If we still could, I thought. Maybe we would find our plane surrounded by tanks and machine guns. Then what? But trying to get out was obviously the right thing to do.

85

'If it is not possible to leave from there,' Leon added, reading my mind, 'we will turn around and head for Croatia. It is not far along the coast, and there they don't like Serbs like Bobrik so much.'

Another ex-Yugoslav country, one with a different history. Hopefully, more welcoming, too.

Leon pulled out his phone then and made the first of many calls. I guessed he was checking on his people, and on his businesses. His world had just fallen apart a little more, and he was doing his best to cope with the aftermath.

I switched off and let the adrenaline die down. I didn't feel good about what had happened back there, but I wasn't going to dwell on it. Not now, not yet. The guy I had shot would have shot me a moment later, and if I hadn't stopped the pair of them right there and then, Leon and Lenka would no longer have been with us. There wasn't much doubt about that.

Losing the yacht didn't bother me too much, either. Leon could probably just buy another one, if he wanted to. The people aboard at the time were a different matter. There must have been quite a few casualties, but there was nothing I could have done to avert that. So there was no point me worrying there, either.

Even so, I wasn't happy. Far from it. Our visit to Montenegro had been a disaster, yet another one to strike the Podolsky empire.

I concentrated on what was happening now. Not in the spirit of mindfulness, exactly. More because now and the very near future might be all the time we had left.

The cloud had lifted and the land was bathed in moonlight. I could see now how extraordinarily mountainous the country was that we were driving through. In the eerie light, we climbed and corkscrewed our way through a bleak, rocky landscape, until finally we crested a ridge and began the long descent down the other side of the mountain.

Lights began to appear in the distance. Civilization? I fervently hoped so. But what else might we find? An army road block and men looking for us with machine guns seemed a strong possibility.

It didn't happen. The army wasn't there. Maybe Montenegro

didn't have one, I couldn't help thinking with relief. There was no special police presence, either. And Leon's plane was ready, engines running, waiting for us.

I was very happy to climb out of the Range Rover and get into the plane. The drive through the mountains had been a bit hair raising, especially given that I was anticipating a road block around every corner. But Leon had done well, and got us out of there before anyone could organize to stop us.

'Will Bobrik be looking for us in Kotor?' I asked as the plane rose above the lights and headed for the safety of the cloud ceiling.

'I think so,' Leon said, nodding. 'We needed to get out fast.'

We had certainly done that, and now we could relax a little and count the cost of our expedition to Montenegro.

'So what's the damage?' I asked, nodding at the phone still in his hand, which must have been red hot by then.

He shrugged. 'It is not yet certain. The crew and captain were ordered off the boat before the explosion. So maybe they are all OK. But I don't know for sure. They will tell me later.'

That was something. We were badly in need of some good news.

'So what now, Leon?'

'I have been sending out instructions to my people to close most of our businesses down for the moment. Put them into suspension. We must sort out this problem with Bobrik before any more lives are lost.'

Amen to that. I couldn't have agreed more. It was a relief to hear him say it.

'And us?'

'Us? I think Lenka and me will return to Prague for the moment. You will go to join Olga in England, to the house in Northumberland. Work there should begin now. Maybe, also, you can visit our IT centre in England.'

'Oh? I didn't know you had one.'

'There is much you don't know, Frank,' he said with a wry smile. 'And the time is coming when I must tell you more.'

That would be nice, I couldn't help thinking.

Chapter Eighteen

WHEN OLGA AND I left the plane at Newcastle Airport in the middle of the night, we were met by a man I hadn't seen before and ushered into a waiting vehicle for the journey north. Olga introduced the man as Dag. She began talking to him in Russian immediately, and I let them get on with it. There would be plenty for her to tell him – though not, perhaps, everything – and I needed to rest and think. A lot had been happening lately.

It bothered me that I didn't really know what was happening. Two powerful Russian businessmen were engaged, literally, in a deadly conflict. The one I was helping seemed to be the innocent party. Perhaps I should just focus on that. But it would have been nice to know what the other side, "the enemy", wanted out of all this.

Whatever it was, Bobrik was waging a pretty determined and bloody campaign to get it. My feeling was that it couldn't just be about a small hotel in Prague, or property in Montenegro, either. It was more likely that it was about something to do with Russia itself. I had no idea what. I would just have to wait for Leon to tell me. But when?

Olga turned to me at last. 'Dag says we will be there in about an hour. Maybe less.'

I nodded. 'Fine.'

'It will be good to see the old house again.'

'Yes,' I said after a moment's hesitation.

'What?' she said with a chuckle. 'You don't like it?'

'Olga, at this moment, I would like anywhere that could offer me a hot bath and a comfortable bed – even that falling-down old house!'

'Poor Frank!' she said, giggling. 'We have made you so tired.'

I smiled, but I didn't really feel like it. Too much had happened, none of it good, since I had last slept. My wounded body was stretched, and aching and sore. My spirits weren't too good, either. I had killed a man just a few hours earlier. Admittedly, it had been him or me, but still....

So I wasn't in a celebratory mood. I would rather have been going home to my cottage at Risky Point, in Cleveland, than to a mouldering old dump in north Northumberland. That was how I felt just then.

Several of Leon's staff were in occupation at The Chesters, as I learned the house was called. They seemed to be a sort of advance guard, there to protect and help Olga, as well as to look after the property. One man seemed to be the specialist renovation man. Others were perhaps security guards, labourers, general dogsbodies. Men who were trusted, anyway, and part of Team Podolsky. They were a quiet, friendly bunch, and seemed pleased to see us return. I could get along with them, I soon decided.

The part of the house that was habitable was actually quite comfortable, probably because the original owners had lived in it themselves until very recently. Then Leon had made them an offer that had caused them to drop whatever it was they had been doing, grab the money and flee – no doubt to somewhere warm and dry, where the wine was inexpensive, and where olives and oranges grew on trees. No doubt they had had enough of living in penury in a stately home that had seen far better days. Not everyone can afford to keep an ancient pile in the condition it deserves, and that English Heritage require.

Olga herself showed me to a bedroom, and then asked if I was hungry.

'Tell you what, Olga. I'm going to get some sleep, and then in an hour or two's time – say about eight o'clock – how about we have breakfast together?'

'You're tired,' she said, nodding appreciatively.

'And so must you be. Let's both get some sleep before we talk or eat. OK?'

'That's very wise, Frank.'

I didn't know about wise, but it seemed a sensible thing to do. It was also about all I was capable of doing anyway.

Far too soon, I woke to the sound of the wind rattling the big sash window in my room. It sounded like a noisy little storm was approaching. I lay still and listened for a couple of minutes, luxuriating in the warmth and softness of the bed, and with no inclination at all to bring my time in it to an end. I could have done with a lot more sleep.

This wouldn't do, I decided reluctantly, having glanced at my watch. Just about eight already. I pushed the quilt aside and got myself upright. There was a bathroom a couple of doors along the corridor from my room. So I collected a towel and cautiously opened the door, ready to see if a hot shower was a possibility.

As soon as I got into the corridor, I realized that everyone else was probably up and about already. I could hear happy, comforting sounds from the kitchen. People were rattling pots and laughing indecently loud at such an hour. I was in danger of missing out on whatever was going on.

I frowned and decided there wasn't time for a shower. A splashed face would have to do for now. Anything more than that could wait until I'd found some clean clothes. The ones I was wearing looked as if they had been stolen from corpses on a battlefield.

'Here you are, Frank!' Olga exclaimed. 'Did you sleep well?'

'For two hours, yes, thank you.'

I stared at her. She was suspiciously fresh and relaxed looking. 'How do you do it, Olga? You've had no more sleep than me, and just look at you!'

She shrugged. 'It was enough. I am too excited to sleep anyway. I can't wait to get started with our project. This old house has waited so long for someone like me to come along.'

I had to smile. Her enthusiasm and good spirits were infectious.

'For now, Frank, Petr is our cook. What would you like for breakfast?'

I settled for scrambled eggs, toast and coffee. Petr, who spoke a little English, was happy to oblige. In fact, he seemed happy to have another customer. Perhaps cooking was the best part of his day.

As I tucked in, Andrei, another of the Russians arrived. This one was the architectural expert. He spoke excellent English, and admitted to having earned professional qualifications in London. We spoke briefly. Then he dragged Olga away to look at some plans and drawings. He seemed to have been around for a while, no doubt nursing the project along until a Podolsky arrived on the scene.

I met two other resident Russians. They seemed to be there to operate as general help, which designation no doubt included a security brief. One, Dag, had been our driver to and from the airport. Milan I hadn't seen before. They both looked fit and capable men. No doubt, they wouldn't have been there otherwise.

Leon must have had a word with them about me, because they seemed to accept implicitly that I was their boss when it came to security. They nodded gravely when I told them to continue doing what they had been doing until now, and that I would speak to them again when I had had a look around and decided what else needed to be done.

That done, and breakfast out of the way, I took myself off on a tour of the house and grounds. I needed to see what I had let myself in for. I suspected strongly that it would turn out to be more than I had realized when I accepted the job. The Podolsky world, I had come to understand, was like that: complicated.

Chapter Nineteen

IT HAD ONCE BEEN an imposing house, The Chesters. Horse-drawn carriages ferrying wealthy and important people would have raced up the gravel drive, and come to a halt on the gravelled circle in front of the impressive entrance. Liveried servants would have rushed out to greet the new arrivals and usher them indoors to the warmth of the great hall, where a log fire would have been blazing halfway up the chimney. Furs and hats, and full-length coats, would have been shed and warming drinks served. (Mulled wine, perhaps?) Then they would have been whisked away to the many rooms in the vast stone edifice that had defied Northumbrian winters for the best part of 1,000 years.

It wasn't like that now. When I first inspected it, the house had a roof still to cover most of the main section and one of the two wings, and the walls were upstanding. Some of the windows had glass in them, too. But the good news stopped right there.

Apart from the wing we were using, much of the interior had deteriorated to such an extent that the house was pretty well a ruin. Ceilings had collapsed, staircases come away from walls, floors had buckled, and doors sagged on broken hinges. Overall, the building was damp, decidedly wet even, in places, and it smelled of mould and decay. It was really depressing.

Only the west wing, where we were installed, was at least partly habitable. The rooms I had seen there so far were fine, to be fair, but they numbered a mere dozen or so. The house's other ninety-odd rooms had long ago been abandoned.

Having made a quick overall tour, I stood in the disused main entrance hall and considered what I had learned and seen. I wondered what Leon had paid for the place – and why he had. What on earth was he doing here? Was it a bolthole, some sort of safe refuge for if, or when, things got too hot for the Podolsky clan in Europe? I recalled him suggesting as much to Lenka at one point.

If he really was intent on putting the place to rights, though, it was going to be a big and expensive job. At a guess, it would cost him several million in sterling. Double figures, probably, by the time the conservation guardians had had their say.

It would take time, too, a lot of time. Architects and designers would need to be brought in to do their stuff. Then there would be local authority planners and building inspectors to satisfy. English Heritage, too, given the consents needed for anything to do with an historic building, which was what The Chesters very definitely was. And all that was before anybody even spoke to a builder.

Some of the preliminary spadework might already have been done, of course. But had it? I shook my head. No idea.

What about the attendant publicity? It would be impossible to do all this work in secret. This was England, for God's sake! How did public openness and transparency fit in with Leon's business and security needs?

My feeling was that the Podolskys were either very brave or hopeless romantics – or very desperate.

Then it occurred to me that if the project was to be undertaken without his involvement becoming widely known, Leon was going to need a frontman. I wondered if he had someone in mind for the role. For a moment, I even wondered if it might be me. Why not? I was reasonably local, and he seemed to trust me.

Forget it! Ridiculous. I wouldn't do it anyway, even if he asked me.

Perhaps I was being too fanciful about his motivation, I thought. Leon was in the hotel business, after all, as well as in so much else. The Chesters could just be his latest project of that sort, a country house hotel in yet another foreign land. He probably already had some sort of arm's length company to front projects like this, one that was complete with experts to handle all the technical stuff and the public relations.

I smiled with satisfaction, and with relief, at having worked all that out. Then I got on with thinking about security arrangements. That was the job Leon had actually hired me to do.

I started at the outer edge of the house grounds, disregarding the farmland beyond that might well be part of the estate still. Somewhere like this you didn't want high security fencing topped with razor wire or a high-tech wall. That wouldn't be allowed by the planners. But you did need some sort of boundary marker that was both obstacle and deterrent, as well as a line on the ground.

I decided to recommend a heavy duty timber fence. It would have solid timber rails with a six-inch face securely fastened to posts at least as thick and sunk in concrete well below ground. The fence didn't need to be high and obtrusive. A couple of feet would be quite enough. That would stop conventional vehicles getting up close to the house. It would even slow down an attack by heavy-duty industrial or military vehicles, not that I was considering fantasy scenarios.

Such a fence wouldn't stop armed men, of course. For that, Leon was going to need an armed response unit on duty 24/7, backed up by a combination of CCTV and sensors. Good communications with people inside the building, too. I would leave it to him to decide how far to go down that road. Maybe he would feel the risks were negligible here compared with Prague or Kotor.

After that, he would be well advised to install bulletproof glass on at least all the ground floor windows. Good locks on the doors and windows were also essential. Then we would need to make sure there was no easy way into the building from the roof, which was a common mode of entry, even to museums and galleries, never mind hotels.

All this was pretty routine stuff for me in my capacity as a security adviser and consultant. Most of my clients wanted to protect business premises, often industrial facilities, but I had also taken on private houses and a few galleries and museums. What made this case different was the nature of the potential threat. I had not had to deal previously with people who were capable of machine-gunning a hotel and blowing up a millionaire's fancy yacht.

None of this would probably happen here, of course, but you couldn't rule it out altogether. So, as well as dealing with physical security issues, I also wanted to advise Leon on how best to organize his soft defences and develop contingency plans. All in all, there was plenty for me to think about.

When I felt like I'd done enough thinking for one morning, I decided to go and see what Olga was up to. She might have very different ideas about the potential threat level.

Chapter Twenty

OLGA WAS STILL ENGAGED with Andrei, the architect, when I found her. She looked up and smiled, and with what looked like a reflex defensive gesture, she moved a sheet of paper over a plan they were studying together.

'It's all right,' I told her. 'I won't look.'

She laughed, embarrassed. 'I'll show you the plans another time, Frank. By the way, Leon is coming back later today.'

'Oh? Anything else happened over there?'

'I hope not.'

I smiled and left them to it.

Leon was doing an awful lot of going backwards and forwards, I couldn't help thinking. He was going to wear himself out. If somebody didn't shoot him first.

He had a lot on his plate. There was no doubt about that. As well as damage limitation to his business and properties, he would be trying to work out how to stop further Bobrik attacks. I didn't envy him. The attacks were on such a broad front it was virtually open warfare.

As I wandered back outside, I wondered if Bobrik would ever bring the battle here. It seemed unlikely, but you never knew. You just couldn't tell. The man appeared to have unlimited resources, and had demonstrated an ability to deploy them effectively. Travelling for people like him and Leon was easy these days, as well. With their super yachts, these oligarchs could take their base with them – unless somebody blew it up, of course.

The more I thought about it, the less likely it seemed that Bobrik would give up after Prague and Montenegro. There was something he wanted very badly indeed from Leon. My feeling, my growing feeling, was that he would follow Leon to the ends of the earth to get it. That wasn't a comforting thought.

Trying to establish an effective security system for The Chesters wouldn't make much sense until I knew what we were up against. What could we expect? Burglary or a break-in were one thing, but a major armed assault would be something else altogether. I would do what I could, but I needed to know more about what was going on if I was to be really effective. I would have to press Leon again. What on earth did Bobrik want?

*

The Chesters was located in a small, sheltered valley that itself was an offshoot of the main River Tweed valley. Much of the land before you when you stood at the front entrance was flat farmland, part of the river's floodplain. Sheep and cattle wandered over it in numbers, but were kept away from the lawn and gardens by a ha-ha, an ancient, sunken trench, like a dry moat, lined with stone walls. I wondered if Leon was a farmer now, as well as everything else he was. It wouldn't have surprised me.

To one side of the house there was an old copse of woodland, a shelter belt of Scots pine to blunt the power of the wind that would no doubt sweep down the valley for much of the year. A hundred yards behind the house the land rose steeply to open moor. Low down on the slope there were thickets of gorse and bramble, hawthorn and stunted sycamores. Dark cloud, hill fog, swathed the upper slopes. The view would be lovely in May. Now, in November, it was an ugly mess that as Leon's security adviser I couldn't ignore.

I headed up the slope, to undertake a recce. I soon decided that if you wanted a good vantage point to monitor the house, you wouldn't be short of choice up here. Likewise for potential sniper positions. Otherwise, though? Well, given what had happened so far, perhaps not too worrying.

Bobrik seemed to favour the blitzkrieg mode of attack, full-on assault from troops equipped with heavy-duty vehicles and massive firepower. That was very definitely something you couldn't do from the hillside above the house. If he were to come at all, my guess was that it would be via the road up the valley, all guns blazing.

To satisfy myself about local geography, I studied an Ordnance Survey map I had borrowed from the house and pressed on up the hillside until I reached the moor. It was much as I had expected: sodden heather, mounds of dead bracken and patches of reed stretching away into the misty distance. The map suggested it would be much the same for about five miles, until you reached the next valley.

Bobrik wouldn't come this way – if he ever came at all. I turned to make my way back down. At least I knew now what it was like up here.

Back at the house, Olga offered me coffee and invited me to look at the plans she and the architect had been studying.

'We will repair the whole building,' she said, 'and make it like new again.'

'That sounds wonderful, Olga,' I said cautiously. 'But won't it be a big job?'

'Oh, yes! Very big.'

Her enthusiasm made me smile. She was really into this.

'So how are you going to approach it?'

'Well, Andrei has found some very old drawings and plans. We will use them to restore everything. First, we will fix the roof and the walls, and the windows, and then the detailed work inside the building can start.'

'When will this be? Next summer?'

'No, no! We will start immediately.'

'In this weather?'

'In this weather, yes. It is not so bad here, I think. A little wet, perhaps, but not so cold.'

'Very wet, Olga, and getting wetter – and cold enough.'

She shrugged, undaunted. 'Andrei says he will start by bringing in the builder to cover the whole house in ... in plastic?'

'Plastic sheets.'

'Yes,' she said thoughtfully. 'A timber frame with plastic sheets. Then the men can be dry while they work, and we won't need to wait until summer.'

I supposed they could do that. It made sense, if they wanted to get a move on. Working under cover would be more pleasant for the men, and it would allow them to replace the roof without the interior of the house getting any damper than it already was.

Again, though, thought of the cost made me shudder. A scaffolding frame for the entire building, to last many months, could set the Podolskys back half a million quid. Perhaps more. It was a good thing they weren't short of money.

I looked at the plans and studied the detailing for the windows and the entrance doorway. Fine sandstone carvings. Beautiful decorative work. Graceful stone pillars. It could be done, all right, but it would certainly cost plenty.

The only thing nagging away at me was the thought that these were not the plans Olga had seemed so anxious to hide earlier that morning. Those had been blueprints. These were not.

Over lunch, Olga apologized for not showing me around the property herself, and asked if I had seen everything I needed to see.

'I think so. I've got a good feel for the house now, and I have some ideas to present to Leon about security.'

'That's good. He will be pleased.'

'I need to know how the house is to be used, though. I haven't been told that yet, and I do need to know. It will affect my security proposals.'

'Leon,' she said firmly, nodding. 'Leon will tell you.'

I took some more of the delicious borscht soup Petr had made, and probed further. 'It's not just to be a family home, is it?'

'What makes you say that, Frank?'

'It's too big, for one thing. Even with all your staff, you wouldn't fill it. My guess is that it will be a country hotel. Am I right?'

For a moment, her face had looked clouded, anxious even. Now it cleared and she smiled. 'Yes,' she said. 'I think so.'

Well, maybe. But she had agreed so readily that I doubted it. More than ever, I wondered what they had in mind.

Perhaps, I thought, they hadn't even got that far. I wouldn't have been too surprised to learn from Leon that it was simply a restoration project – for both Olga and The Chesters.

Leon arrived that evening, looking and sounding cheerful. It was good to see him.

'Has Lenka stayed in Prague?' I asked.

'She has.' He sighed, shrugged and said, 'There is much to do there.'

I was sure that was true.

'Any comeback from Montenegro, or from Bobrik?'

'No, nothing. All is quiet.'

My guess was that Leon was working flat-out on some way of responding to Bobrik, but he wasn't ready to tell me about it yet.

'We should eat,' Olga interrupted any further conversation. 'Petr has been cooking all afternoon.'

'Wonderful!' Leon cried, his eyes sparkling. 'What have you got for us, my old friend?'

So that was that. For the moment, once again, business was sidelined.

Later, Leon took me aside to discuss what I had been doing.

'I've done as much as I can for the moment, Leon.'

I briefed him on my thinking, and he agreed readily to all of it.

'You've done well, Frank. So much progress in such a short time.'

'Well....' I shrugged. 'I do this for a living, Leon. It's not new to me. But I can't do much more until I know more about the threat level, and for that you need to tell me more about what's going on with Bobrik.'

'We have been at this point before,' he remarked with a mild reproof.

'You're right. We have. But my point still stands.'

I was determined not to let him put me off, or avoid the question, again.

'We need to talk about whether Bobrik is likely to come here, and what force he will bring with him if he does. If you're not prepared to talk to me about that, Leon, then frankly I'm wasting my time – and yours.'

He sighed. 'You're right. I should tell you more. Let's sit down in a quiet corner.'

We did that. Then Leon looked me straight in the eye and said, 'It's a fight to the death, Frank. Bobrik will not leave me alone until he gets what he wants, and I can't give him what he wants. So I must kill him, or be killed by him.'

He paused, and then added, 'We hope he will not come here. We hope he will not know about this place. But who knows? There, is that enough for you?'

'It's a start,' I said firmly. 'But it's not enough, no. What is it he wants from you?'

'Everything!'

'All your businesses?'

'And more. Otherwise he will lose the support of his biggest backer.'

'Who is...?'

'The man in the Kremlin,' Leon said with one of his engaging smiles.

'Ah!' I said after it had sunk in. 'I should have guessed.'

'Yes, Frank. Perhaps you should. Tomorrow we will make a journey, and then you will understand even more.'

Chapter Twenty-One

WE WERE AWAY EARLY the next morning. Dag was driving the Range Rover. Olga sat up front with him. I sat in the back with Leon, who was being very mysterious about the whole thing. I asked him once where we were going and got such an enigmatic response that I didn't bother asking again. This was a story he wanted to tell in his own way. So long as he actually told it, I didn't mind how he did it. I just wanted it done.

There was frost on the ground that morning. Overnight, the wind had fallen away, the rain had stopped and the sky had cleared. So now the fields and fence posts, like the road itself, all had a coating of glistening rime. Christmas card weather. Even Leon seemed to be pleased by the change.

'This is better,' he declared. 'Is it often like this here?'

'Our winters won't be the same as the ones you're used to, Leon. We don't have anything for more than a few days at a time. Rain, snow, frost, heat waves, we can get the lot – even in January.'

'Maybe that is better,' he said reflectively, as if he was

considering borrowing the English weather template and taking it away with him.

'Bobrik is back in Prague,' he added. 'He looks for me once more.'

'You need a way of putting a stop to it,' I said with a grimace. 'You can't go on like this. Innocent people could be killed next time.'

'No. You are right. Once, I thought he would tire and amuse himself some other way, but not now. He is a greedy man, and he is driven.'

I wondered what that meant. The conflict seemed to be about more than accumulating yet more wealth, of which both Bobrik and Leon appeared to have more than enough. If the Kremlin really was behind Bobrik, as Leon had said, then it was in some way political. That made it seem even worse.

I assumed we were heading into Newcastle but as we sped around the Western Bypass and kept going, I realized I'd got that wrong. Where to, though? I was damned if I was going to ask again. It was when we left the A1 and cut across country, past the Nissan factory in Washington, to join the A19 that I became suspicious. Surely he wasn't taking me home?

Later still, when we topped a rise and industrial Teesside, with the Cleveland Hills as the backdrop, came into view, I gave in and asked.

'Are we going to Middlesbrough?'

'Near there,' he said.

Got that wrong. Where, then?

'What's it like?'

'Where? Middlesbrough?'

He nodded.

It was a good question. What was Middlesbrough like?

On the spur of the moment, without notice of the question, all I could come up with was, 'An industrial town that's seen better days. Steel and chemicals built it, and the global economy has brought it down.'

Leon nodded. 'So I understand. The cost of making steel is

lower in India and Brazil, and even in Russia, than here.'

That summed up the economics of it better than I could have done. Now, and for some time past, "the infant Hercules", as Queen Victoria's Prime Minister, William Gladstone, once famously called Middlesbrough, was on its knees. It would come back, though. One day. Maybe. You had to hope.

At least it was a better place to live now that it wasn't covered in smoke from the blast furnaces and the forges, the coke ovens and the steam engines. People lived in better houses, as well, and were better fed and more healthy. Full time employment and prosperity? Well, you can't have everything, can you?

We turned off the A19 just past Billingham, close to the Newport Bridge, and ran along north of the river, through the old industrial villages of Haverton Hill, High Clarence and Port Clarence. We went to the edge of the modern industrial area of Seal Sands, where the petrochemical industries have let rip. Miles and miles of weird looking metal structures, stretching over the marshes and the area alongside the River Tees that in pre-industrial days was called Samphire Batts.

'Are we going to see if there's any seals around?' I asked him facetiously, puzzled by our route, and curious about our destination.

'I'm told there are still a few near the mouth of the river.'

'It's true,' I admitted. 'There's a nature reserve there they seem to like, and they still come up Greatham Creek. But what do you want to show me?'

Leon just smiled, infuriatingly.

We slowed to turn off the main road and then drove a hundred yards down an access lane and through a gate in a high security fence that the driver opened with an electronic pass. We parked outside a two-storey red brick building that had a lot of darkened, one way glass in the windows.

'What's this?' I asked suspiciously.

'You'll see,' Leon said with a chuckle.

I was growing tired of his little mysteries. I was close to wanting to get done and get away home.

'For chrissake, Leon! Where the hell are we?'

'This is my IT headquarters,' he said with a chuckle.

'Your *what*?'

'Come on! Let's look around. I haven't been here before, either.'

He strode off towards the front door. Mystified and disgruntled, if admittedly more curious than ever now, I followed.

Olga was alongside me, smiling happily at my display of impatience. 'Frank!' she chided gently. 'This is not like you.'

'Maybe not,' I grunted sourly. 'But I don't like being kept in the dark. I don't work that way.'

'Please be patient with us.'

'Yeah,' I said with a scowl.

At the entrance, I paused and looked back. Whatever the place was, I was impressed with the security I'd seen. Professionally speaking, someone had done a good job here.

The perimeter fence was more than it looked at first glance, a lot more. Just inside the high outer fence of strong steel-mesh, there was a low fence of heavy-duty steel girders set on steel posts embedded in concrete. That was not unlike my proposal for The Chesters, although I was proposing less visually intrusive heavy timber instead of steel, in deference to the rural environment and aesthetic considerations.

Inside the low fence stood another high fence, this one consisting of fancy-looking metalwork that was thick with sensors, cameras and lights. I didn't have that in mind for The Chesters, but it was good security all the same.

So you might be able to smash through the outer fence in a heavy vehicle but then the vehicle would be stopped by the steel girders. If you climbed over them and tried to tackle the inner fence on foot, your every move would be illuminated and recorded. For all I knew, you might be fried, as well, by the current that was undoubtedly running through the metal work. And you would probably bring a squad of security personnel along at the double.

Better to come in by helicopter, then. Except, when I glanced skywards, I could see the network of criss-crossing wires that would prevent it. I wondered if they could be retracted for an authorized landing.

I shook my head. 'Some security you've got here, Leon.'

'Not me. Martha. This is her baby, although she was following Olga's instructions.'

That name again!

'Martha?'

He just grinned and waved his electronic pass at the front door. With a hiss, the heavy steel door opened. I followed him inside, wondering more than ever who the hell Martha was.

Chapter Twenty-Two

IT FELT LIKE WE were entering a space capsule. The outer door hissed shut behind us, trapping us in a vestibule. Then Leon held up his pass again to get us through an inner door. I couldn't imagine the White House war room having better security than this. Leon didn't really need advice on home security from the likes of me.

I paused to gaze around once we were through the second door. We were in a big, open-plan room containing more computer screens than I had ever seen in one place. The screens were all alive. Not with pictures, but with text and numbers. Half a dozen young people moved between the screens and worked at keyboards. Somebody laughed. Laughter? Here? It seemed totally incongruous.

Leon wore an infuriating smile, and was obviously enjoying himself.

'OK, big shot,' I growled. 'You win. What's going on here? Is this where you calculate your wages bill, and work out your profits?'

'In part,' he said with a chuckle.

Then he pointed at a glittering hi-tech sign on one wall: **LEONOMICS**.

'*LEONOMICS*?' I said, feeling faint.

He just grinned again.

'This way, gentlemen,' Olga said, bustling past us.

'Come,' Leon said, taking pity on me. 'Let's hear what Olga has to tell us.'

We followed her up a staircase to an office that had a desk with a computer screen, of course, and some easy chairs set around a coffee table. The interior wall was full-length glass, giving a good view of what was happening down in the main room. A man emerged from a room down there, carrying a bundle of computer printout. He looked up, saw us and raised a hand in salute. Olga waved back.

'Is that Josef?' Leon asked.

'It is.'

'He's good?'

'Very good. The best,' Olga added.

Leon nodded thoughtfully.

'Sit down, please,' Olga said.

We did. Olga pressed an intercom button and said, 'Josef, can you have someone bring us some coffee, please? Thank you.'

Leon leant back in his chair, laced his fingers behind his head and smiled at me. Big shot!

'And all this is yours?' I said at last, trying hard not to sound impressed.

He nodded with evident satisfaction. 'All of it.'

'So what is *LEONOMICS*?'

'It's an online financial analysis company, with a global sub-scription service. We deal with inquiries from around the world relating to economies and markets – price movements, currency fluctuations, forecasts, and a lot of other things as well.

'People pay a standard subscription fee, for which they get a certain level of information and analysis. If they want more, such as custom-built reports, they pay extra.'

Well, he'd told me when we first met that he had global busi-ness interests. Now I could hear the ching-ching of coins dropping into the cash register. Every minute of every day, all around the world. The little hotel in Prague was no more than a hobby.

'I'm impressed,' I said reluctantly. Then another thought came to me. 'But you said you'd never been here before.'

'It's true. I haven't.'

He waited a moment, seemingly enjoying watching me trying to cope with that one as well.

'Tell him, Olga,' he said, feeling sorry for me.

Smiling, Olga said, 'The business, the company, has been in existence for a few years, Frank, but this building complex is new. I helped with the design, and we moved in just a few months ago.'

'Olga is our IT expert,' Leon said firmly. 'She knew what was needed.'

I nodded. 'So where was the business located before?'

Leon sighed ruefully and said, 'We have moved several times, and we may well need to move again at some point.'

I took a wild guess. 'Because of Bobrik?'

He nodded. 'Him, and others.'

'They want the business?'

'Not really. They just want to destroy it.'

I must have looked puzzled again because he said, 'Tell him, Olga. Tell him the rest of it.'

'The *LEONOMICS* business is not all we do here,' Olga said. 'In some ways it's not even the most important thing we do here.'

She broke off to take delivery of a tray of coffee mugs from a young woman. I waited, more or less patiently, wondering what on earth was going to come next.

'Cream?' Olga asked, looking up at me.

'No, thanks.'

'Sugar?'

'No, thanks.'

She poured sugar into Leon's coffee as if it were a highly desirable novelty, or something very rarely seen. Then she stirred it vigorously before passing the mug to him.

'So what else do you do here?' I asked.

'Hm? Oh, yes. We run an online newspaper for Russian readers.'

'Oh?'

Is that it, I was thinking. Another online newspaper. What's all the fuss about?

'Does Bobrik want that, too?'

Leon snorted and shook his head.

'No?'

'The man in the Kremlin doesn't like it,' he said slowly.

'Ah! So they want it shut down?'

This time Leon nodded.

'And they're using Bobrik to do it?'

'Exactly.'

We were getting somewhere at last. It was politics.

Olga chimed in then. 'What we do is important, important for Russia. In the long run, the country will be a democracy. We are trying to help that day come sooner rather than later.'

That set me thinking. How long was the long run? Longer than we would be alive, probably. Especially if the Kremlin wanted it shut down. The people in power in Moscow don't like political opposition, and they don't mess about. They never have done, not since Tsarist times.

'*LEONOMICS* pays for the newspaper,' Olga said. 'So the business is important, too. But the newspaper, the bulletin, is what we are really all about here. It offers people the right of free speech – dissidents, opposition figures, people who disagree with them, and people who disagree with everyone.

'In elections we take sides. We say who we support, and who we want to win. So, as well as a commitment to free speech, we make a stand. The people who read what we have to say like that. They appreciate it, and want more of it.'

And the Kremlin will hate it, I couldn't help thinking, and won't want any more of it. Might even move heaven and earth to put a stop to it. In fact, they were well down that road already.

'So, this place,' I said, waving an arm around. 'Here, in this area that was once called Samphire Batts. Maybe it's not permanent?'

'Probably not, no,' Leon agreed with a shrug. 'But then we

107

will move somewhere else. We have contingency plans. Samphire Batts, though?' he added thoughtfully. 'I like that. We can use the name.'

'Good luck!' I paused before saying, 'Now I think I'll just go home. Don't come to the door, Leon. I can find my own way from here.'

He looked disappointed.

'Leon,' I said gently, 'you can't take on a whole state, not that one anyway. They'll kill the whole bloody lot of us!'

'Well, they haven't yet,' he said with the old grin back in place.

'It is not so simple,' Olga said. 'The Kremlin doesn't have a single voice, however it appears from outside. It's a Tower of Babel. We give those who don't like what is going on hope, hope for the future.

'At present, there are people there – sons and daughters of the old KGB – who are using Bobrik to try to destroy us. So far they have not succeeded. We may close down somewhere, but then we pop up again, like ... like ...'

'In this country,' I said, seeing her uncertain frown, 'we say like dandelions.'

'Thank you, Frank,' she said without a hint of irony. 'Like dandelions. What are they?' she added with a frown.

I couldn't see that that had got us very far. Wordplay, when what the other side was using was swordplay.

'Frank,' Leon said, 'If we stop Bobrik, we take away their main weapon against us.'

'Stop Bobrik? You mean that?'

'I do,' he said grimly. 'It is our best chance. Maybe not for you, though. You were right. This is your chance to walk away from us and get on with your own life.'

It was true. Now he'd levelled with me at last, now I knew what was going on, and what the stakes were, I could take a sensible decision.

I thought about it. The money was one thing. Leon would pay me what I asked. I knew that. He already had, in fact. But this wasn't only about money. There was danger, and risk, too.

Probably more than I had ever encountered. Compared to the opposition, Leon was a pygmy warrior, and I was a grain of sand in the shoe. We were nothing, infantrymen – at best – standing up to tanks and battleships. Talk about a one-sided contest!

'In or out, Frank?' Leon pressed quietly.

There was an atmosphere in the room now that hadn't been there before. It wasn't a good one, either. They thought they knew what my answer was going to be. I was back on home soil now, and I owed them nothing. More than that, I was aware now of the scale of their undertaking. It didn't make sense. No good could come of what they were doing. It wasn't sustainable. Disaster was a certainty.

'Frank?' Leon said, sharply now. 'In or out?'

'In,' I said. 'Count me in.'

Chapter Twenty-Three

THERE WAS A SOMBRE atmosphere in the car on the way back to Northumberland. The driver, Dag, was pretty taciturn at the best of times, and now he really did take the opportunity to concentrate on the road. Leon was far away, no doubt concentrating on what he needed to do next. Olga was perhaps doing some complicated algorithm in her head. I had plenty to think about myself but I was still building a picture, and I needed to talk.

'Leon, I'm guessing The Chesters is being prepared as a fallback position, in case the IT centre at Samphire Batts gets hit?'

He pursed his lips and shrugged. 'In part,' he admitted. 'We need to have contingency plans. But first came the house. We wanted a retreat, and Olga liked the idea of refurbishing the old house when she heard about it.'

'Somebody told her about it?'

He nodded.

'Who?'

'Martha.'

'Who's that?'

'Does it matter?' he asked sharply.

I let it go.

A few minutes later I said, 'You've probably been in this position before?'

'Position?' he said, looking puzzled.

'Contingency planning: preparing for the worst, hoping for the best.'

'Oh, yes!' He chuckled. 'If Samphire Batts – as you call it – goes down the tubes, we must be ready. Like we were on other occasions.'

'Where were you based then?'

'Prague was last. Before that, other places. Bobrik hit us hard. But we were ready. So we moved.'

'To Teesside?'

'Yes. It was necessary, and if it becomes necessary again we will move once more.'

'Expensive business.'

He shrugged and lapsed into silence. It didn't last long.

'You see, Frank, we lost a lot of good assets in Russia. Confiscations, compulsory purchases at ridiculous prices, and so on. The state gradually wore us down. Some assets we managed to retain, but many were lost. Whole industries – chrome mining, for example. Uranium mining. We needed something that wasn't tied to a geographical location. We needed to be able to operate outside Russia with an asset they couldn't take from us.'

'Hence *Leonomics*?'

'Exactly. They don't even know about it. They know only about the online newspaper, *Leon's World*.'

'But they suspected something?'

'They knew I had to have a way of making money, although they didn't know how I did it. So they enlisted Bobrik to find out. They gave him immunity from prosecution for things they knew about him if he cooperated, and they promised to make his business life in Russia easier. So he cooperated.

'He found out some of what we were doing, but not all of it. And he suspects, rightly, that my dear sister, Olga, with her skills, is at the heart of it.'

'So that's why she was abducted?'

'I think so. We were lucky to get her back.'

I thought about what he had said and made a suggestion.

'Leon, if they know about the newspaper, surely they will discover *Leonomics* before long? The names are too similar.'

That worried him. I'd found a surprising blind spot in his thinking.

'Change the name,' I suggested. 'It's easy to do.'

He nodded and looked relieved. 'Why didn't I think of that?' he asked. 'Frank, you are a genius!'

'It's true,' I admitted. 'The man in my shaving mirror tells me that every day.'

Our laughter attracted Olga's attention. She turned to us, smiled uncertainly and said, 'The builders will arrive in three days.'

'The house,' Leon said with a grimace. 'They may find that, too, eventually, but we will be ready to move once more. They will not defeat us, not Bobrik, not Putin himself. We are strong. We will prevail!'

I didn't know about that. I wasn't so confident. But I certainly hoped he was right.

Later, at The Chesters, Leon came to see me. 'I'll be leaving first thing tomorrow, Frank.'

'So soon?'

He yawned and added, 'The business requires it. I could do with a rest, but....'

'Where to this time?'

He shrugged, as if to say that the least known, or said, the better. Again I let it go. Leon wasn't confiding in me as much as he had at first, but I could understand that. His life was spent on the edge, and the edge right now was particularly sharp. He would have a lot on his mind. I went easy on him.

'See to the security here, Frank. I trust your judgement on

what is required. Talk to the builder. Get him to order anything you need. Pay top prices if necessary. Time, speed, is very important. Oh, and make sure Martha knows what you're doing. OK?'

I nodded. 'Martha?'

'She's in charge here, or she will be when she arrives.'

He spun away from me then before I could ask any more questions. I stepped after him, but already his phone was out and he was talking to somebody else. I let it go again. I was cool, chilled – for now, at least.

Martha, eh? In charge. For somebody who wasn't here yet – who I had never even met – she seemed to be a very influential person.

Well, I thought philosophically, it looked like I was soon going to find out who she was at last. I couldn't wait.

Chapter Twenty-Four

FIRST THING THE NEXT morning, I set out to see Leon before he disappeared. I found him in one of the sitting rooms, in a whirlwind. Talking, gesticulating, ending one phone call, starting another. I waited patiently. In a quiet interlude he grinned at me.

'A lot of activity?' I asked.

He nodded. 'Chaos, actually. We put in a big shift last night, and we'll be putting in another today. My people at the IT centre are being run ragged.

'More problems with the US dollar, and with the US credit rating. The expectation is that Standard & Poor's are going to down-rate the US again.

'Meanwhile, of course, our friends in the Eurozone are not doing very well, either. So we have clients all over the world who are worried to death about where to move their investments to. So, yes, we're busy.'

I think that was when I realized that *Leonomics* really was a serious business, and not a tax dodge or just some egotistical little game for the Podolskys.

'What are you telling your clients?' I asked out of curiosity.

'It all depends on their particular circumstances, and on events as they happen. For a while, there, we were advising them to get into gold, but the price of gold spiked pretty high after Brexit. They'll not lose out, but gold isn't really such a great option anymore.

'Futures, we're telling them. Especially the basic foodstuffs – wheat, rice and so on. And oil, as well. That's started to go up again now OPEC is getting its house back in order.'

He shrugged, smiled and said, 'So what's on your mind, Frank?'

'A couple of things, Leon, security issues. I wanted to catch you before you leave. First, I'm concerned about patterns. You're going backwards and forwards between Prague and Newcastle. If that doesn't stop, someone over there will notice and wonder what's so great about Newcastle in winter.'

Leon nodded. 'I should have thought of that myself. Just too busy, I guess. Right. I'll use different airports – where?'

'Edinburgh and Carlisle come to mind. Then there's Leeds-Bradford. Manchester. Even Durham-Teesside.'

'OK. Anything else?'

'There is, actually. This Martha. Who is she – family?'

Leon shook his head. 'Martha works for me. She will manage the project. It's what she's good at. Talk to her when she arrives, Frank. Don't worry!' He glanced at his watch. 'Now I gotta go!'

And then he was gone, leaving me vaguely dissatisfied. That old thing about Russia came to mind: a riddle wrapped up in an enigma. You could apply it to Leon himself, as well as to his homeland.

Martha hit the ground running. She arrived at the same time as the builder and his main men, and was immediately pounced on by the architect and Olga. The whole lot of them went into conference in a room that had been set aside for the purpose. I stayed clear. My turn would come.

Initial impression? Martha was a ball of fire. Thirties-something, trim figure, tall, long dark hair – radiating energy in a brisk, no-nonsense way. She was in charge and knew it, and so did everyone else.

Not my kind of woman, but I could see the attraction for Leon. He wanted someone capable to run things here in the UK when he was away. It looked as though he'd found someone.

I had coffee in the kitchen with the two security guys assigned to me.

'Know her?' I asked.

Roman, who spoke a bit of American English, grinned and said, 'Sure. She's the boss!'

'So I understand. Is she Russian?'

He shook his head. Boris, the other guy, just grunted. So she wasn't Russian.

'What is she?'

They looked at each other and shrugged. They didn't know.

Having got that subject out of the way, I turned to more practical matters. I told them I wanted the two of them to monitor who came on site once work got started. Nothing over the top, but I wanted them to watch and count heads, and make sure who was who. I would talk to the builder and get started on some physical security.

They were experienced and capable men. I had no doubts about their ability to spot things that were not right, and people who were not what they seemed. Locally, between us, we could cover security around the house. It was what was going on in the wider world that worried me. I just couldn't believe that Leon's activities would be unseen by somebody connected to Bobrik. Russian intelligence agencies had always had a long reach.

'All will be good,' Roman said with confidence. 'Leon knows what he is doing.'

I hoped he did.

*

Martha found me gazing up at the hillside, wondering how easy it would be to get up and down it in the dark.

'Hi! I'm Martha. You must be Frank Doy, the security guy?'

She sounded English, southern English. So that was one question answered.

I admitted she'd got the right man, and we shook hands.

'Did Leon tell you I would be managing the project?' she asked, all business.

'Yes, he did. When you've got a spare half hour, I'd like to talk to you about the security arrangements I want to see put in place.'

'This afternoon, perhaps?'

'Sure.'

'It's going to be a busy day, Frank. I want to clear the way for the builders to start on site as soon as possible – tomorrow, hopefully. There's a lot to do. But I also know how important security is. So we'll talk again soon.'

Then she was off and away, already moving down the items on her agenda. My first impression had been confirmed. Martha had arrived like the proverbial tornado.

Chapter Twenty-Five

BY THE END OF the morning, preparatory work had started on site. I watched as the builder, James Cummings & Son, brought in men to erect scaffolding and tarpaulins. By the end of the day, *The Chesters* was pretty well cocooned in plastic sheeting, just as Olga had said was to happen. I didn't know if that was down to Martha or to an incentive scheme. Either way, work on the building could now proceed regardless of the weather.

True to her word, Martha called me in to see her during the afternoon. She had set up an office in a small room that had been disused until then.

Andrei, the Russian architect, gave me the nod. 'Martha

wishes to see you now,' he told me, making it sound like reporting to the headmistress's study.

'OK, Andrei.'

'Now,' he instructed, making it an imperative, and making me wonder if he'd had his head chewed off.

I smiled, decided not to react and went to see what the boss wanted.

She was immersed in voluminous paperwork already, but looked up as soon as I appeared.

'Thanks for coming in,' Frank,' she said.

'That's OK. We need to get at it.'

'I've been looking at the cost profiles and manning schedules,' she said without further preamble. 'They're both over the top.'

'Oh?'

'You've got two guys working security with you. I need one of them. Keep Roman. I'll use Boris.'

I grimaced. 'There's a lot to do here, Martha.'

'Indeed there is,' she said crisply. 'And I don't believe security concerns are top of the agenda right now, not out here in the wilds of Northumberland. We're running into the coldest part of winter in the next couple of weeks, and I want to make sure work is well under way by the time the snow comes.'

I shrugged and wondered how good she was at forecasting the weather. It didn't snow every winter, even up here.

'So what else do you need, Frank?'

I thought it best to focus initially on installing the hard security, rather than the soft stuff that people do.

'Well, I need to talk to the builders about the perimeter fence that we need to erect to stop an approach by vehicles. It will—'

'Leave that for now,' she said impatiently. 'We don't need that immediately. Let work on the house get started. Then talk to Cummings about it.'

'Leon accepted the need for it,' I said mildly. 'He told me to go ahead.'

She shook her head. 'Leon left me to manage the project.'

'Well, you're the boss,' I said with a shrug.

She nodded to confirm it, and then switched track. This was not going how I had anticipated.

'Then there's project costs. Your daily rate is on the high side, Frank. I want to cut it back some.'

I shook my head. 'That's my standard rate, and it was agreed with Leon.'

'Leon isn't as aware as he should be of local payment structures. We need to cut back.'

It was time to dig my heels in. 'It's not going to happen, Martha. That's my standard charge-out rate.'

'We're not paying you that much, Frank – and that's final.'

'You'd better find someone else, then.'

'That's easily done, Frank.'

'Then do it.' I got to my feet and added, 'Something you should know, Martha. I really don't need this job. I didn't want it in the first place. I'm only doing it as a personal favour to Leon and his sisters.'

'I don't see it like that,' she said with a shrug. 'Business is business.'

'Good luck,' I said, as I turned to leave. 'I hope it works out well for you.'

I left her to it. Strangely, perhaps, I wasn't particularly annoyed. Surprised, certainly, and irritated, but not indignant or outraged. Nothing like that. To be honest, Martha had done me a favour. As I'd told her, I hadn't been eager to take the job in the first place. So I could get my life back now.

There was no way I was prepared to stay anyway, not with Martha in charge, and already moving the goal posts. She might be a big operator in her world, but I never have been well suited to the ways of big business. It was one reason why I preferred to work for myself, rather than for someone who could offer me a pension plan.

Still, I thought ruefully, the money Leon had been going to pay me would have kept me afloat for quite a while. Pity about that.

It didn't take me long to pack my stuff. I didn't have much that was worth taking with me. There hadn't been much opportunity to replace what I'd lost at Leon's place in Prague. What little there was went into my pockets. Prague. I smiled wryly to myself. How long ago and far away all that seemed now.

That done, I went looking for Olga, to say goodbye. She wasn't there. Roman said she had gone into Newcastle with Andrei. So I shrugged and asked him to run me into the village five miles away. I would have preferred to get him to run me home, but I didn't want to risk him being reprimanded by Martha for exceeding the travel expenses budget.

Once there, I thanked Roman for his support and wished him well. He seemed surprised I was leaving at first, but soon recovered.

'Martha, eh?' he said with a sympathetic grin.

I returned the grin and patted him on the back.

After Roman had left, I headed into The Black Bull to dawdle over a pint and work out what I was going to do next.

Chapter Twenty-Six

I GOT SETTLED IN and had a meal in the bar. The place had a pleasant atmosphere. Local people having a quiet night out, for the most part. There was a football match on the telly for those who weren't interested in food.

I sat by myself in welcome solitude, reflecting on an extraordinary few days. Already it seemed like a dream, a bad dream much of it. I just hoped things would work out well for the people I liked who were still taking part in the dream. I would keep my eyes and ears open. Somehow, I would have to discover the outcome. I might even talk to DI Bill Peart, my old pal in the Cleveland police. Something was bound to break eventually. This was England, after all, not the Wild East.

The rattling of a nearby window told me it was turning into a cold, wet night. If I listened hard, ignoring the telly, I could hear the rain beating against the glass. In here, though, in this comfortable warm bar, it was heavenly. I didn't think many of the pub's customers would be leaving soon. Probably not for a long while. Me, neither. So I relaxed and enjoyed the sense of being off-duty. Then at 10.30 I called it a night and shuffled off to my room, well content.

I wasn't ready for sleep, though. Too much to think about, too many loose ends. So I sat in a chair and listened some more to the rain and the wind outside. What a night! I felt sorry for anyone who had to be out and about in it. No doubt there were a few hardy souls diligently pursuing their chosen calling. Shepherds perhaps, or a mechanic running a breakdown and recovery service. Fishermen, maybe. There were always people who had to be out even on a night like this.

Just as I was about ready to flop into bed, there was a brisk knock on the door of my room. What? Had I forgotten to tell them downstairs what time I wanted breakfast, or whether I wanted kippers or a "Full English"? I smiled wryly and got to my feet.

'Yes?' I said, opening the door. Then I stopped and stared with astonishment.

'Martha!'

'Good evening, Frank. May I come in?'

Without waiting for my reply, she stepped forward. I moved aside.

'What is it?' I asked. 'What have I forgotten?'

'What are you doing here?' she responded, turning to face me.

'Getting a good night's sleep, I hope.'

'Here?'

'This is fine. It was too late to go any further anyway.'

She nodded and glanced around.

'What do you want, Martha?' I asked impatiently.

'Come back to The Chesters with me.'

I smiled and shook my head. 'No way!'

'I would appreciate it if you would.'

I stared hard at her. She seemed to be perfectly serious.

'Look, Martha, you and I didn't hit it off, and I can't see that changing. You've got a job to do, and I'm happy to be out of something I never really volunteered for in the first place. Get someone else.'

She gave a big sigh and flopped into the only chair in the room. 'It's not that simple.'

'Oh, I think it is.'

She shook her head and sighed. 'I've just had my arse kicked by Leon. He said I have to get you back.'

'Or what?'

'Or look for another job.'

I laughed at that. It was the funniest thing I'd heard for a long time.

'It's not funny,' she protested. 'Leon meant it. I'm to give you an apology, let you do what you think fit, and assure you that you will be paid every penny of what you and he agreed.'

'Even though it's far too much, in your view?'

She shrugged but didn't say anything.

'Like I've told you, Martha, I don't want the damned job! I don't really care what the pay is. I don't want it. OK? I'm glad to be out of it – after some of the toughest, ugliest days of my life. I'm going home in the morning.'

'How will you get there?'

'What?'

'You haven't got transport, have you? How will you get there?'

'That's the least of my worries. Don't you worry about that. I'll sort something out in the morning.'

I wandered over to the window to give myself breathing space. I was angry now. I wanted rid of her. But how to do it without physical assault?

A big four-by-four went by. A Toyota, I thought, a Land Cruiser. It was followed by a truck, a pickup. What I would give for either one of them. At the moment I was stranded. How would I get home? Phone for a hire car, presumably. In the morning.

'How did you find me?' I asked over my shoulder.

'It wasn't difficult. I asked Roman where he'd taken you, and started from there.'

There weren't many places I could have gone, I supposed. The village had a pub, but not much else. Not even a shop. I wondered if the old stone church would still be open, but that would only be on a Sunday – and not every Sunday.

A couple of cars went past. Farmers returning home from a night in some other pub. Foresters even. What was wrong with their local? The Black Bull seemed fine to me. It had everything you could want – food, telly, dartboard, even beer.

'What do I have to do to persuade you to change your mind?' Martha asked. 'You seem to be important to Leon, and he wants you back on site very much. Do I have to grovel? Is that what you want?'

'You could always get yourself another job, Martha. Have you thought of that?'

She didn't answer. She was brooding. She couldn't get her own way for once, and didn't like it. She didn't know what to do about it, either.

'Leon said to pay you what you ask – give you a pay rise, if necessary.'

I sighed. It was exasperating. I couldn't get through to her that I was finished with the whole damn lot of them.

As another pickup went past the window, I wondered what the big event they were all coming home from had been. Something special, in late November. A pie and peas supper? The local hunt ball?

'You'd better go, Martha. You have my answer. I'm not going to change it.'

I turned away from the window and gaped with astonishment. Martha had removed her coat and sweater and now was unfastening her bra.

'Will this change your mind, Frank?' she asked, straightening up, her breasts pointing at me dangerously.

'What the hell...?'

'I mean it,' she said, stooping to pull down her jeans.

'For God's sake!' I grabbed the coverlet from the bed and threw

121

it over her. 'Get out of here!' I said angrily.

Then I turned back to the window, something suddenly jarring me even harder than the provocative sight of a wonderful female body.

'How did you get here?' I demanded.

'By car. How do you think?'

'Did you pass anybody on the road – any person or vehicle?'

'Of course not. There's nobody who lives up the valley. Not a single farm or cottage. Nothing until you get to The Chesters. Surely you know that?'

'We've got to go back,' I said, turning back to her. 'Get dressed!'

'What? What do you mean? You'll come with me, after all?'

'A whole procession of vehicles has headed up the valley while I've been talking to you, Martha. Where the hell are they going, do you suppose? Get dressed!'

She understood then. She grabbed her clothes and dressed quickly. We were out of there in two minutes.

'Do you think...?' she began as we headed for her car.

'No time for that,' I snapped. 'Let's just hope we're not too late.'

Martha drove. She knew the car and I wasn't about to ask her to surrender the keys.

'Who's there at the moment?' I asked as she let out the clutch and we took off.

'Andrei's there. And Roman and Boris.'

'Not Olga? Dag, Petr?'

'Olga's gone to join Leon in Switzerland. The men have gone to Newcastle.'

Thank God Olga wasn't there! So just the architect and my two guys. No-one else. Good, and bad.

Martha could drive. A car, I mean, as well as other things. I couldn't have got us up that road as fast as she did.

'What are you expecting to find?' she shouted over the noise of the racing engine.

'No idea,' I said, shaking my head.

That wasn't true. I was living on hope. My fear was that Bobrik had somehow discovered what was going on at The Chesters. If he had, what happened next wasn't in doubt: carnage and destruction. I just hoped it wouldn't be like that.

'You know the IT centre on Teesside?' I asked.

She nodded. 'Of course.'

'Heard from them tonight?'

'No. There was no reason.'

'Phone them.'

She glanced at me, and I could feel the question she didn't ask.

'Go on – call them!'

She fiddled with the phone set-up on the dashboard. It lit up and she pressed a speed dial button.

The phone began to ring. It rang for a long time before she stopped it. I felt her glance at me again.

'Who, or what, did you phone?'

'The twenty-four hour reception desk that's manned every day of the year.'

I grimaced.

'They should have answered,' she said, as she ripped through the gears and the engine roared.

'If things were OK, they would have answered.'

'It's connected, isn't it?'

To this, here, she meant. She didn't need me to reply. Things were looking bad.

As we clattered across a badly potholed section of road, she said, 'What the hell went on when you were away in Europe with Leon?'

'He hasn't told you?'

She shook her head.

'It's a long story,' I said, and left it at that. Leon could tell her what he wanted her to know.

I could see Martha's face clearly now, I suddenly realized. There was more light in the car. There was more light everywhere, in fact. I could see things off to the side of the road. Not well, but I could make out the outline of trees and walls. We rounded a bend in the road and I saw why. The sky ahead was lit up like a football stadium with a game in progress.

Martha braked to a stop. We both stared.

'Oh, God! It's the house,' she said aghast.

I didn't bother replying. My stomach had plummeted. I grimaced and felt sick.

We gaped for a few more moments. Then I said, 'Drive on, but slowly. Let's get closer.'

'Oh, the poor men!' she said breathlessly.

I didn't think there was much to wonder about in respect of them. Not now. Neither side was in the habit of taking prisoners in this war.

Chapter Twenty-Seven

WE FOUND THE FIRST body just before we reached the pinewood and the vehicles parked alongside the road. Martha braked. I got out to look. It was Boris. He'd been shot. There was a lot of blood on his chest.

'Is he dead?' Martha asked fearfully.

'Yeah. Turn the car round, ready to get out of here. I'll look a bit further.'

I made my way quickly along the road, flinching at times at the roaring and crackling of the fire. When I reached the edge of the wood, I stopped. I could see everything there was to see from there. The house was ablaze, and in the light from the flames, I watched the figures milling around in front of it for a few moments.

Their work was done now. They were getting ready to leave. It was hard to believe how fast they had been, and how quickly they had disposed of a thousand years of history. There were two more bodies on the grass in front of the house. I wasn't in any doubt who they were, or that anyone else in residence would have ended up the same way.

I turned and jogged back to the car. There was no time to

waste, not if we wanted to live. There was nothing anyone could do here now except sweep up when the flames died down.

I literally bumped into Martha. She clutched my arm as she emerged from the shadows of the wood. 'What's happening?' she demanded.

'I'll tell you later. No time now. We'd better get out of here before anyone spots us.'

As we turned a bend, I saw that we were too late. Not all the attack party were gathered around the house. Two or three figures were clustered around Martha's car. I grabbed her and pulled her back into the trees. A shout and torches pointed in our direction indicated we hadn't been quick enough.

The men began to move fast in our direction. Martha didn't need any persuading. I pulled her after me and we set off through the wood, changing direction as we ran. My one thought was that we couldn't afford to be caught. I knew there wouldn't be any discussion or argument. We would be collateral damage.

I found a path I recognized and we ran hard along it, desperation lending wings to our heels. The path took us the length of the wood. Before breaking out into the open, we paused a moment, both of us heaving for breath.

'You OK?' I gasped over my shoulder.

Martha nodded and said something that might have been a yes. I held on another second or two before we left the shelter of the wood, trying to listen for sounds of pursuit. It was impossible. The roar of the raging fire was all I could hear. They weren't close behind, but I didn't doubt they would be there.

The way ahead was clear in the light from the flames. I scanned the route up the hillside that I had scouted earlier. Back then, I had worried about strangers coming down it. Now the strangers had arrived, and it was our escape route.

I turned my face away from the heat of the fire and led the way across the open ground to the lower slopes of the hillside, running fast. To my relief, Martha seemed to have no difficulty keeping up with me. It was a desperate time. Any moment might bring discovery, and disaster.

As we climbed, I glanced back a couple of times without seeing anyone following close behind. I just hoped they'd given up. There was a chance they had. Their priority now would surely be getting out of there fast before people came to see what was going on. And there was no doubt people would come. The light from the fire would be visible for many miles, and at night especially there are always watchful eyes on the lookout for unusual happenings.

'Where are we going?' Martha gasped when we paused halfway up the hillside.

'Up to the moor,' I panted. 'We can get across. Five miles, and we're into the next valley.'

'What then?'

'No idea.' I gasped hoarsely, fighting for breath. I sensed she was thinking about her car, and I wanted to put a stop to that. 'We'll just have to see. Come on!'

She was still staring downslope.

'We can't go back down there, Martha. They'll kill us!'

'What about the others?'

'Dead. Tell you later.'

I was thankful she didn't complain or object. She got on with it then, and together we forced our way up the hillside. No flagging. Martha surprised me with her strength and resilience. She did well.

I looked back when we got to the top. There was no sign of anybody following, and we'd have been able to see them if they had been. The whole valley was lit up by the towering flames.

'That lovely old house,' Martha gasped. 'I can't believe it!'

Nor could I. But I just shrugged. I was in no mood to wax sentimental about The Chesters. Some good men had died tonight.

'What about my laptop?' she demanded, sounding distracted.

'Buy another one.'

'But it had all the plans for the house on it!'

'Well, they wouldn't be much use now, would they?' I said brutally. 'Think yourself lucky you're not down there with it.'

'My iPad, as well. And my clothes – my car!'

'For chrissake, shut up, Martha! We've got more to worry about than that.'

'Why? What do you mean?'

'Leon's enemies play for keeps. We're not safe yet. We've got to get away from here.'

'But where can we go?'

I shook my head wearily. 'A bit at a time, if you don't mind. Let's just get across the moor first.'

I was right about that. We didn't need to worry about much else for the next few hours. Once we were away from the edge of the escarpment, and the light from the fire, darkness closed in on us. Under low cloud, in the middle of the night, with intermittent rain, visibility was just about zero. I tried to keep us going in a straight line but it wasn't easy, or even possible in places. There were too many holes and ditches to fall into, boggy stretches to wade through, and other, sometimes unidentifiable, obstacles to overcome.

We both stumbled and fell many times, and we both got very wet. Thankfully, the temperature was not sub-zero, but in our condition and in the rain and wind, hypothermia was a real danger. As for the risk of broken legs and sprained ankles, avoiding them was going to be a matter of luck. We simply had to keep moving.

At one point, Martha fell heavily behind me. I winced, fearing the worst, when she yelped, and I turned to help her back to her feet.

'Are you hurt?'

'Not too badly.' She gave a brave little laugh and added, 'Why? What would you do if I was – leave me, or carry me?'

I gave her a hug to encourage her and said with relief, 'For the moment, that's a hypothetical question. I don't need to answer it just yet.'

'Oh? You're a prevaricator?'

'You bet!'

'You'd be no good as a manager.'

'Something I never aspired to be.'

'Just as well.'

127

'That's enough of that. Come on! Keep moving.'

The exchange seemed to have lifted us both. I smiled in the darkness. Who would have thought Martha had a sense of humour?

It took us over three hours to get across the moor. When I'd thought of the route as a possible line of escape, I'd estimated two hours max, but I hadn't reckoned on what it would be like in the dark on a wet night. I hadn't reckoned on Martha's company, either. Possibly I could have done it faster alone, and certainly I could have done it a lot faster in daylight.

Martha did well, though. Scarcely a complaint escaped her lips, and she kept going. I didn't bother asking about her feet, which were clad only in light shoes and bound to be wet and cold. Wet feet can be a serious problem, but there was nothing I could have done about hers.

Suddenly we found ourselves going steadily downhill on a broad, gravelled track. I couldn't really see it, but I could feel and hear it under my feet. It was a welcome change.

'Easier going than floundering through wet heather,' I remarked.

'A lot easier. What's that light, Frank?'

I'd had my eye on that for a couple of minutes. It looked like the external light on a farmhouse.

'Somebody must have forgotten to switch it off before they went to bed,' I suggested.

'Or they're up awfully early.'

She could be right, I realized. I'd lost track of time, but now it was the early hours, rather than late at night.

Martha was right. As we drew closer, I could see movement around a building, almost certainly a farmhouse. A dog barked. A door slammed. A vehicle started up. Then the vehicle moved towards us, and stopped. It was a van. A man got out to open a five-bar gate.

He saw us in his headlights and shouted, 'What are you up to?'

'You won't believe this,' I called back. 'We got lost while we were out walking – lost on the bloody moor!'

He studied us for a few moments before saying, 'Do you want a lift?'

My heart lifted.

'That would be great!'

'I don't believe it, either,' Martha whispered beside me.

We moved closer and waited for the man to drive the van through the gateway. I shut the gate for him.

'Thanks,' he said through the open window. 'Jump in. I know what it's like in these hills. No mobile signal, either, is there?'

'None at all.'

We both got into the van and joined him on the front seat.

'Don't bother about them,' he said, as I fiddled in the dark with seat belts. 'I'm going into Berwick. That any good to you?'

'Perfect,' I told him. 'Anywhere near the railway station?'

'I can drop you right outside.'

He glanced sideways at us and said, 'You'll have had a rough night, up there?'

'I don't even want to think about it,' Martha said quickly, 'never mind talk about it. It was the worst night of my life,' she added.

'Aye, well. We all have one or two of them behind us. You'll soon get over it.'

'You're up early?' I suggested, anxious to get the discussion away from us, and what we'd been doing.

'No more than usual. It's the job.'

'Oh?'

'I do a daily bread round for a bakery in town. 154 miles. Shops and hotels, and that. I start off at this time every day of my life, except Sundays.'

I began to relax. 'There was I, thinking you must be a shepherd, up this early.'

'I'm that, as well,' he said with a chuckle. 'I start on the shepherding when I get back from the bread round.'

'Lucky for us,' Martha said.

Amen to that, I thought. Better a workaholic than an alcoholic any day.

Chapter Twenty-Eight

IT WAS STILL DARK when we were dropped off at Berwick railway station. In the street lights Martha looked a mess. Sodden, exhausted and dirty, she looked very different to the woman who had landed at The Chesters with such an impact. I probably looked much the same, but in my case it wasn't so far from normal.

We thanked the driver and he waved us goodbye as he set off to start his day's work.

'What now?' Martha asked.

'What you do next, Martha, is up to you. No doubt you have ideas and plans, as well as responsibilities. Feel free to get on with them. Me? I'm going home.'

'So this is the parting of the ways?'

I just shrugged.

'Where's home – your home?'

'Cleveland.'

'And that's where you're going?'

'Just as soon as I can.'

I could see she didn't know what the hell to do. She was trying to get herself together, but it was a struggle.

'I have nothing with me,' she said plaintively. 'No money, no phone. Nothing! Just a bunch of car keys.'

'Maybe you'll find a car they fit.'

She grinned. At that point I stopped being awkward. She had nothing, while I had everything I needed in my pockets. Finally, I felt sorry for her. More than that, I actually had a grudging respect for her. She was doing her best, and had been ever since she had come to my room in The Black Bull to eat humble pie.

'I know we got off to a bad start, Martha, but ...' I shrugged, paused and then said, 'Why don't you come with me? Come back to my place, and have a rest and sort things out.'

'Home with you?' she said cautiously, sounding very uncertain about that.

'Yes. It's not much, but it is home – my home. You're welcome to be my guest, until you've sorted something out with Leon.'

'Thank you, Frank.' She hesitated and then stepped forward to kiss me on the cheek. 'In the circumstances, I would like to do that.'

I paid for tickets with a card and we caught a fairly early train that came through not long after. It was from Edinburgh, and bound for King's Cross. Many of our fellow passengers were headed for work, or meetings at least. Men and women dressed in conventional business suits who were poring over laptops, smart phones and the contents of briefcases. One or two were actually reading newspapers – real ones, printed on paper.

Neither of us seemed to have any taste or energy for small talk. It had been a long, hard night. So we sat quietly with our own thoughts and stared out of the window until we got off at Newcastle, and took the Metro to the airport.

'Cleveland, Ohio?' Martha asked.

I smiled and shook my head. 'I want to pick up my car. It's in the long-stay car park at the airport.'

'Isn't it expensive to keep your car there?'

'Very.' I shuddered at the thought and added, 'I'm going to send the bill to Leon.'

'Because? What's Leon got to do with it?'

'It's a long story.'

'You said that once before.'

'Well, for now, let's just say he diverted me. Without his intervention the bill would have been quite modest.'

She nodded and settled back in her seat. 'I'm really looking forward to hearing the long story,' she said, closing her eyes.

I could have bought Martha a ticket to London, and got rid of her. Once there, she would soon have been able to re-orient herself and get back to what she did best. Possibly. That is, if someone didn't shoot her on the street where she lived first. Bobrik had proved he had a long reach, and I wouldn't have been surprised if he knew all about Martha.

This way, I could keep an eye on her for a time, and keep her out of harm's way. Most of all, though, we had a lot in common now, namely last night's shared experience. It didn't feel right just to walk away from each other. Besides, she had information I needed. I wanted to talk to Leon, but I didn't know how to do that. I was hoping, and assuming, Martha did.

So we picked up my car, an old Volvo I had acquired on a recent job, and I gritted my teeth and used a card to pay the exorbitant exit fee from the car park.

'Nearly as much as the car is worth,' Martha commented. 'Sorry!' she added hurriedly. 'No insult intended.'

'It's OK. I'm not sensitive. This is the best vehicle I've had for a long time. Until I got it, my only transport was an old Land Rover I seem to have been restoring most of my life.'

'Land Rovers are good. Get a new one.'

'Yeah. When my boat comes in.'

Get a new one? The exchange left me thinking I might have done just that if the job at The Chesters had worked out. Fat chance now.

'What do you normally do for a living, Frank?' Martha asked, as if she was wondering why I hadn't already taken her advice.

'This and that. Investigations, security.'

'Independent? Self-employed?'

'Yeah.'

'Then Leon came into your life,' she said softly.

'Very well put!'

I had to laugh at that. At the same time, I wondered if something similar had happened to her.

Once we got round the Western Bypass I left the A1 and, just south of the Nissan factory at Washington, headed across to the A19. We didn't have much to say for the next half hour, but it was a companionable silence. As we came to the edge of the Durham plateau, and Teesside with the backdrop of the Cleveland Hills came into view, I broached a topic that had been on my mind for a while.

'I should tell you I'm not planning on visiting Leon's IT centre, by the way. Whatever happened there last night, there'll be a lot of people investigating on site by now. We have nothing to add. So we're better off keeping out of it.'

'OK.'

I was a little surprised she didn't argue, but she must have seen the sense of what I was saying. A small problem, and the local staff would have sorted it. A major problem, and the place would be crawling with police, and with fire and rescue personnel. Perhaps anti-terrorist teams, as well. We could have added little, if anything, even if we hadn't both been shattered by the night's ordeal.

'This it?' Martha asked a half hour later, as I pulled off the road and onto the track that led the short distance to Risky Point.

'It is, yes. This is home.'

I stopped and we piled out of the car. It was an icy morning down there. Different weather to what we'd had in Northumberland. Ice on the track, and a sugar coating of frost across the grass sward and the roofs of my cottage and Jimmy Mack's. I could hear the sea quietly murmuring at the foot of the cliffs. Normality, it felt like. Heaven.

'How wonderful!' Martha said quietly, under her breath.

I smiled, pleased, and led the way indoors.

Chapter Twenty-Nine

'I SUGGEST A HOT bath,' I said, 'while I look around for something for you to wear while your stuff is in the washer. Then I'll show you around.'

'That's very kind of you, Frank.'

'My middle name, kindness,' I said. 'Be off with you!'

I showed her to the spare bedroom and the bathroom, gave her a robe and let her get on with it. To avoid falling asleep on my feet, I got the wood-burning stove going. Then I hunted for something for her to wear. There wasn't much I could offer. Tracksuit bottoms, tee-shirt and sweater was about the best I could come up with. And thick woolly boot socks. At least everything was clean.

I dumped the clothes outside the bathroom door. After that, I made myself a coffee, watched the stove heat up and thought about how good it was to be home. Then I tried to do some contingency planning.

It was hard to know where to start. I concentrated on not thinking about what had happened at The Chesters. The need now was to work out what happened next, rather than to dwell on how Bobrik had managed to generate so much carnage.

I thought we ought to be safe enough here, at Risky Point. For a while, at least. Until somebody worked out who I was, and where I lived. We had to make progress before that happened.

'Thank you!' Martha called down the stairs as she collected the clothing I'd put out for her.

'There's not much in your size, unfortunately.'

'These things are perfect until my clothes are washed and dried.'

When she came downstairs I showed her where the washer was and left her to get on with it. She didn't need me to load it for her.

'Go and have a bath or a shower yourself,' she said. 'I can manage now.'

'Sure?'

'Sure.'

So I did.

By the time I was done, Martha had scrambled together a meal for us from what she had found in the fridge, cupboards and freezer. I gazed at the table with astonishment. I hadn't realized there was so much food in the house.

'Hot soup first?' she suggested.

'Wonderful!'

'Then pasta, with salami and a bunch of vegetables I grilled. And baguettes from your freezer.'

'Amazing! I'm beginning to see you in a new light.'

She put out her tongue and grinned. Enough said. But I

couldn't believe it was the same woman.

We were both hungry, and got stuck into the meal. Afterwards, I made coffee for us both.

'What now?' I asked, as we sat either side of the stove with steaming mugs.

She sighed and said, 'I've been thinking about that. We need to contact Leon asap.'

'I agree. Can you do that? Do you know where he is even?'

'He's in Switzerland, with his family.'

'His sisters, you mean?'

She shook her head. 'With his wife and two children.'

I probably looked surprised, but I was actually quite shocked.

'What?' she said. 'You didn't know Leon has a family?'

I shook my head. 'He never mentioned them – only his sisters.'

'Well, he does like to keep his private life private.'

It made sense, I supposed. He would hope to keep them out of the battle. Good luck with that! I doubted Bobrik would either be ignorant of the arrangement or feel inhibited.

'You said Olga was there, as well?'

'Yes. She went because things were becoming difficult at the IT centre even before whatever happened last night.'

'In what way?'

'The computers there were being hacked, slowing down a lot of processing. When that happens, which it does from time to time, Olga can keep things going from their place in Switzerland.'

'Nice.'

I was thinking how extraordinary the Podolsky empire was. Leon hadn't been kidding when he told me it was global.

'So contact him?' I suggested.

She nodded. 'Let me finish my coffee first.'

Cool, calm and collected again, Miss Big-time Project Manager, or whatever she was. But I was glad she was here. There was a lot to do, and I couldn't do it all myself.

Martha used my computer to make first contact, one of Leon's email addresses being in her memory. A short time later his reply gave her a phone number to call. She did that, and launched into a version of what had happened at The Chesters. It wasn't the full version. That would have taken far too long. But she told him the gist of it. Then he wanted to talk to me.

'Where were you, Frank, when all this was happening?'

It was a terse, potentially judgemental question. Leon was not happy with his security adviser.

'Not at The Chesters, Leon. I had already resigned, and was off site, well away.'

'Martha fired you, I understand?'

'It was heading that way. I jumped before I could be pushed.'

'I told her to reinstate you.'

'Yeah, well. That hadn't happened. By the time she reached me, it was too late for us to do anything but get the hell out. We were lucky, Leon. You may not think so, but we were. Others were not.'

'So I understand. You did well. I would hate to have lost Martha as well as the others.'

I inferred that losing me would have been acceptable, but perhaps I was wrong. Perhaps indignation had got the better of me.

After a lengthy pause, he said, 'The IT centre got hit by hackers, as well. Pretty well wiped out for the moment.'

'Bad as that, eh?' I grimaced. 'This has to stop, Leon. You – we – can't go on like this. None of us can. We've got to find a way out.'

'Let me think about it.'

He hung up. That was it.

I looked at Martha and grimaced. 'I don't think he's very pleased – with either of us, or with what's happened.'

'What did he say when you told him it has to stop?'

'He said he wanted to think about it. Then he hung up on me.'

She nodded. She seemed to understand that. So could I, in a sense.

'I suppose, if there were easy answers....' I mused.

'That's right.'

If there were, they certainly hadn't been found so far.

'I'm going to sleep on it,' I said. 'I don't know about you, but

136

I've had it. I'm bushed.'

'Me, too,' Martha admitted.

So we called it a day. I went to bed, too tired even to speculate about what tomorrow might bring.

Chapter Thirty

SOMEHOW, OVERNIGHT, MARTHA ENDED up in my bed. I jumped when I felt a foreign body slide in next to me.

'Cold,' she murmured, 'and can't sleep.'

'Not scared, though?'

'Not much, no.'

'That's all right, then.'

But it wasn't. Not really. One thing led to another, when what I really needed was a good night's sleep. But we did get to sleep eventually.

Next morning we were up by 8.30, which was a surprise, given recent events. Before nine, while we were still finishing breakfast, there was a knock on the door.

'Who's that?' Martha demanded, jumping to her feet, alarmed.

'It'll be Jimmy Mack, my neighbour.'

She nodded but remained tense while I went to the door.

'I saw you were back,' Jimmy boomed heartily.

'Morning, Jim! Yeah. Got back last night.'

'Everything all right? Good holiday?'

Where to start? I took the simple approach.

'Yes, thanks.'

'I thought you said you would only be away a couple of days?'

'Well....'

He laughed. 'No need to explain! I know you've got company. I'll call again later.'

'OK, Jim. See you later.'

I returned to the kitchen.

'He knows?' Martha said.

'Knows what? He knows nothing.'

'It didn't sound like that. Anyway, who is he?'

'He's an old fisherman. Lives in that cottage next door. He's my neighbour, like I said – my only neighbour, here in Risky Point.'

I could see she was still worried Jimmy might be one of Bobrik's agents. So I told her about him.

'Jimmy's lived here all his life, as did his father and grandfather before him. And, no, he's never been anywhere near Russia!'

She grinned at last. 'OK,' she said. 'I get the point.'

'Good. Now, what are we going to do today? Wait for Leon to call back? Or are you going to call him again?'

'First,' she said, 'I'm going to see if my clothes have dried. If they have, I'll get changed. After that, we can talk some more – if that's all right with you?'

'Martha, anything's all right with me where you're concerned.'

'Now?' she asked, head on one side cheekily.

'Especially now.'

We laughed at each other. Then she got up, gave me a quick kiss and went looking for dry clothes that actually fit her.

While Martha was getting dressed, I switched on the desktop computer and took a look at the BBC news page. There was nothing on the national page about a fire in Northumberland, which wasn't really surprising. The Chesters was about as far off the beaten track as it's possible to get in England.

I couldn't find very much on the local page for the North East, either. Just a one-liner about a fire at an historic house in Northumberland. An investigation into the cause was expected to start today, with suspicion resting on leaking gas bottles used by builders who were working on the site.

'No mention of dead bodies?' Martha said over my shoulder.

I shook my head. 'The investigation won't find any, either. It was a pretty intense fire.'

'Of course they'll find ... Oh! Perhaps not?'

I shook my head. 'Tidier to keep it as an investigation of a fire.

A murder investigation might throw up all sorts of problems, and involve the Met, MI5 and God knows who else.'

Martha grimaced. She was out of her depth now things had turned nasty. Being a high-flying project manager was one thing; what had happened at The Chesters was something else altogether.

I turned, studied her and said, 'You know, I think I prefer you in one of my tee-shirts.'

'With or without tracksuit bottoms?' she asked coquettishly.

I grinned. That was better. We couldn't afford to wallow in the trough of despond.

'So, what now?' I asked. 'Keep our heads down, and wait to hear from Leon?'

'Not much else we can do, is there?'

'Probably not, no.'

My mind flew back to The Chesters. The builder would talk to the police, and anybody else interested, about the work he had been going to do. He would deny all responsibility for the fire, of course. Not his gas bottles. No way!

Investigating that would take time.

Meanwhile, concern would grow about the people who had been living, or staying, at the property. Investigating that would take time, too. Then there would be time spent trying to identify and locate the owner. All that could rumble on while we waited to hear from Leon how he wanted to play it.

We could, of course, contact the police right now and tell them what had happened the previous night, but that wasn't a very attractive option. Arson, Russian gang warfare, murder, and foreign excursions would then be right up there centre stage. The police would have a five year investigation on their hands, at least, and anyone involved – including me – would be dangerously exposed while that went on. Either that or we would all be locked up.

Besides, the legal process would inevitably falter once the core problem was eventually found to be well outside British jurisdiction. My feeling was that it would be in everyone's better interests to try to bring this story to a close pragmatically and quickly, rather than legally. Enough people had been killed. It was time to draw a line.

I didn't expect everyone to share my point of view, but it was one I was determined to put to Leon.

While we waited to hear from Leon, I took Martha down the rough track that leads to the little beach at the foot of the cliffs. It was slippery and hard going, but she managed. She even enjoyed the outing.

'It's beautiful here,' she said, as we stood at the water's edge. 'Cold, but lovely.'

I could only agree.

On the way back up the cliff, I became aware of engine noise in the sky. I glanced seawards and saw a helicopter a mile or two out from the shore.

'Air-sea rescue?' Martha asked, seeing what I was looking at.

'Maybe. A training flight, perhaps.'

The chopper was heading towards us, and soon I could see it wasn't yellow, the colour of the RAF's Air-Sea Rescue craft. It didn't look like a regular RAF chopper, either. Then I recalled that the maritime rescue service had recently been privatized. I had no idea of the colour preferred by the company that had picked up the contract.

My thinking changed again when we reached the top of the cliff and stepped out on to level ground. By then, the chopper was circling overhead, as if it was searching for something close to where we were standing.

'What are they doing?' Martha asked.

Jimmy Mack had come out of his cottage, and he, too, seemed to be asking that question as he looked towards me and shouted something.

'Landing,' I said with astonishment. 'He's coming down right here!'

Chapter Thirty-One

PERHAPS I SHOULDN'T HAVE been astonished, but I was – even more so when I saw Leon climb out of the chopper, duck his head and begin to jog towards us.

He grinned when he reached us. 'A cup of hot coffee would be good,' he said, being his usual irrepressible self. 'How are you both?'

'Better today, thank you, Leon,' I said, shaking his hand. 'Coffee? I'm sure we can manage that.'

He kissed Martha and gave her a hug. She seemed pleased to see him, but perhaps was not as surprised as I was by his arrival.

'So this is where you live, Frank?' Leon wheeled round to admire the view. 'It's certainly different.'

To what? I wondered.

'Come on!' I said. 'Let's see about that coffee.'

By then, the pilot had switched off the engine and the noise level had abated. I gave Jimmy Mack a wave to reassure him that all was well. He just shook his head.

'So where the hell have you come from?' I asked Leon, once we were sitting around the kitchen table.

'From my yacht,' he said with a grin.

'Which blew up in Montenegro, remember?'

'My other yacht, the *Kursk*. I'd had her stationed in the North Sea.'

'Just in case?'

He nodded.

'And how did you get to your yacht from Switzerland – or were you never in Switzerland?'

'Yes, I was there, until ...' He glanced at his watch and continued, '... until a few hours ago. It is not difficult to move around quickly these days, Frank. You should know that.'

If you have the money and the resources, I thought.

141

'Humour me, Leon. Just tell me how you did it. I'm curious.'

'I flew to Rotterdam, and took a helicopter from there to the yacht. OK?'

'Then another one to here?'

He nodded agreement. 'I didn't want anyone in Rotterdam who might have been watching to know where I was going, out of respect for your privacy, Frank.'

'Thank you, Leon. I appreciate it.'

I would have appreciated it even more if he had stayed away from Risky Point, but I couldn't tell him that. He was here now, and he'd gone to some trouble to hide his trail. Besides, we needed to talk.

I poured the coffee. Martha, who had scarcely said a word so far, distributed the mugs around the table.

Leon looked from one to the other of us speculatively. 'So are you back on board, Frank? Or are you still resigned, or fired, or whatever it was that happened?'

I had to smile.

'OK. Don't tell me. I can see how things stand between the two of you now.'

'You can?' I said with some surprise.

'Sure I can. I've known Martha a long time.'

I had to laugh then.

Martha looked furious. 'Leon,' she said, 'we've had a terrible time, and barely escaped with our lives. A lot of people died! We don't need jokes.'

'OK, OK! You don't have to tell me anything – but I still know,' he added with a smile that seemed to infuriate Martha even more. 'Now, what happened the other night? Tell me again.'

So we took turns putting him in the picture, and did it properly. This time, he got the full story.

'So three good men dead,' he said sombrely.

'That we know about.'

He grimaced and nodded. 'You did well to get out yourselves.'

I said nothing. We had done well, and we'd been lucky. That much was obvious.

'It was thanks to Frank,' Martha said quickly. 'I was paralysed by shock. I had no idea what to do, or where to go.'

'No, no!' I insisted. 'I'm not having that. You were fine, Martha.'

Leon glanced from one to the other of us again and nodded. 'Not your game, Martha. That's why I brought Frank in.'

Turning to me, he added, 'Would it have made any difference if you had still been on site?'

I shook my head. 'The only difference is that Martha and I would probably have been dead, as well. There were too many of them. I couldn't have held them off any more than Roman and Boris could.'

He didn't react. He knew the truth of it. Bobrik didn't go in for half-measures. Blitzkrieg was more his style. Overwhelming force, and sudden impact.

'What about the IT centre?' I asked.

'In chaos. Hackers have devastated the systems. We'll get it back up and running, but it will take time. For now, Olga is operating with key personnel on backup systems.'

'In Switzerland?'

He nodded.

I sighed. 'Leon, like I said before, this has to be stopped. You can't go on like this.'

'Frank is right,' Martha chimed in.

'Easy to say,' Leon mused, 'but hard to do. We have come here today to talk to you both, and to see if we can find a solution.'

I was a bit slow on the uptake, but after a second or two I frowned. 'We?' I said.

'Me and Lenka.'

'Lenka?'

'Sure. Didn't I tell you?'

I shook my head. 'So where is she?'

'Outside, somewhere. She's the chopper pilot.'

Chapter Thirty-Two

AND THERE SHE WAS, when I stuck my head out the door. Lenka, fussing over something in the cockpit, just like a real pilot.

'Come and have a coffee, Lenka!'

She waved and said something about being too busy. I left her to it, and went back inside. Leon grinned at me, enjoying the disruption he'd brought to Risky Point.

'OK, Leon,' I said, dropping into a chair. 'Let's get down to it. Here's what I think. One, you either possess or can do something that Bobrik wants very badly indeed. Two, you don't want to give it to him. How am I doing so far?'

'Pretty good,' he said with a nod. 'Carry on.'

'You're going to have to negotiate with him – properly this time, not like in Montenegro. You have to find a compromise that will satisfy you both. Otherwise, there'll be no end to it – the killing and destruction. As well as yourself and your staff, Leon, you have a family and innocent bystanders to think of. This has to stop.'

'I agree,' Leon said. 'So what do you suggest?'

'For a start, tell me what Bobrik wants.'

'He wants to stop us publishing our online newspaper.'

'Because the Kremlin objects to it, and getting the thing stopped will buy him favour with the Kremlin?'

'Yes. That's right.'

It didn't seem enough. All this death and destruction because of an internet news organ? How many people would read the damned thing anyway?

'OK. What else?'

'He wants to destroy *Leonomics*.'

'Because it's helping to keep you afloat financially?'

Leon nodded. 'Essentially, yes.'

'Anything else?'

He pursed his lips and shook his head. I didn't buy it. It wasn't enough.

'There has to be something else, Leon.'

But if there was, he wasn't saying. All he added was that any favours Bobrik did for the Kremlin would help protect his business assets in Russia. It just didn't seem enough. This vendetta was so vicious, it was hard to believe there wasn't more to it.

'Is that really all Bobrik wants?' I asked. 'Is there nothing else at all he wants?'

'He also wants me dead,' Leon said flatly. 'Me, personally.'

There was that, of course. I'd forgotten about that.

'And I want Bobrik dead!' Lenka snapped, as she came into the room.

I sighed. 'This is not getting us very far, Leon,' I said, frustrated. 'You've got to offer him something as a negotiating token, something that's important to him.'

Just then there was a knock on the door. I went to see who it was. Jimmy Mack, of course.

'I'm busy, Jim,' I said with irritation.

'That helicopter,' he said stubbornly, standing his ground.

'What about it? Is it blocking your view?'

He glared at me, affronted, and said, 'It's moving. But I don't know why I'm bothering telling you. It can go over the bloody cliff for all I care!'

'Sorry, Jim. You've caught me at a bad time.'

I looked outside. The chopper didn't seem to have moved much to me, but it was rocking in the wind that had got up. Maybe it should be tied down. Or whatever. I had no idea what you were supposed to do with the damned thing.

'I'll get the pilot,' I said.

I called Lenka to come and check things. Jimmy took a good look at her, and then wandered away with a thoughtful expression on his face. He was impressed, I could tell. In his day girls didn't do stuff like this.

I walked with Lenka over to the chopper. She looked around and said everything was OK for now, but she would stay out here with it. They would be leaving soon anyway.

Then she blurted out something surprising. 'You were right,

145

Frank. There is something else, something between Bobrik and the Podolsky family.'

'Oh? What's that?'

'Leon's wife. She was with Bobrik first, but he used to beat her badly. Leon rescued her, and her son.' She shrugged and added, 'Now they are with Leon.'

I was taken aback. 'Are you talking about his family in Switzerland?'

She nodded. 'Leon also has a son and daughter of his own now, with her, but the older boy is Bobrik's.'

I sighed and shook my head. 'Thank you for telling me, Lenka.'

'There is more, Frank. Bobrik and me. He did bad things to me once. It is why I hate him so much. I would kill him if I had the chance!'

I grimaced, but didn't ask. I didn't need details. In one sense, I already had too much information. But at least I seemed to have been given what might be the key to the whole sorry business now.

'Don't trust Martha, Frank,' Lenka added. 'She is not what she seems.'

I stared at her, astonished, but she just turned and walked away.

Chapter Thirty-Three

'LET'S TAKE A WALK, Leon,' I suggested when I went back inside.

He looked surprised. 'We don't really have time, Frank.'

'He wants to talk to you in private,' Martha piped up disapprovingly. 'Without me.'

I didn't deny it. Martha could pout and implicitly object all she liked.

'Frank, anything you can say to me, you can also say to Martha. She knows everything.'

'Which is more than I do.' I shrugged. 'OK, if that's how you want it. Leon, I didn't know your wife used to be with Bobrik. In fact, I didn't know you had a family in Switzerland until yesterday, when Martha told me.'

He smiled. 'Frank, how long have we known each other? There hasn't been time to tell you everything about myself.'

'Fair enough,' I admitted. 'You're right. Still, this changes things for me. I can see now why Bobrik is so hell-bent on destroying you. It makes sense at last.'

'I'm glad you think so.'

'Not sense in the normal meaning of the word. I just mean it helps explain what's been happening. It doesn't really change anything, though. You still need to negotiate a settlement with him.'

'He was cruel to Elizabet, who was then his wife. You know that?'

'Lenka told me.'

'Did Lenka also tell you that he raped her so badly she was in hospital for a month?'

I grimaced. 'Not exactly.'

'He is an evil man, Frank. I want you to know that.'

'OK. But we still have to bring the feud to an end.'

He nodded. 'I know that. But what if he will not negotiate?'

'Then shoot the bastard!'

The discussion became sensible again. When I reminded Leon that we still hadn't thought of anything to offer Bobrik, Martha came up with a proposal.

'There's always Svoboda, Leon. You could offer him that.'

He looked puzzled. 'Svoboda? Have we still got it?'

'Yes.'

'Well, well.'

'What is it?' I asked.

'A gold mine,' Martha said.

Nice! A gold mine Leon owned but seemed to have forgotten about.

'You're sure we've still got it?' he repeated, sounding puzzled.

147

When she said she was, he shrugged and looked mystified. 'I thought we lost all the gold mines when the state took them over.'

'We did – all except that one.'

'Where is it?' I asked.

'Siberia,' Leon said, 'where most of the other Russian gold mines are.'

'Well, Amur Oblast,' Martha qualified. 'The Russian Far East. Leon kept ownership when the others were expropriated because the authorities didn't realize the company set up to run it was one of his.'

'We'll lose it eventually, though,' he pointed out, 'when they discover their mistake.'

'So?' Martha said.

'There you are, then,' I said. 'You have nothing to lose, Leon. Offer him that, just to get him to the negotiating table.'

Leon looked thoughtful. 'If he was short of cash, he might be interested.'

I grimaced. 'He doesn't seem to be, does he?'

'No. And he's got plenty more salted away offshore.'

'How do you know that?'

'Olga traced his investments portfolio. Most of it's in Cayman.'

'Most of it?'

'Ninety per cent.'

'Really?' I said slowly, thinking aloud. It took a moment before the idea came to me. 'So he's very vulnerable. Leon, do you think…?'

'Get her!' he snapped, jumping out of his chair. 'Martha, get Olga. Meanwhile, I want to know what the situation is at the IT centre. How soon before they're up and running again?'

He grinned as he took out his phone. 'Thank you, Frank! You might just have found the solution. We'll go after his money.'

'Great minds think alike,' I said modestly, grinning back.

It was all checked and arranged in double-quick time. The IT centre was back online. Olga would leave Switzerland and return to Samphire Batts, with Lenka ferrying her by helicopter on the last stage of the journey. First, though, Lenka would fly Leon to the IT centre, where he would wait for his sisters.

Simple, when you had the resources.

'What about The Chesters?' Martha asked.

'Forget about it,' Leon said brusquely. 'It's gone now, and we have too many other things to worry about.'

So then there was just me and Martha left at Risky Point. Well, us and Jimmy Mack.

I walked Martha over to Jimmy's cottage, so the two of them could get acquainted, figuring that might stop him being so damned nosey.

'Polish?' he asked her after I had made the introductions.

She shook her head. 'English.'

'English?' He looked dumbfounded. 'Well, the other one was Polish, wasn't she? The pilot, I mean.'

'What did you think of her as a pilot?' I asked him before Martha could correct him on that score as well, and perhaps get him wondering even more.

'Not bad,' he said thoughtfully, as if he knew a lot about flying helicopters. 'She took it up and away without any messing.'

Martha took my hint. 'So you're a fisherman, Jimmy?'

'I am, like my father before me, and his father before him.'

'I know nothing about fishing,' she said innocently. 'I often wondered how it was done from those little boats. Cobles, are they called?'

Well, I could see Jimmy's eyes light up. 'Oh, it's a complicated business,' he said, wiping his mouth with the back of his hand as he relished the opportunity. 'You have to be born to it. Would you like a cup of tea, pet?'

'I'd love one,' she assured him.

'I'll catch you up later,' I said hurriedly. 'One or two phone calls to make.'

'Aye. Away you go, then,' Jimmy said complacently. 'We'll be all right here, the two of us.'

Chapter Thirty-Four

THE WORD FROM LEON came early the next day in a terse phone call. We were wanted back at Samphire Batts just as soon as we could get there. Martha jumped up, ready to go.

'Hang on!' I told her. 'Let's just think about this for a moment.'

'He wants us there, Frank – now!'

I shook my head. 'What are we going to do there? What's the hurry?'

She sighed impatiently and looked frustrated. I took her in my arms and said, 'Think about it. Are you sure you want to do this, Martha? You've already been through a lot for Leon.'

'So have you.'

'I signed on to provide security for The Chesters. Sadly, I failed. Now I have to ask myself if I want to continue to be involved with the Podolsky family. So should you. It's a very dangerous commitment.'

'I know that. I've worked for Leon for a long time. You're right. It's high-risk. You think we should review our involvement?'

'I do. We need to think it through carefully, Martha.'

'OK. I've done that.'

'And?'

'I'm going to Samphire Batts, to the IT centre. Are you coming with me?'

I gave her a rueful smile. 'Nothing's going to change your mind, is it?'

'No.'

'All right, then. Let's get our stuff together.'

The decision, or the speed of it, went against my better judgement, but I was just as much caught up in the nexus of Podolsky intrigue as Martha was. Neither of us was going to back out now, it seemed.

It was early afternoon when we got there. Inside the centre, the atmosphere was electric. We could sense it as soon as we got through the doors. Martha looked at me and I nodded. Something was happening, or about to happen.

Plenty of people not in the know would have been carrying on with their usual work for *Leonomics,* but even they must have been aware that something special was afoot in the building.

Leon greeted us and then went to join two people he referred to as his money men – one a young man, the other a middle-aged woman – who were closeted in a big room stacked high with an impressive bank of computer equipment.

Next door, Olga was working alone at a terminal. I guessed she was being given the space and time, and no doubt all the computer power and expertise she needed, to try to divest Bobrik of his offshore investments.

'Olga is supposed to be good at this kind of thing,' I said quietly.

Martha nodded. 'Most people in her field would probably say she's a genius.'

'Where did she learn the trade?'

'She started off in Moscow, at the university space agency, I believe. Then she spent several years in California – NASA, Stanford U, Silicon Valley.'

'All the good places.'

'For what she was interested in, yes. Then she came back to Europe to help out with the family business.'

Lucky Leon, I couldn't help thinking. From what I'd gathered, Olga's skills were probably responsible for a large part of the family's wealth.

A technician moved behind a glass wall that separated him from Olga's room. Leon suddenly appeared beside us. He said the technician was monitoring screens that told how well the systems were coping with Olga's demands.

'She is trying to hack into systems that are very well protected,' he told us. 'That requires a lot of intense work, and a lot of computer power.'

'Can she do it?' I asked.

'We will see. A personal view? I believe she can.'

'Of course she can!' Martha added.

We were like spectators at a big-money chess match. Rapt but silent. It was a game for the knowledgeable, a not to be missed occasion. We had to be there, all of us.

Nobody said anything else for a while. The two money men, the young guy and the middle-aged woman, pored over paper spewing out of a printer and checked screens that stood on tables along one side of the room. Leon was in his element. Not much violence at the moment, but all the tension and slow-building excitement in the world.

If I hadn't been there, I would have guessed it would have been like an operating theatre in a hospital. But it was nothing like that. Operating theatres are crowded and noisy, with people reading off monitors, anaesthetists doing their thing and sur-geons giving a running commentary on what they are doing for the benefit of the assistants and trainees alongside them. This was more like a church, a cathedral even, in a solemn moment. Just about the only sound was the clicking and clattering of Olga's keyboard, coming through the open door from her office.

A young guy appeared and poured us each a glass of water from a dispenser near the door. I nodded and thanked him. The others said nothing. Olga didn't seem aware of anything except the screen in front of her. A few minutes later, another young guy brought in a tray of mugs of coffee. If he expected to be thanked, he was out of luck. Not a word was spoken. With bowed head, he passed the mugs around and departed.

I waited, like the others, caught up in the intensity. If it worked, we might be able to do the next thing in the sequence. Then, at the end of the sequence, Leon and his family just might be able to get on with their lives unhindered, and I would be able to go home. All that seemed a distant prospect at the moment, but it was what we were about.

By chance, I was the only one in that outer room who saw the moment when Olga's work come to an end. Leon's eyes were closed, as he practised whatever form of relaxation therapy worked best for him. Martha had drifted off somewhere. The two money men were poring over a computer printout that required their attention. My own attention had switched away from a print of the Transporter Bridge, the Middlesbrough icon, and back to what I could see of Olga's right shoulder and forearm, wrist and hand and fingers. It was the fingers I noticed first. They stopped moving.

I waited. Moments passed, long moments. Olga's fingers remained still. Then she turned her head slightly, looked over her shoulder and caught my eye. She nodded and gave a faint smile. I smiled back, and released the breath I hadn't realized until then I was holding.

Olga stood up and walked into our room. Leon looked up inquiringly. The others in the room stood, quite still, and waited.

'It is done,' she said.

Leon, a big grin on his face, whooped and leapt to his feet to grab her in a bear hug. Martha yelped with delight. The money men dashed through into the office Olga had just vacated. I smiled and congratulated her. She nodded at me again and walked out of the room, visibly exhausted.

Leon was all for getting the champagne out. Instead, Martha organized some fresh coffee, which seemed far more sensible. We had a long way to go yet, and I was already thinking of the obstacles and threats ahead of us.

When the festivities had died down a bit, I got Leon to tell me the details.

'We took a few hundred million dollars from him, Frank. Olga has emptied his petty cash!'

I nodded appreciatively. That would give Bobrik something to think about. Hopefully, it would also make him more amenable.

'The next step,' Leon said more soberly, 'is to get him to the negotiating table. That's where you come in, Frank.'

Leon couldn't do it himself, he said. He needed someone else, an outsider, to talk to Bobrik and persuade him to meet. I said I was prepared to try. Why not? That should be easy compared with all the other things I'd done for Leon.

'Let's give him a day or two to learn of his losses,' I suggested.

Leon agreed.

'Meanwhile,' I added, 'you can work out how to use Bobrik's money to pay for some of the damage he's caused.'

He flashed me a grin. 'Exactly!'

'Another thing,' I said. 'I'll need someone at the negotiating table with me, if we get that far, someone who has all the information, and who knows how things work in Russia.'

'Of course.' Leon grinned again and added, 'Will you ask her?'

'Me?'

'Well, you know Martha better than I do by now.'

Chapter Thirty-Five

SURPRISINGLY, BOBRIK WAS CURRENTLY in the UK. Leon conjured up a phone number for him, which I rang. I didn't expect to speak to him in person, but I was confident my message would reach him.

'I am speaking on behalf of Mr Podolsky,' I said carefully.

I ignored the cynical laughter at the other end and continued, 'I have an offer to make to Mr Bobrik.'

'What offer?'

From the accent, I judged I was talking to another Russian tough guy.

'Mr Podolsky would like to bring the current difficulties between himself and Mr Bobrik to an end. He is prepared to make a generous offer in order to help bring that about.'

'Yeah?' the voice said suspiciously. 'So what's he offering?'

'A very valuable asset. A gold mine. Check with your boss. When you've done that, call me back on this number and let me know if he is interested in meeting to discuss the offer.

'As a sign of good faith, I'm willing to let him choose the time and place for a meeting, but it must be in a public place. And it will be just him and me – no-one else.'

I ended the call. It was up to them now. We would have to wait and see. Leon knew that. He nodded and got up to leave the room.

'Well done,' Martha said with approval. 'You handled that well, Frank. Brief and to the point. He'll want to know more.'

I shrugged. 'Let's see if it works. We might need a Plan B.'

Two hours later the phone rang. I answered.

'Are you the guy I spoke to a while ago?'

'I am.'

'The boss wants us to meet, you and me.'

'I need to talk to him.'

'You can talk to me first. Then we'll see.'

I let a second or two go by before agreeing. 'OK. Where and when?'

'The American Diner on the A1, just south of Gateshead. Do you know it?'

'I've seen it. Never been in it, though.'

'I'll meet you there. Four this afternoon. OK?'

'Yeah. Who am I meeting?'

'Don't worry about that. I'll find you, if you sit with a coffee.'

That was it. The phone went dead.

'OK?' Martha asked anxiously.

I shrugged. 'Maybe. Who knows? That was Bobrik's guy, not Bobrik himself. He wants to meet just outside Gateshead, on the A1.' I glanced at my watch. 'I'd better get moving.'

'I'm coming with you.'

I shook my head. 'You're not. You can't. It's just him and me meeting.'

'That was for the meeting with Bobrik.'

'It's the same thing.'

'Either I come with you, Frank, or I'll follow on behind. I'm not letting you go alone.'

Shit! What to do?

'OK,' I said with a sigh. 'You can come with me, but I'll drop you off before the actual meet.'

She wanted to argue, but I said, 'Agree to that, Martha, or I don't go myself.'

Reluctantly, she agreed.

Next I briefed Leon.

155

'You going to be OK with this, Frank?'

'Should be. I'm just the messenger, remember?'

'Messengers don't always come out in good shape.'

'Thanks for that, Leon. Just what I needed.'

He patted me on the shoulder. 'You'll be OK. He needs to get back the cash he's lost in Cayman.'

That was how I saw it, too. It was a thought to cling to as I made my preparations.

The American Diner at a service station on the A1, just outside Gateshead, was exactly as you might expect. A little bit of Stateside traditional popular culture. Long, low and shiny tin on the outside, with colourful and extravagant neon lighting to show it at its best at night. Rows of booths with plastic bench seats and little formica tables on the inside. Elvis and Little Richard, alternating, singing their hearts out in the background.

It was nearly empty when I arrived. I sat down at a table overlooking the parking lot for lorries and vans. A waitress in the smart uniform smock that was the house style came over. I ordered coffee and a cheeseburger and fries. Healthy eating was a long way from my mind just then. I needed some nutrition, and some caffeine.

It had been a cold, clear, sunny day, but the sun was going down now as we neared nightfall. On the A1, traffic was building up towards the rush hour peak. I watched the streams of vehicles carrying people homeward, their working day done. Amazingly, plenty of people seemed to have jobs, despite the recession.

Recession? What recession? Well, the same one there seems to have been in the North East all my life. Only London and the South East don't really have recessions. But down there they have other problems, ones I wouldn't want to live with. Too many people, for one thing. What we call overcrowding and traffic congestion would be a quiet day in London.

I ate the cheeseburger and fries, which were good. I drank the coffee, which I also liked. Having considered ordering another burger, I reluctantly decided just to order more coffee. Elvis on the juke box was warning me off. Anyway, I needed adrenalin more than I needed more extra super-saturated fat, or whatever it is that makes good burgers dangerous in the eyes of the food police but so very tasty.

A young couple got up, paid their bill and left. They separated in the car park, each going to their own vehicle. A middle-aged couple did exactly the same thing. Bobrik's man had chosen well. This was a place for people on the move, and for people who didn't want to be noticed or remembered.

He came through the door. I hadn't seen another car arrive, but here he was. Blue jeans and a black leather jacket, biker style. Bald, burly and tough looking. Forty-ish. He didn't look much in the mental department. Just a bruiser. Hired help, that was all. My first impression.

He made his way directly to my table and sat down. I nodded.

'Nice place,' he said, glancing around with apparent approval. 'I like it.'

'Well, you chose it. Too American for me.'

He laughed at that. Must have thought it was good.

'So what do you want to talk about?' he asked when he stopped laughing.

The waitress came and hovered before I could get another word out. He looked up at her and said, 'Coffee.'

She looked insulted by his lack of courtesy, and I wondered if she would spit in his coffee before she brought it over. I waited until she had moved away before starting my spiel.

'Mr Podolsky wishes to bring the long-running feud with Mr Bobrik to a close. To help achieve that, he is prepared to make Mr Bobrik a generous offer: ownership of a gold mine that has a good record and plenty of profit left in it. In return, he wants to be assured that attacks on his family and property will cease.'

He stared at me and said, 'That's it? That's the offer – all of it?'

I nodded.

He brooded a moment or two, moving the salt and pepper cellars around with one hand while he did his thinking. I watched the tattoo on the back of his hand. It changed shape as the hand moved, starting off as a tiger and becoming something else – a horse, it looked like. I wondered how long it would be before the novelty wore off, and you got sick to death of a tattoo like that.

Then, abruptly, he said, 'We need more information about the mine.'

'That can be arranged, once we get an indication the offer is acceptable in principle.'

'In principle?' he said, chuckling at the idea.

The waitress arrived with his coffee. I watched as she put it down. He didn't touch it, or thank her. Consistent as hell.

'What's it to you?' he said when she had gone. 'Where do you stand in all this? Who are you anyway?'

'I have a job to do. I've been engaged by Mr Podolsky to help with security.'

'That right?' He looked even more amused. 'Like at that big house of his that went up in flames the other night? Were you helping look after that?'

I gave him a stony look that was supposed to tell him all I was interested in discussing right now was the Podolsky offer.

'Tell you what,' he said carefully in his American English. 'Podolsky can go fuck himself! How's that?'

'I'll tell him,' I said, nodding.

Then I put a twenty pound note on the table and slid out of the booth before adding, 'He'll probably tell me to urge you to get Bobrik to check his investment accounts in the Cayman Islands.'

'What the hell's that supposed to mean?'

I sat back down and leant forward.

'Look,' I said patiently, 'this vendetta could well end up with everyone penniless – and dead – if it goes on much longer. Think about it. And contact me again if Bobrik decides he wants to talk about an alternative future, one where everybody lives and makes some decent money – and is able to keep it.'

He stared at me for a moment. Then he moved his coffee cup away, untouched. He didn't like coffee, it seemed. Not this coffee, anyway. He didn't even like the smell of it. The horse on the back of his hand quivered, nostrils flared. They made a fine pair, him and the horse.

'What was that about … Where was it again? The Cayman Islands? What's that got to do with anything?'

'Just check,' I advised.

'We'll check. What else you got?'

'I think you'll find that's quite enough,' I said, smiling knowingly.

He made to get up, his coffee still untouched. Then he paused. 'I know who you are, Doy,' he said, staring hard. 'You think about that.'

'I will,' I assured him. 'But I would still advise you to check on the Cayman Islands.'

He finished getting up and walked away, something weighing heavily on his mind.

The waitress came across, picked up the note and said, 'I'll get your change.'

I shook my head. 'Keep it.'

She raised her eyebrows in surprise. 'Are you sure?'

'Yes. I don't want to fill my pockets with change.'

She smiled. 'Didn't your friend like the coffee?' she asked, nodding after Bobrik's man.

'He doesn't like anything very much,' I told her. 'Don't take it personally.'

She laughed. I got up again, and followed Bobrik's man through the door.

Chapter Thirty-Six

THERE WAS NO SIGN of Bobrik's man when I got outside. I walked over to the car, got in and waited until Martha joined me a minute or two later.

'How did it go?' she asked.

'We'll have to wait and see. He was coming on strong, but my advice to check their Cayman investments stopped him in his tracks. Let's see what they have to say when they've done that. Did you recognize him, by the way?'

She shook her head, disappointing me.

'He didn't seem anything special,' I added, 'but he must be close to Bobrik.'

'Probably,' Martha said with a yawn. 'I'm cold and hungry. Can we get something to eat?'

I grinned at her. 'Priorities, eh?'

'You bet! It might have been very nice inside that diner, but it wasn't where I was standing.'

'Where was that?'

'Amongst the rubbish bins out the back.'

'Tut-tut! The things the modern project manager has to do.'

'Just drive, Frank. Drive until you see somewhere decent to eat.'

In the event, I didn't see anywhere really worth stopping. I just grabbed a burger for Martha and coffee for us both at a service area. Then we sped on down to Teesside. Leon was waiting for us at Samphire Batts. He was calm and listened patiently while I told him what had happened.

'So it's wait-and-see time?' he suggested when I'd finished.

'That's about right.' I grinned and added, 'Let's see how they react to losing all their money in Cayman.'

'Badly, I should think,' Leon said with a grin of his own. 'Bobrik never did like losing.'

'And he's lost a hell of a lot this time,' I pointed out.

'Too bad, eh?'

We tossed it around for a minute or two. Then Leon said, 'The guy you met, he didn't give a name?'

I shook my head.

'What was he like?'

I described Bobrik's man as best I could. 'He didn't seem top drawer, if you know what I mean.'

Leon nodded. 'And that was how Martha saw him?'

'Well, she didn't disagree.'

'Nothing else, Frank?'

'I don't think so. I would guess he's seen the inside of a prison, but I don't suppose that will surprise you. The most distinctive thing about him was a tattoo on the back of his hand.'

'A tiger that shifts, and becomes a horse?'

'Exactly!' I said with surprise. 'You know him?'

'Congratulations, Frank!' Leon said with a chuckle. 'You just met Yevgeni Bobrik, and survived.'

'The man himself?'

Leon nodded. 'You're lucky he didn't shoot you.'

'He got pretty close to it, I think.'

'Don't let him get that close again.'

Something puzzled me. After all, I had seen Bobrik once before.

'I didn't recognize him. He had hair when I saw him in Montenegro,' I pointed out.

'So he's shaved it off?' Leon said, shrugging. 'A master of disguise!'

I was annoyed with myself for not seeing through such a simple deception. Then again, Martha hadn't recognized him, either.

'Don't let it trouble you, Frank. But don't be deceived, either. Bobrik is a very cunning guy, and he's relentless. Now let's wait to hear what he thinks about Cayman.'

Martha joined us then. We all got coffee and retired to a small conference room to consider gold mines.

Leon was in relaxed mode. I sensed that he felt all was not lost, after all. In fact, things might even be moving slightly his way. Or perhaps he just felt better to be hitting back at last, instead of being perpetually on the receiving end.

'Remind me about Svoboda, Martha,' he said lightly. 'If I had forgotten I owned it, it can't be terribly valuable.'

'I think you're wrong, Leon,' Martha said quietly. 'The stats are really quite impressive. The mine was started in 2001. Currently, annual production averages 38,000 tonnes of ore mined and stockpiled, and over 30,000 ounces of actual gold.'

Leon whistled. 'That much?'

'Indeed,' Martha affirmed.

161

If Leon was mildly surprised, I was ... well, gob-smacked wouldn't be putting it too strongly. Forget about hotels and financial consultancies, Leon, I felt like saying. Forget about political online newsletters, too. Gold mines are where it's at!

'And this mine is in Siberia?' I asked.

Martha shook her head. 'The Far East, beyond Siberia. It's in the Amur Oblast of the Far Eastern Federal District, or region.'

She consulted her papers and added, 'The projected life of the mine is another forty years, but it might well go beyond that.'

'If the deposit is bigger than we initially thought,' Leon said thoughtfully, 'which is often the case.'

Martha agreed.

'Quite a valuable asset, then, Leon,' I suggested breezily. 'When he hears it, Bobrik should find your offer interesting.'

'Let's hope so, Frank,' he said with a smile.

Chapter Thirty-Seven

WE DIDN'T HAVE TOO long to wait. Bobrik – as I now believed him to be – called late that night, just before midnight.

'Doy?'

I readied myself to deal with an angry tirade.

'That's me. How can I help you?'

'By setting up a meeting with Podolsky.'

'I can do that.' No mention of Cayman. No screaming down the phone. Just a calm, quiet voice. That suited me. 'Where and when?'

I had discussed this with Leon. He was prepared to let Bobrik choose the venue again, but this time there would be a proviso.

'Not here. Prague,' Bobrik said without hesitation. 'I want my lawyer present.'

'Can you give us three days to get there and sort out the paperwork?'

'Three days, yes.'

'Good. Now we have a condition to propose.'

'What?'

'The meeting should be somewhere like a big hotel, and we want it to be arranged and managed by a third party we both trust who can guarantee security.'

'There's no need for all that. Podolsky and me know each other well.'

'Exactly. We don't want a repeat of the Montenegro fiasco. We want the meeting to be organized by either Blatko or Vorodin, Russian gentlemen resident in Prague who you both know.'

He chuckled. 'What is this?'

'They are people with an interest in the meeting being peace-ful – no bloodshed, in other words. You can choose which one you want to do it, and we will ask them to make the arrangements.'

I held my breath and waited for him to explode with rage. It didn't happen.

'Both,' he said after a short pause. 'Approach them both.'

'We'll do that,' I assured him, but by then he had already ended the call.

I switched the phone off and turned to give Leon a smile and a thumbs-up. Leon nodded and walked out of the room.

It was already the next day. We would have another day here, and a day spent in moving to Prague and setting the meeting up. Then there would be the meeting, the negotiation – or whatever the hell everyone wanted to call it.

I have to admit I was out of my depth. It would have suited me better if the meeting had been held here, or anywhere else in the UK. When it came to a city like Prague, I had no idea how things worked there. Also, I couldn't imagine who could provide the kind of security Leon wanted. The G8 organizers, perhaps? Events in Montenegro and since had given me a realistic idea of the scale of the challenge.

But it was what it was. The decision was not mine. Prague. In three days' time. Security in some hotel to be provided by two men of whom I had never heard. I just hoped Leon knew what he was doing. I was certain Bobrik did.

Meanwhile, I kept out of the way. Leon was busy dealing with some of the problems Bobrik had created for him around the world. Martha was even busier preparing information and documentation for the Prague meeting. Olga, I gathered, was keeping the online newspaper up to date. Lenka had disappeared altogether. I gathered she had gone on ahead to Prague, charged with contacting the people who Leon hoped would provide security for the meeting.

Everyone seemed to have a job to do. Everyone except me. I was at a loose end. I considered returning to Risky Point for some R & R, but reluctantly decided against it. I was afraid I might miss something if I did. Events moved fast in the Podolsky world. And you could say I was caught up in the excitement of it all. Bill Peart would undoubtedly have said something else, something more judgemental – and might well have arrested me. So I had to avoid him, and avoid being visited at home by him.

What I did do was reflect a lot on what had been happening. The Chesters was finished with, of course. No point spending time thinking about the old house in Northumberland. It was gone, along with its history, its contents and some good men. Perhaps justice would take its course eventually, but that wouldn't be soon and in any case, wouldn't help anybody much even if it did.

Far more significant, and urgent, was the impending negotiation with Bobrik. I wasn't happy about the meeting being held in Prague, but there was a sense in which the venue was appropriate. It was where Leon and Bobrik both had major interests, and it was where I had first stepped onto their stage. If Messrs Blatko and Vorodin really could guarantee security, perhaps it would turn out to have been a good thing. "If". I had my doubts.

Another big question was whether Bobrik would accept what was on offer. Would he take the gold mine and be satisfied, or would he still want that and everything else as well? Could he be persuaded to stop his campaign to destroy the Podolskys?

At least we had got him to the negotiating table. The Cayman trick had done that. We would start there, and take one step at a time.

Hopefully, we could avoid another Montenegro-style flare up. But just who the hell were Blatko and Vorodin? How could they possibly guarantee a peaceful negotiation?

Leon smiled when I put the question to him.

'Blatko and Vorodin are the two biggest Russian criminals in Prague,' he said succinctly.

'Ah!' I shook my head in disgust. 'Why didn't I guess? Bigger than you and Bobrik?'

He gave me a hurt look. 'Frank, Frank! You think of me like that?'

I just shrugged. How the hell did I know what he really was? I knew about his legal businesses, some of them, but were they all there was? Then there was the small matter of his disregard for the law when it suited him. But he came from a country where that was the norm. So why single him out for criticism?

'Bobrik is a criminal, yes,' Leon insisted. 'I am not. I try very hard not to be! But sometimes others make that difficult.'

I thought of the executions I had witnessed, and decided to keep quiet. I'm not very good at observing legal constraints myself. Half the time, Bill Peart wants to lock me up.

'OK, Leon,' I said wearily. 'That's you. What about these two characters who you and Bobrik think can arrange security? Can they? Really?'

'I believe so, yes. After all, it is in their own interests.'

'Both Russians, you said?'

He nodded.

Of course. How else would both Leon and Bobrik know them?

'They each have very many business activities, some legal, some less so. And some definitely illegal.'

'Nice guys. What sort of businesses?'

'Oh!' Leon blew out his cheeks and waved his arms. 'You know, Frank. The usual things.'

'Drugs? Prostitution? People trafficking?'

'Some, Blatko especially. Vorodin is more of a financial

criminal. He finds ways to manipulate stock markets and cash flows, I believe.'

'Maybe he should be in the government.'

'I think so, yes,' Leon said, taking me seriously for a moment. 'But here, not Russia. In Russia it is too difficult. There is too much competition,' he added with the old familiar grin.

I was growing tired of all this. In fact, I was tired full stop. I had been on the go for a long time. So had Leon, of course, but he was more used to this life than I was.

'OK, Leon. Priorities. What can these two characters do to help us?'

'It is simple, Frank. They are well-established in Prague. They like it there, as do I. It is in their interests to stop the Russian business community drawing attention to itself, and forcing the authorities to take action against us all.'

'But what will they actually do?'

'I don't know,' he said, spreading his arms in a gesture of helplessness. 'But I do know they will come up with something between them. Bobrik knows that, too. We can trust them.'

Trust them? I shook my head and went to look for Martha.

Chapter Thirty-Eight

I FOUND MARTHA IN the room she had requisitioned, where she was busy with screen, phone and even paper files.

'How are you doing?'

'Hi, Frank. I'm OK, thanks. Busy.'

'I can see that. I've brought you a cup of coffee. Take a couple of minutes off to drink it.'

She hesitated.

'Take it,' I instructed. 'Everyone else has coffee breaks.'

She smiled. 'Thanks, Frank.'

'How are you doing with ... Svoboda, is it?'

'OK. I'm getting there. There's a lot to do, though. The lawyers are not used to working this fast.'

'Even the ones that work for Leon?'

'Even them. But we want our proposal to be properly backed up with title deeds, etcetera. So they must get on with it.'

I sat down and sipped my coffee. 'Where, exactly, is the gold mine? You did tell me. But remind me.'

'The Russian Far East.'

'Beyond Siberia, you said?'

She nodded. 'That's right. But it's handy for the Trans-Siberian Railway. It's actually in the Amur Oblast, if you know where that is.'

'Very vaguely. Not that I've been.'

'No more have I. Even Leon hasn't been for a few years. Anyway, it's in the south, on the border with China.'

'And it's just been left to its own devices, to get on with producing gold?'

'Exactly. That was the safest way, given that the State had found ways of confiscating Leon's other mines.'

I shook my head. Business couldn't be easy in a country where the writ of law didn't run very deep, and in any case was applied differentially. No wonder Leon wasn't always too bothered about observing it himself. He'd learned the hard way.

'How big is it?'

'The mine? Oh, it's not one of the big ones. Polyus has the biggest. Their new Natalka mine produced 500,000 ounces in its first year, and will soon be up to 1.5 million ounces. In total, it has 60,000,000 ounces of reserves. But that's State-owned. Any deposit with more than fifty tonnes of ore is claimed by the State.

'Svoboda is nothing like that. Total proven reserves are about three million ounces, and it produced 36,000 ounces last year.'

I did some quick mental arithmetic. Given that the current price of gold was not far short of $1,200 per ounce, the outcome was pretty impressive, small mine or not.

'So last year, Svoboda produced gold worth about $43,000,000?'

Martha screwed her face up in concentration. 'Something like that. Turnover, of course. Not profit. And you have to remember the price of gold is lower right now than it was a few years ago. At 2011 prices, that output was worth more like $65,000,000.'

'No wonder Bobrik is interested! He could soon replace the money Olga emptied out of his Cayman accounts.'

'Indeed.'

'I'm surprised Leon wants rid of it.'

She grimaced. 'In an ideal world.... But Russia is not ideal for investors without friends in Moscow.'

'And especially not for political opponents?'

'That's about the size of it,' she said with a shrug. 'There's no way Leon can do business in Russia. It's a pure fluke that he still owns this mine.'

I wondered if Bobrik could do better. He must think he could. Otherwise, he wouldn't be prepared to talk about it.

The other explanation, of course, was that he was desperate after Olga had cleaned him out in Cayman. One way or another, it looked like being a tricky negotiation in Prague.

'Is Bobrik really going to stick by the rules?' I wondered.

'Leon thinks he will. He believes even Bobrik won't dare go up against the men organizing the meeting. If he does, he can say goodbye to everything he has in the Czech Republic, and certain other countries as well. Bobrik may be big, but he wouldn't be able to stand up against the combined forces of Blatko and Vorodin.'

'They sound like the Mafia!' I suggested with a chuckle.

Martha didn't smile at all. 'That's exactly what they are, Frank. And in their world, strange as it sounds, trust is everything. Break that trust, and you might as well spend your remaining time on Earth organizing your own funeral.'

'Their version of trust, of course.'

She nodded. 'Exactly. Now kindly piss off, Frank, and let me do my job!'

I kissed the top of her head and left her to get on with it.

Chapter Thirty-Nine

PEOPLE BEDDED DOWN AROUND the building for what remained of the night. From somewhere, sleeping bags and quilts were found and distributed, as if it wasn't such an uncommon experience for the staff of the IT centre.

'We do a lot of work at night,' Martha confided, as if she was one of them.

'Not me,' I said shortly, grabbing a sleeping bag. 'I'm at my best in daylight.'

She grinned, announced that she still had things to do and took off. I found a quiet corner and got my head down. I thought I might add something for sleep deprivation when I finally gave Leon my bill for expenses.

The next morning, soon after eight, Leon, Martha and I headed out to the Durham Tees Valley International Airport not far away at Middleton St. George, halfway between Stockton and Darlington. Leon's executive jet was waiting there for us.

'I'm surprised the pilot could find his way here,' I remarked as we headed across some pretty bland open country cloaked in mist.

'Oh, he's used to picking me up in out of the way places,' Leon said.

I smiled. I could imagine that. Working for Leon would never be easy. There would be plenty of smaller and poorer airports than this one to be visited.

Martha moved up front with the driver, which gave Leon and me in the back seat a chance to talk.

'Tell me more about the men who are guaranteeing security for the meeting,' I invited.

'You think it should be you looking after security?' he asked with a smile.

'No way! I have no leverage in Prague.'

'Well, they do, fortunately. Even Bobrik knows that, which is why he agreed so readily. I have told you about them. What more

169

do you want to know?'

'More detail. Who they are. What they are. How come they have such influence.'

Leon paused, probably to sanitize the character reference he was about to give them.

'Vorodin is a financial genius. He finds ways to bribe and corrupt government ministers and officials. He launders money for the criminal community and deals with stolen art treasures, and so on. And he buys and sells things in ways that are illegal in any civilized country in the world.'

'Nice guy! And he's based in Prague?'

'In the Czech Republic, yes. Where he actually lives I don't know, but that country is where his business is based.'

'What about the other one – Blatko?'

Leon gave a heavy sigh. 'He is different. He is involved in drug smuggling, arms trading and people trafficking, as you wondered. Prague is a natural transhipment point between east and west Europe. So it suits him, too, to be based in Prague.'

It was something to think about. Why was Prague so much more congenial than, say, Moscow? Freer politically, perhaps? The rule of law, instead of the rule of one man and his cronies? Who could tell?

'And you know them both, Leon? What does that make you – and me, for associating with you?'

'I don't know them well personally, but I know who they are and I have met them. As I told you, the Podolsky businesses are legal. What my compatriots do is their business,' he added stiffly.

I decided not to push him any further. It was going to be a long enough day, even without the two of us falling out.

'We're here!' Martha called over her shoulder.

Indeed we were. And Leon's plane was here, too, and all ready to go.

Formalities were pretty minimal and we took off within a few minutes of arriving at the small and quiet terminal.

'Two hours,' Leon said with satisfaction. 'We will be there in two hours.'

I nodded. Leon gave up his seat to Martha and went forward to talk to the pilot.

'How are you doing?' I asked her.

She smiled and said, 'OK. I think I'm on top of things now.'

'Good. Ready to negotiate?'

'I think so. Shall we discuss tactics?'

We did. But the reality was that the situation did not lend itself to complex positioning. We had a proposal to put. Then we would respond to what the other side had to say about it. After that, we would be able to sense if we had the makings of a deal.

'We are going first to the Presidium Hotel,' Leon advised me as we walked out of the terminal in Prague and looked for the car he had ordered.

'Nice name. Nostalgic – especially for you Russians.'

He grinned. 'It used to be called the Red Star Hotel.'

'Even better. So that's where the meeting will be?'

'Yes. Tomorrow. We go there now because Blatko and Vorodin want to meet each side separately, in advance.'

To tell us the rules of engagement, presumably. It made sense. I wondered again if they really would be able to ensure that Bobrik played by the rules. I still had my doubts. But if they could, they had to be something special.

The Presidium Hotel was a massive block of 1960s concrete set on the banks of the river Vltava, not far from the city centre. In summer, the lawns sloping down towards the river would be alive with sprinklers and flower beds. Right now, they were buried beneath mountains of decaying snow from the recent blizzard.

We were met in the entrance by a couple of tough-looking men. They had a few words with Leon and then walked us through an atrium stretching up to the sky and into an elevator that whisked us to the tenth floor. Once there, we were led along a walkway that bordered the atrium to what was obviously a very expensive suite, where Blatko and Vorodin were waiting.

Leon addressed them briskly in Russian before turning to introduce Martha and myself. We shook hands with our hosts, and, with some alarm in my case, accepted kisses on both cheeks,

Russian style. Then we all sat down around a conference table. This was where the big meeting was to be held, I gathered.

One young woman brought round a tray of shot glasses containing what I assumed was vodka. Another occupied herself at a side table pouring tea from an enormous samovar, which was bubbling contentedly and emitting gentle puffs of steam. We were being given a traditional welcome.

Blatko proposed a toast that I didn't understand, and we all raised our glasses and drank. The women who had done the serving disappeared. The two men who had brought us here took up positions at a discreet distance from the table, guarding the door and their employers. Then Vorodin took the chair and made a short speech.

I didn't really know what he was saying, but I paid diplomatic attention. Martha, I noticed, did even better. I even wondered if she understood what was being said.

I studied our hosts. Surprisingly, Vorodin, the alleged financial genius, was a thuggish looking man. Middle-aged, short and heavily built, he could have been a superannuated Olympic weight-lifter. Perhaps he was a great poker player, though, because his expressionless face gave nothing away. What he thought of us, and the entire situation, remained a mystery.

Blatko, the drugs, arms and people trafficker, was also a surprise, but in an entirely different way. He was younger and slimmer, and with his sunny smile, altogether more presentable and attractive. Also, he was the one who spoke English.

Just as I was thinking it was a waste of time my being there, if the whole conversation was to be in the Russian language, Blatko turned his smile towards me and said, 'Welcome, Mr Doy. I admit to being surprised that Mr Podolsky's close adviser is an Englishman, but I respect his choice. To save time, I will let him tell you later what I have been saying, but I want you to know that you are not being overlooked.'

I nodded to acknowledge his courtesy and he turned back to Leon. Martha, I noticed, received neither a word nor a smile. It gave me the impression that women were not rated in their world, but Martha took it on the chin and didn't object.

Afterwards, Leon's car collected us and we set off to his villa on the outskirts of the city. I noticed that the driver took considerable care to assess whether or not we were being followed, and engaged in some complicated evasive manoeuvres.

At one point, two powerful cars came up behind us. At a slow speed, they occupied both the lanes going in our direction. It was a rolling road block that allowed us to speed off at high speed and stopped anyone who might have been following.

I glanced at Leon.

'Don't worry, Frank. We are simply being careful.'

I nodded. 'I'm not worried, Leon. Just surprised, and impressed.'

He sighed and said, 'We are used to such things.'

The Podolsky family, I assumed he meant. It was how they lived.

'So what did Voronin say?'

'Only what I expected to hear.' He shrugged. 'Both he and Blatko are anxious to bring hostilities to an end. The conflict threatens their own business operations. For that reason, they have accepted this task. They expect, and demand, that both parties enter negotiations in a spirit of partnership and cooperation.

'Non-cooperation will not be accepted, or tolerated. They are both determined to avoid it. Any transgression will be met with appropriate sanctions. That's all. We meet tomorrow at noon.'

'Appropriate sanctions,' I murmured. 'What might they be, I wonder? Will thought of them be sufficient to restrain Bobrik?'

'Oh, yes,' Martha assured me earnestly. 'There is no doubt about that.'

I glanced at her, surprised by her intervention. She looked away.

Leon nodded agreement. 'Yes, indeed,' he affirmed. 'Only a fool would discount the combined power of Blatko and Vorodin in this city.'

'But Bobrik is backed by the Kremlin,' I pointed out.

'And so are they,' Leon responded with a steely glint in his eye. 'So are they.'

Chapter Forty

LEON'S VILLA WAS A good place for us to retreat to after the pre-liminary session at the Presidium. It would probably have been a good place to retreat to at any time. Comfortable, safe, warm, well-staffed, it felt good to be there. Not exactly homely. It was too big and luxurious for that. But it was home for Leon, and I was happy to be there with him.

We got ourselves installed and ate a late lunch. Then we got down to business. By then, Lenka had arrived to join us. She seemed in good form.

'Well done!' Leon told her. 'Persuading Blatko and Vorodin to host the meeting can't have been easy.'

Lenka shrugged and yawned, but I could tell she was pleased by the compliment.

'I just told them we were about to start a fire-bombing cam-paign of Russian-owned premises in Prague,' she said airily. 'If they wanted to stop it, they had to act now.'

I stared at her. 'Tell me you were joking?' I demanded.

Lenka just stared back at me. It was worrying. By then, I knew nothing was beyond her.

'Well, it seems to have worked,' Martha said quickly. 'That's the main thing.'

I wasn't sure it was, but I let it go.

'What about the security arrangements?' Leon asked.

Lenka scowled. 'OK, I think. They agreed to evacuate the entire tenth floor, and to guard every way of getting onto it.'

'Can they do that?' I asked.

'Yes,' Lenka said.

I wondered how easy it would be.

'Frank,' Leon said patiently, 'they own the Presidium. They can do whatever they like.'

So that settled one question.

We sorted out various other matters over the next hour or two. Then we were joined by Leon's Czech lawyer, Dalibor, a big cheerful man who brought some welcome humour to our gathering.

'The tenth floor of the Presidium?' he said dubiously when Leon explained where the meeting was to be held the next day.

'It is safe enough,' Leon pointed out.

'Possibly,' Dalibor said even more doubtfully.

Turning to me, he said, 'This is your first visit to Prague, Mr Doy?'

'Not quite. I was here for a few days just the other week.'

'Ah! So you are aware of how we Czechs dispose of our political opponents?'

'Elect them to Parliament, as we do in Britain?'

'No, no! We defenestrate them. It is our custom.'

I must have looked blank for a moment. Martha explained. 'They push them out the window, Frank. Historically, I mean.'

'Good God! Do they really?'

Dalibor nodded vigorously. 'It is true. It is also why holding a meeting on the tenth floor of any building in Prague is not such a good idea, in my opinion. Better, I think, to hold the meeting on a barge on the Vltava, preferably one with French cuisine and wine.'

'And risk drowning?' Leon queried.

'Ah!' Dalibor raised a hand, conceding the point. 'I knew there was some reason not to do that. Perhaps the Presidium is best, after all.'

Dalibor was obviously one of those lawyers who liked to hear themselves talk. He was good at holding the floor, which might well be exactly what we would need tomorrow. I began to warm to him.

With his excellent English, and apparently good Russian as well, Dalibor was also to be the interpreter Martha and I needed in the first part of the meeting, before the principals joined the discussion. I wasn't sure Martha needed an interpreter, but I certainly did.

I had asked Martha if she knew the Russian language. No, she had told me. Just the odd word or two. I assumed she was being modest. At the meeting with Blatko and Vorodin, she had seemed quite comfortable following the discussion in Russian.

I didn't pursue it with her, but it reminded me how little I knew about Martha. Next to nothing, in fact. Our acquaintance, such as it was, had been very brief and recent. If she hadn't obliged me to resign from my role at The Chesters, and then come to the Black Bull to try to persuade me to change my mind, I might not have got to know her at all.

She'd been lucky, I couldn't help thinking. If she hadn't sought to change my mind, she would have been on the heap of the dead at The Chesters, along with Leon's other employees. Very lucky, when you thought about it.

I wondered if Bobrik had expected her to be there, at The Chesters, along with the others. Probably. He seemed to know an awful lot about Leon's arrangements. So why wouldn't he have known about the old house, and who was working on it?

That set me to wondering where Bobrik's information came from. How could he keep abreast of things in Leon's world? Was he being informed? Was there a mole in Leon's camp? Disquieting though the thought was, I had to wonder.

Later, when the briefings were over and the others had dispersed, Martha and I spent some time together. Over a beer we chewed over what we had learned and what was still to come. I wasn't too happy, and Martha spotted that.

'What is it, Frank? Worried about tomorrow?'

I sighed. 'To some extent. Mostly, though, I'm just worried about what I'm doing here. Where do I fit in? What can I offer that other people in Leon's team can't? You, for example.'

She smiled. 'You really don't know, do you? You haven't figured it out yet.'

I shook my head.

'It's about trust, Frank. Leon trusts you, trusts you to be on his side, and to be sensible and effective. You have proved that to him time and time again, starting with that fracas outside his hotel here in Prague, going on to Montenegro, and then to The Chesters.'

I smiled, without feeling amused. 'None of those episodes was a success, though, was it? Damage limitation, mostly.'

'But that's it! When things went wrong, you stepped in effectively. Each time, it could have been so much worse. Leon is an astute man. He knows what you did, and he appreciates it.'

'A fat lot of good I'll be tomorrow, though. Negotiating through a Czech interpreter, a man who seems to see it as his role in life to be jolly and entertaining. You're the one with the knowledge and the detailed information, not me.'

'You will bring gravitas to the proceedings, Frank. I can do some things. But, much as I hate to say this, when things go wrong – as they surely will again tomorrow – you're better than me. You can respond mentally and physically – again I use the word – more effectively. Leon knows that. It's why he wants you there.'

I smiled, if reluctantly. 'You're wasted,' I said. 'You should be a high-earning psychotherapist who makes people feel good about themselves. Maybe in Manhattan.'

'Am I good for you, Frank?' she asked coyly.

'Oh, yes,' I said, taking her in my arms and smiling sincerely now. 'You're very good.'

And so she was, to a point. But in the small hours, when she was asleep and I was still awake, I stared at her relaxed face and wondered who she was.

Increasingly, I was aware that she was a stranger. We had shared some hectic hours together, some of them frankly terrifying, and we were good together in bed, but what did I really know of her? Not much. Not much more now than when I had met her for the first time at The Chesters.

She worked for Leon, and she was a valued employee with capabilities that were important to him. Based in London, and British, she seemed to be one of his go-to people when there was a project to manage, someone who could be left to get on with picking up and running a new venture. That was about it, all I had been told or given to understand. But there was more to Martha than that, and some of it I was beginning to figure out for myself.

One thing was my growing belief that despite what she said, Martha understood Russian. She probably spoke it as well. I had seen her intelligent face light up as she followed the discussions in the pre-meeting. Nothing odd about her having a language capability, you might say, but I was surprised Leon hadn't mentioned it.

Then there was Lenka's mysterious word of advice. Did that come from jealousy, or did she know things I didn't? Jealousy, probably. I knew myself that Lenka didn't like outsiders getting into the family's inner circle.

I slipped out of bed without disturbing Martha and wandered over to the window. Still a snow-covered landscape out there. Being able to see the outside world gave me some reassurance and slowed my racing mind. It gave me a sense of perspective, too. I couldn't stay cocooned in Leon's world. I had to stay grounded, and have my own take on things if I was to make sense of them.

Something bothering me a lot was how Bobrik seemed to know so much about Leon's affairs and intentions. Once again, I was thinking about insider information, and about the possibility of there being a mole in Leon's retinue. Surely not?

I sighed and shook my head. Some things were beyond me to know. I would have to accept that, and try to sleep. Like Martha!

I smiled fondly and gazed across the room at her. How did she do it? She had even more on her mind than I had. She was the one with all the knowledge about the gold mine.

It was impossible to forget, as well, how much her world had been turned upside down lately. She had arrived at The Chesters all ready to go on her new project – and look at what had happened! In a few hours everything had changed, and she had found herself an endangered refugee, running for her life.

How lucky she had been, though. Coming to persuade me to withdraw my resignation had meant she wasn't murdered along with the others. In that sense, it couldn't have worked out better for her if it had been planned. I shivered uneasily, not liking that insidious thought one little bit. I returned to bed, and eventually to sleep, troubled by where we were going with all this. I just didn't believe things would work out well at the Presidium.

Forty-One

MARTHA AND I TRAVELLED to the Presidium with Leon and Dalibor in a posh Lexus saloon. I wondered if the car had bulletproof windows, and rather hoped it did.

'What a beautiful morning!' Dalibor said, glancing around admiringly at the wintry sunshine.

Martha, very subdued, ignored him. I gave him a thin smile, wondering if the man had any idea what we were heading into. Perhaps Leon hadn't told him. I felt like asking him if he knew there was a good chance we might all end up riddled with bullets today.

'Good luck, all of you,' Leon said tersely before we got out of the car. 'Call me when you can.'

As we headed towards the entrance to the Presidium, I glanced over my shoulder and wondered where the Lexus was taking Leon.

'A hotel around the corner,' Martha said, divining my thoughts. 'He will wait there.'

Not far, then. Good. We might need him soon. I had limited confidence in the ability of Blatko and Vorodin to prevent the violence Bobrik was capable of unleashing.

The two men who had escorted us the previous day met us with nods of recognition outside the entrance and shepherded us inside. The hotel was very quiet. Only a few people were sitting around in the atrium dining area as we passed through. Breakfast had finished, and lunch didn't seem to have started. I was surprised and said something to Dalibor along the lines of it being my impression that Czechs ate lunch early.

'The kitchen is closed because of a technical problem,' he said with a wry smile. 'Today, guests are advised to eat lunch elsewhere – or miss it altogether.'

I raised my eyebrows.

'Yes,' he added quietly. 'It is for us, I believe.'

I revised my opinion of Dalibor. Perhaps he did know what we were walking into.

The conference room was as I remembered it: one big table, chairs around it for ten people, a couple of big potted palms, facilities for making tea and coffee, and big sliding glass doors giving access to a wide balcony overlooking the Vltava. Waiting for us were our hosts, Blatko and Vorodin.

I was impressed with the stage management. As we entered the room, Bobrik's contingent appeared from the other side. Our hosts were clearly intent on being even-handed. I took some comfort from that, but it was early days yet.

Once again, Vorodin made a short speech in Russian to welcome us all formally. Then Blatko took over. He made the introductions, in both Russian and English, and with the help of four attendant men, got us seated at the table. Coffee and tea were served by two young women who discreetly withdrew from the room as soon as their task was completed.

Then Vorodin went through the rules of engagement once again. There wasn't a lot to say, but what there was said it all. I didn't really need Dalibor's translation, but I listened intently anyway.

'It is in all our interests,' Vorodin said firmly, 'to bring hostilities between the two parties to an end. Mr Blatko and myself are determined to do what we can to help bring that about.

'As previously agreed, the delegates here now will seek amicable agreement. Once that is established, the two principals will be summoned to endorse the agreement. Then,' he added with a smile, 'our lives will be able to go on happily in this beautiful historic city.

'Finally, let me repeat that Mr Blatko and myself will take the most serious view of any transgression of the rules of engagement. You are here in good faith, accepting our hospitality, and proceedings will be conducted in an appropriate manner.'

By which, he presumably meant, we were not to start fighting or shooting each other – or else! That was fine by me.

'Gentlemen – and lady –' Vorodin said in conclusion, 'that is all I wish to say. Now I turn the proceedings over to you.'

As previously agreed, I made my pitch on behalf of Leon. It was simple enough. In return for a truce, a cessation of hostilities and agreement to draw a line under all that had happened, it was proposed to transfer ownership of the Svoboda gold mine in the Russian Far East to Bobrik.

I listed the headline figures for the mine covering age, longevity, output, reserves, and so on, and then invited Martha to present a more detailed account. She did that rather well, with Dalibor translating. She spoke crisply, and judged the pace of her delivery superbly. I was impressed.

The other side listened intently, as if they were waiting to hear what the catch was. They were led by a guy called Brodsky, who looked to me like a streetwise lawyer from Moscow. It seemed to go well enough.

Brodsky nodded at frequent intervals and asked Martha a few questions that kept the interpreters busy. His sidekick, whose name I had missed, weighed in with a couple of points of detail that Dalibor translated and Martha fielded. Vorodin seemed to take a keen interest, Blatko less so.

As I say, it seemed to be going well, but I wasn't sure. This was partly because I was distanced from the nub of things by the language barrier. It was like peering through murky water, trying to get a clear picture of a fish you are targeting. Probably the Russian poker faces, or chess faces, didn't help, either. So I found it hard to get a feel for things.

It began to seem too easy somehow, too relaxed. Early days, perhaps, but there was none of the heated argument I had anticipated. It was a question and answer session, not a real negotiation. Nobody, absolutely nobody, was getting het-up or in any sort of tangle. Good, in a way, that people were so cool, but it felt strange. As I say, I was uneasy.

Men had died in this feud, quite a few to my knowledge. A dozen, at least. A score, actually, when you added up Montenegro and The Chesters, not to mention casualties I knew nothing about. And for what? Could it all have been avoided by seating people around a table, discussing things sensibly, like this? I had my doubts.

While Martha was engaged in a long, tedious explanation of transportation arrangements in the Russian Far East, I pushed my chair back and stood up to ease my limbs. I moved slowly over towards the window, aware that Vorodin and Blatko, and no doubt all four of their men, would be watching me like hawks. I didn't care. I needed to get away from the table for a moment.

I stared down at the river. A couple of pleasure boats, floating restaurants, were moving slowly upstream, heading for the system of locks that would get them past the artificial rapids the Vltava encounters in the centre of Prague. It was a tortuous journey. That wouldn't trouble the skippers and crews, of course, or the tourist passengers, either. This was the best stretch of river to be afloat on in Prague, the historic heart of the city, with the castle high up on one bank and the Old Town on the other shore.

Tortuous. These interminable discussions were, too. Then it struck me. This wasn't a negotiation at all. It was the delivery of set-piece speeches in the form of a question-and-answer session. It was as if the business had already been concluded, perhaps even before the meeting started.

I returned to the table, listening intently. What were they talking about now? The process for refining gold from the ore extracted in a hard-rock mine. They had finished with transport. Now this. They could have got it, this information, from Wikipedia!

I interrupted Martha, impatient to bring this to some sort of conclusion.

182

'Forgive me, Mr Brodsky, but time moves on, and I am anxious to complete the main business of the day. May I suggest this level of detail can best be settled in later sessions between our technical advisers?'

Looking daggers at me, Martha said, 'Frank, it's important!'

Despite that, I was determined to impose my agenda and my timetable on the meeting.

'I know it is, Martha, but I would like to hear Mr Brodsky's response – even if it is only in principle – to our basic proposal for ending hostilities.'

'Frank—'

Thankfully, Dalibor intervened at that point. 'I think Mr Doy is right,' he said with an apologetic smile. 'I myself am due in court very soon, and won't be able to stay here for the duration of the technical discussions, I'm afraid.'

Martha looked ready to blow a blood vessel. Somehow she desisted. She shrugged and pushed her chair back from the table, signalling that she was giving way, if reluctantly.

'Mr Brodsky?' I said gently.

It looked as if he had been caught unawares by this shift, and he twisted uncomfortably in his chair for a moment while he worked out what to say. I noticed that Vorodin was taking a keen interest in Brodsky's discomfort.

Through their interpreter, Brodsky said yes, they were prepared in principle to accept the offer of the mine, with one caveat. They insisted on the funds that had been taken from the Cayman account being restored. Otherwise, there could be no deal.

I mulled that over for a moment, eager to create the impression that the qualification was one I was prepared to entertain, which, of course, on behalf of Leon, I was not.

Then Martha beat me to it. 'Yes,' she said, 'that is fair. I'm sure Mr Podolsky will agree to that.'

'No, Martha!' I snapped, scarcely able to believe my ears. 'That is not acceptable. Definitely not.'

'Frank—'

I held up my hand and turned to face Blatko, who had been following our exchanges and was looking amused by the breakdown of our negotiating position. I said that we required an adjournment. There needed to be consultations with my principal.

'Very well,' he said, glancing at his watch, and then at Vorodin, who nodded. 'We will allow you a thirty minute recess. If you cannot return to the table by then, the meeting will be brought to an end, and the negotiations abandoned.'

I nodded my thanks and got to my feet. Dalibor followed. Martha was reluctant to leave the table, but acquiesced with poor grace. We were shown to a nearby room, where we could speak amongst ourselves, although perhaps not securely.

'Frank,' Martha said, 'I have never been so humiliated! How dare you?'

'Shut up, Martha. Your behaviour in there was completely unacceptable.'

I pulled out my phone.

'Who are you phoning?' she demanded.

I ignored her and made the call.

'Leon? I want Martha taken off the team. She has just tried to give away our negotiating position. I've called for an adjournment while we sort things out.'

To his credit, Leon reacted calmly. 'Tell me what happened, Frank.'

I told him.

'Is Dalibor there with you?'

'He is.'

'Let me speak with him.'

I handed the phone over, and listened to Dalibor giving his assent to whatever Leon was saying or asking.

'Well?' I demanded when I got the phone back.

'Martha is to leave immediately,' Leon said quietly. 'Let me speak to her now.'

Together with Dalibor, I returned to the meeting and tried to pick up the pieces.

'Your caveat is not acceptable,' I told Brodsky. 'The Cayman funds will not be returned. They will be used to pay for at least some of the damage caused to Mr Podolsky's property and businesses. For example, the destruction of his yacht in Montenegro, the hotel here in Prague and his historic property in England.

'We very much doubt that the funds will be sufficient to cover the cost of all the damage. Even so, we still offer to transfer ownership of the gold mine.'

Brodsky was shaking his head.

'No? You think it is not enough?'

'Not enough,' he said, struggling in broken English.

'Then we are done here,' I told him. 'This meeting is over.'

Chapter Forty-Two

IT'S FAIR TO SAY I was fuming when I left the meeting, and the building. I couldn't believe Martha's behaviour. It was nothing short of sabotage. Why the hell had she done it?

Leon's car picked me and Dalibor up outside the hotel and took us to where Leon was waiting. We said very little to each other on the way. I think Dalibor was just as bemused as me.

The car dropped us off outside a small hotel a few streets away. There, Dalibor shook my hand and wished me good day. He said he would speak to Leon later. In the meantime, other business was pressing. I nodded and thanked him for his support.

He gave me a wry smile and said, 'What's that saying the Americans have? Shit happens?'

I grinned and shook his hand.

Leon was waiting in the coffee shop on the ground floor of the hotel. He looked weary.

'How did it happen?' he asked.

'No idea. Where's Martha?'

He shook his head. 'I don't know. Sit down, Frank, and tell me again.'

I took a seat and told him the story.

'Brodsky insisted that, as well as the mine, they wanted the full return of the Cayman funds. I told him no, that the money would be used to pay for some of the damage they had caused. He repeated their position. Martha supported him. So I asked for an adjournment, and walked out.'

I leant back in my chair, and added, 'So where is she?'

'I don't know,' Leon said again. 'She didn't come here. Lenka is looking for her.'

'Lenka? She's around? It's a pity she wasn't with me and Dalibor. Bloody Martha!'

Leon nodded. 'It sounds like she compromised our position.'

'She certainly did. I couldn't believe it when she said we would agree to return the Cayman funds. She wouldn't stop when I challenged her, either. She argued like a wildcat.'

Leon waved to a waiter, who brought us both coffee. It gave us a breathing space. My fury began to subside.

'I wonder what got into her?' Leon said quietly as he stirred sugar into his coffee.

'That's my question, as well,' I said bitterly.

'You feel betrayed, Frank?'

'Well....'

'Me, too,' Leon said.

I took a sip of my coffee and then sat back. My poor old brain began to function on something other than rage.

'You know, Leon, I haven't said anything before. In fact, I hadn't even worked it out properly. But I'd been starting to wonder about Martha. I know, I know!' I said hurriedly as his eyebrows went up in surprise.

'Yes, we slept together a couple of times. I admit it. I like her, or I did. We seemed to get on well together. We went through some tough times together, as well.'

'But?' Leon said quietly. 'Is that a "but" I hear?'

I nodded. 'Yes, it is. It bothered me that Bobrik seemed to

know so much about the Podolskys, and their business interests. Everywhere we went, everything we did, we couldn't turn around without Bobrik being there. I began to wonder if there was a mole in your camp.'

'An informer?'

'Yeah. Someone who knew a lot. I don't know many of your people, and most of the ones I've met seem to have got themselves killed. So who could it be? I didn't think it could be family, and once I started thinking about it Martha came into the frame.'

Leon nodded slowly and waited for me to continue.

'Then I thought about how Martha and I first met, and how lucky it was for her that she came to visit me after I'd left The Chesters. If she hadn't done that, I thought, she would probably have been killed, along with Andrei and the others. It couldn't have been better for her if it had been planned.

'Then yesterday, at the preliminary meeting, I sensed that she understood Russian. She didn't need anybody to translate for her. And finally, today, she broke ranks and tried to scupper the negotiations.'

Leon was silent as he studied what I'd said. I could see him testing the idea of Martha as a traitor.

'It doesn't make sense,' he said eventually. 'Why would she do that when she has a good job with us? She has been almost part of the family.'

By then, I was beginning to think the same thing myself. I was just stringing a lot of coincidences together. The only thing I was sure of was that Martha had screwed up our negotiation.

'Well, she certainly let you down today,' I said wearily. 'Me, too.'

Leon's phone danced on the table. He picked it up. I overheard some excitable babble in Russian. Leon asked a couple of questions and gave some instructions. Then he switched the phone off.

'I wonder,' he said slowly. 'Perhaps you are right, Frank. Svoboda is worth at least ten times what Martha said. Perhaps more. That was one of my accountants. I had him check a few things about the mine.'

'And you think she knows that?'

He nodded. 'She does. Once you look at the figures, the account-ant said, it is obvious. And Martha has access to the same data he does.'

I grimaced. My perspective changed again. It looked as if Martha had done a good job for Bobrik. The only thing that puzzled me was why she had come out into the open now, in the way she did, in the meeting. What was that about?

I thought for a few moments more. Then I said, 'I'm going to look for her.'

Chapter Forty-Three

WHERE, THOUGH? WHERE TO look?

I had no idea, but I believed Martha wouldn't be far away. She couldn't be. Lenka would probably have picked her up if she had taken off somewhere. My guess was that she would be around the Presidium still. So that's where I went.

The catering department was open for business again. However the management had explained the default of kitchen and res-taurant, there were plenty of diners there now. Whatever meal they were partaking of at three in the afternoon, they seemed to be enjoying it, too. I made my way through the restaurant and entered the coffee shop, where I sat and ordered an espresso, and then glanced briefly at a newspaper someone had abandoned.

Then I thought about Martha. She would have been in a highly agitated state when she left the meeting, summoned by Leon, her career probably in ruins. Whatever had possessed her?

By now, I had calmed down enough to persuade myself that she had been very stressed and had acted out of character. She had no longer been the high-powered, up and coming project manager of a global business. For some reason, the situation had got on top of her. She had blown it.

Even if she had been intent on helping Bobrik, she had picked a funny way of doing it. The negotiations had broken up, without resolution. Bobrik wouldn't be pleased, any more than Leon and I were. Something had gone wrong, and she had found herself in a hole.

So where had she gone?

I doubted if she was familiar with Prague. The UK, London particularly, was her beat. She wouldn't have had a personal bolt-hole here to run to. Nor could she have expected to receive an ecstatic welcome from Bobrik. Perhaps she knew, too, that Lenka, or somebody else delegated by Leon, would be looking for her. So?

My guess was that she hadn't gone far at all. She had known she simply had to make herself scarce, and that's what she'd done. But where had she gone?

A lift pinged on the other side of the coffee shop. I glanced at it, and at the perfectly ordinary middle-aged couple who emerged from it, laughing and having such a good time. People often do, I thought cynically. Not me, though. Hell on wheels summed up my relaxing short break in the Czech capital.

My gaze strayed to the lights signalling the lift's progress back upstairs, all the way to the top floor, the tenth. The tenth? I frowned. No. That wasn't right. This hotel had twelve floors. I'd counted them when I was outside.

I thought about it. The meeting had been on the tenth floor. Not the top of the building, but perhaps the highest floor to which there was public access. As the hotel belonged to either Blatko or Vorodin, or both of them, the two top floors might well be set aside for their own private use.

Thinking along those lines gave me an idea. Martha, even in her agitated state, would have known that she would be picked up by somebody if she tried to leave the building. Possibly by Bobrik's men, or by Leon's people – Lenka even. She wouldn't have wanted any of that to happen. But she needed somewhere to go to sort herself out. Why not up there?

It made sense. I left money for my coffee and headed back into the atrium and made for the lifts.

There were two floors above the tenth, where the meeting

had been held. A lift on the tenth floor gave access to them, but I looked for and found the emergency stairs. They took me to the very top of the building. I ignored what were probably prohibitive notices on various doors and kept going upwards until I could go no further. Then I opened a fire door and made my way onto the roof.

That was where I found her, just as I had half-expected, and had hoped.

She was gazing out over the city. I approached her slowly, carefully. But she still heard me coming. Her head swung round.

'Get away from me!' she snapped, pushing out with both hands. 'Don't you come anywhere near me.'

For a moment, I thought she was contemplating jumping. Then I knew she wasn't. She was too self-aware, and too robust for that. I sat down on a ventilator cap and tried to appear relaxed. She stared at me, suspicious.

'OK, Martha. What's going on?'

'Go away, Frank. It's nothing to do with you.'

I waited a moment or two, and then said gently, 'What have you got yourself into?'

She said nothing.

The seconds passed. Half a minute. Longer. Still she said nothing. Nor did I. Waiting is something I can do.

Then, visibly, she seemed to deflate. I watched as she collapsed inwardly. All that anger that was fuelling her attitude dissipated.

'They have my daughter, Frank,' she said quietly. 'Bobrik has her.'

I winced. I should have known something had happened.

'You have a daughter?'

She nodded. 'Alysha. She's seven.'

'You left her with her father?'

'No. Her father and I are no longer together. I left her with her grandmother.'

'In London?'

'Yes.'

All this reminded me again just how little I knew of Martha.

Time had been compressed in our brief acquaintance, and the illusion had been created in our togetherness that we knew each other well.

'I'm not going to apologize, Frank,' she suddenly blurted out. 'I did what I had to do.'

I nodded. I believed her.

'You'd better tell me what happened,' I suggested.

There wasn't a lot she could tell me. The story was simple, and straightforward. She had received a couple of phone calls. They had been the start of it. One had said they had her daughter, and if she wanted to see her again she should keep quiet. The other, from her mother, had said Alysha was missing. It had all escalated from there.

Bobrik wanted information from her at first, and then he had required her support in his corporate war with the Podolsky family. Otherwise, Alysha's body would be returned to her.

I shook my head and felt sick at heart. As Martha had said, she'd had no choice. No-one in her position would have felt they did have a choice. What I didn't know, and didn't ask, was when all this had started. There seemed no point.

'And now I've blown it,' she said bitterly. 'All that I've done. And now it's unravelled. Everything is lost.'

I wondered if she had come up here to jump off, to end it all. Somehow, though, I didn't really believe that. She had come to get away from us all, to salvage her peace of mind. Martha was strong. I took comfort from that. It gave me hope, something to work with.

'First,' I said, 'we have to level with Leon.'

'Oh, no!' She gave a scornful laugh. 'Lenka has always wanted to shoot me. Now she has the perfect excuse to do it.'

I shook my head. 'No. You're wrong. There are things we can do, but we need Leon on side.'

'*We?*' she said then, incredulous.

'Yes. We. We're in it together, you and me, Martha. Don't forget that. We'll go forward together.'

Or not at all, I was thinking. I didn't promise we'd get Alysha back. It would have been an empty promise. I had no idea how or if we could bring that about. All I meant was that Martha should understand that she was no longer alone with this problem. I was with her, and I wanted Leon to be with her, too.

She took some time before she said anything more. I gave her the time. It seemed the least I could do.

'You will help me, Frank?' she asked eventually, still suspicious.

I nodded.

'Why? Why would you help me?'

After all that has happened, she presumably meant.

'Because of all that has happened,' I told her with a wry smile.

We left the Presidium together. I half-expected to be stopped, at least challenged, but nothing happened. Why should it? To Blatko and Vorodin, if they or their people were watching on closed circuit TV, we were minor players of little or no interest to them.

Even so, we left the building carefully and discreetly, using the emergency staircase at first and then the lift to take us to the bottom of the atrium. There, we mingled with guests wandering towards the exit, and left as part of a small crowd. Once outside, we made our way over to the promenade that runs alongside the river.

From there I called Leon. I had Martha with me, I told him. We needed someone to collect us, so that we could join up with him for discussions. He said he would send a car for us.

It was a grim-faced Leon we found back at the villa. Each in our own way, we had let him down, and he wanted us to know that. Perhaps he felt I should have pushed Martha off the roof, instead of bringing her back here.

He glared at her but said nothing. She stared back defiantly. I decided to get in first and nip it in the bud, if I could.

'Leon, Martha has been under unbearable pressure. None of us knew that, but I do now. It explains things.'

Leon's gaze turned towards me. 'Frank?'

'Bobrik has Martha's daughter. He abducted her, and required Martha to do certain things for him if she wanted the child to live. She did the best she could, but back there in the meeting it all became too much for her. She snapped. Frankly, I'm not surprised.'

Leon turned back to Martha. 'Is this true? He has your child?'

She nodded, and was suddenly close to tears.

'Yet you said nothing? To me, you said nothing?'

'I couldn't. Alysha is seven years old, Leon. I want her alive – I want her back!'

Leon shook his head, as if he couldn't believe what the world had come to. I wasn't sure if he was more mad at Martha or at Bobrik.

'Leon—' I started.

He cut me short with a chop of his hand in front of my face. 'Frank, I understand everything. She is a mother. Martha is a mother. Mothers will do anything for their children. It is a great weakness. In one sense, it is a great weakness.'

I still wasn't sure what he would do or say, but I had the sense to keep quiet. He walked over to Martha and wrapped his arms around her for a moment. Then he let her go and turned back to me.

'Suggestions, Frank? Proposals. What are we to do?'

'I've been thinking about that. It's a terrible situation, admittedly, but not without hope. Let me tell you how I see things. You ready to listen?'

'Of course.'

The door opened to admit Olga, who I hadn't seen since she took off for Switzerland. Boy, was I glad to see her.

'Olga!' I said. 'You've arrived at exactly the right time.'

Chapter Forty-Four

'FRANK! AND MARTHA. How are you both?'

Olga was looking radiant. I have to say it. And she brought a calming beauty with her into the room. Martha just gave a wan smile, but at least it was a smile. Leon seemed surprised to see her.

'Where's Lenka?' Olga asked.

'I don't know,' Leon said. 'I expected her to be here by now.'

Never mind that, I was thinking impatiently. It's not Lenka we need right now.

'We're in a bit of a state, Olga,' I said without preamble, 'and you might be able to help us.'

Leon looked questioningly at me. I ignored him. I ignored Martha, too. For the moment, at least, Olga was the only one who mattered. She was the one who might be able to get us out of the hole we were in.

'How can I help, Frank?'

I took a deep breath and plied her with the question distracting me. Either she could, or she couldn't. If she couldn't, then I didn't know what to suggest. I would have to think of something else.

'Olga, can you use your IT expertise to track a mobile phone? I know police and security services can do it, but can you do it, without all their special equipment?'

'The phone is moving? Perhaps because someone is carrying it?'

'Exactly! Can you do it?'

'Yes. I can. But I can do better than that.'

I beamed at her, and then at Leon and Martha in turn. 'Then we're in business,' I told them.

I phoned Bobrik and told him we wished to reconvene the meeting at the Presidium, Leon having previously established that Blatko and Vorodin were amenable to the arrangement. First, though, we needed to be satisfied that Martha's daughter was alive and well. Yes, he said with chuckle. He could understand that. To that end, I suggested Martha should be allowed to see her daughter. If she was satisfied, she could phone and let us know. After that, we would return to the Presidium.

Bobrik was cautious, but he thought it through and agreed. Martha would be collected from a downtown location and taken to see her daughter. Then, if the meeting progressed satisfactorily, and the deal he wanted could be clinched, both mother and daughter would be released. Maybe, I couldn't help thinking. Maybe they would. We would have to take precautions to be sure of that.

But one step at a time. Making Martha a hostage was a means to an end for us. She was more than willing to take the risk, and none of us had anything better to suggest anyway.

Olga gave Martha a phone with the numbers she might need. We also fitted her up with a tracker device no bigger than a small coin, assuming they would take the phone from her and switch it off as a matter of course.

'Remember, Martha,' Olga cautioned. 'You must switch the tracker off if they are going to scan you. Then switch it on again afterwards.'

Martha nodded.

'You sure you're OK with this?' I asked her, worried.

'It's my daughter, Frank. Of course I'm OK with it.'

So that was it. We were ready. I gave her a hug.

Then we pressed the start button.

Leon came with us to the rendezvous downtown along the riverside, where Martha would be collected. Just before he had the driver stop to let us out, he said, 'And you, Frank? Are you happy with the arrangement?'

I nodded. I was as happy as could be expected. 'The other car's in position?'

'It is. Good luck to you both!'

He shook our hands and we got out. The big car moved away, heading to the small hotel he was once again using as an antechamber to the Presidium.

I shepherded Martha across the pavement and we stood half facing the river and the road. The Vltava seemed quiet today. There were plenty of tourists on the Charles Bridge, despite it being bitterly cold in the gusting wind, but none at all on the barges and pleasure boats tied up at the quayside, waiting for summer. The road was busy, though, with a constant stream of traffic. Cars, buses and trams, all with their headlights on, carrying people home in the gathering gloom, as the working day drew to a close.

'How long is it since you last saw Alysha?' I asked.

Martha took a deep breath and shuddered. 'Three months,' she said reluctantly.

Tears were threatening to come. I winced and gave her a hug. 'Don't worry,' I said. 'It's nearly over now.'

She pressed her face against my chest for a moment. Then she straightened up. 'Don't worry about me,' she said. 'I will do what needs doing.'

'I'm not worried at all,' I said, smiling to encourage her.

It wasn't true. I was worried as hell – about everything. The big worry was what happened if our tracking failed? They would almost certainly take Martha's phone away. Perhaps they would scan her and remove the tracker, too. Maybe the safeguards wouldn't work, either. An even bigger worry was that Bobrik would have no intention of letting Martha and her daughter go anyway, whatever happened. So there was plenty to worry about.

With just a few minutes to go, I took out my phone and made a quick call.

'Ready?' I asked.

There was a grunt on the phone. Ready.

Martha looked at me questioningly. I just shook my head. Nothing to worry about.

A big Mercedes pulled off the main road and onto an access slipway leading down to the quayside. It stopped. A man got out and stood waiting.

'OK,' I said, squeezing Martha's hand. 'Let's go.'

She walked over to the car. The man opened the rear door. Martha got in. The man gave me a stare and a nod. I nodded back. The man got in the front passenger seat. The car did a three-point turn and headed back onto the main road.

I watched the Merc disappear into the traffic and stood still for a couple more minutes. Then I walked to the kerb and waited for the car parked in an alley on the other side of the road to collect me. We were off and running.

Chapter Forty-Five

OLGA SAID ON THE phone, 'They are heading out of the city, north towards Neratovice.'

I studied the laptop and could see she was probably right. The red dot she had conjured up on my screen was doing just that, heading fast out of town.

The course was set. We didn't need to be close behind. I spoke to the driver, who slowed down a little.

Olga spoke in my ear again. 'They have taken the phone from her, I think. It has gone dead.'

We had expected that.

'The tracker has also gone dead,' Olga added, sounding calm. 'Perhaps Martha has switched it off.'

I gritted my teeth. Now we were dead, as well, dead in the water.

'Ah!' Olga said. 'It is OK.'

I blew out gently with relief as the red dot reappeared on my screen.

The journey took thirty-five minutes. Then the red dot turned off the main road and into Lipno, a small village a few more minutes away. My Google map indicated that it stopped on the edge of the village, at an isolated property. We continued down the highway, looking for another way into Lipno.

Via unlit country roads and farm tracks that had not seen a snow plough, and in deep darkness, we made our way around and back to Lipno. It was a rough night. A while ago it had begun to rain. That had turned to sleet now, and there was a rising wind.

The driver swore as we hit a huge pothole, and I wondered if it had been a mistake to make this detour into uncharted territory.

My other phone rumbled and vibrated.

'Hello.... Martha?'

'I am with Alysha. They will not allow me to say more.'

'Understood. Is she all right?'

After a brief hesitation, Martha said, 'I think so.'

'Good. I will phone Leon now, and let him know.'

'Frank, I don't believe they intend taking us back to the city. I overheard them talking, and—'

The phone went dead.

I grimaced. I feared she was right. It was why I was here. Bobrik was not a man to be trusted. We had known that. Once he had what he wanted from Leon, Martha and Alysha would have served their purpose. They would be redundant, a nuisance as well as a potential hazard. Best to get rid of them.

I phoned Leon to tell him Martha was with her daughter.

'Good,' he said. 'I will return to the Presidium, and do the business with Bobrik.'

'You might want to wait a little while,' I advised. 'Martha said she doesn't believe they will let her and Alysha go.'

'No, of course they won't. But we go ahead anyway. Do what you can, Frank.'

The phone went dead. I winced. Leon had sounded very calm and accepting. It was hard to believe. This was a critical juncture. He was placing an awful lot of trust in my capabilities. Or perhaps he just wasn't all that interested in what happened to Martha and her daughter. They were not family, after all.

It wasn't good – any of it – but there was no point holding back now. I had to carry on, and hope for the best.

I studied the screen. We were close to the target now. It was just a couple of hundred yards away. I told the driver to stop. I would go on alone from this point. What I would do when I got there I didn't know. Something. I would do something. That was the plan, all of it.

I took out the Glock Leon had given me and checked it once

more. Satisfied with that, I made sure the driver understood his instructions. Then I left the warm, dry interior of the car and waded off into the night, steeling myself against the howling wind and pelting sleet, ready to do what I could.

The road from the village was snow-ploughed only as far as the boundary of the property we had identified. So for all practical purposes, the property was at the end of the road, in winter at least. From a snow-covered thicket of bushes near the entrance, I studied the layout. The main building was a large timber structure, probably an old farmhouse. I noted the distribution of lights indicating occupied rooms and tried to get a feel for how the house was organized.

My guess was that Martha and her daughter would be in the basement, the cellar. All these old houses had them, and that was the safest place in them. It was also the hardest to escape from, of course, and the most difficult to get into. So the basement was where I would start.

Men started loading a truck at the front of the house with boxes and suitcases. I watched for a minute or two. Four men. It looked like they were preparing to depart, to evacuate the house. That spurred me on. Martha and her daughter might not have much time left, if I was right about that. I had to move fast.

I skirted the fringe of shrubs and bushes enclosing an open space that was probably a grassed area in summer and moved closer to an outhouse at the rear of the building. If I could reach that unseen, I should be able to get inside the house and down to the basement.

I froze when four figures came back out of the house carrying stuff for the truck. There wasn't much chance of them seeing me but I didn't want to improve their odds by moving. Somebody said something. Somebody replied. There was laughter. Then another voice joined in.

That was when all my planning and theorizing fell apart. For a moment, I couldn't believe my ears. As Mike Tyson once said, everyone has a plan until they get punched in the mouth.

Chapter Forty-Six

THERE WAS NO DENYING it. The voice was real. Even as I stood there, stunned, my brain was processing what I had just heard, working out what it meant. The last of the voices I had heard was a woman's, and it was one that was very familiar to me. I spent a minute or two going through the *how could she?, I can't believe it!* routine. Then, sick at heart, I pulled myself together.

There was no doubt about it. Martha was not a hostage. She was part of whatever was going on here. She even seemed to have a supervisory role. The men in the group were doing what she told them, and laughing at her jokes. This was the Martha I had met that first day, the ball-of-fire Martha who had arrived at The Chesters like a tornado. It was time to reassess once again. *Martha is not what she seems.* Why, oh why, hadn't I taken Lenka more seriously?

What about the child, Alysha? Was she here? Did she exist even? Or had she been part of the fantasy Martha had sketched in order to get out of a hole? I grimaced, feeling guilty. I'd done Leon a disservice. He had trusted me.

But I still had to get inside the house. If there was a child, that was where she would be. At least now, though, I didn't have to worry about rescuing Martha.

I studied the situation some more. The house was being evacuated. There was no doubt about that. From what I could see, the people here were almost ready to leave. No more boxes were coming out to the truck, and no more suitcases to the car. Maybe I didn't need to get inside. Alysha would surely be coming outside soon – if she existed.

But I pressed on with my approach. I needed to know, to be sure. So I completed my circuit to the rear of the main building and cautiously approached a door in the back porch. It was big, black and probably ancient oakwood. The ironwork – the latch and the keyhole – were what you might have expected to find on an eighteenth century prison door. If the door was locked, it would be well locked with an enormous key.

It wasn't locked. I eased the door open and stepped inside, holding my breath. Dim light from a distant hallway showed me I was in a scullery of sorts. It was where wet weather gear was stored, as well as where big, dirty things could be washed in a huge ceramic sink. I edged around a massive tiled stove that once would have been kept burning day and night by brown coal, warming the house and supplying hot water. Now it was cold and still.

You couldn't say the rest of the house was quiet. Boots clattered on wooden floors. Men in a hurry called to one another. Russian voices. Doors were slammed. Things were dropped and thrown. What sounded like crockery fell and smashed. It sounded like a typical Russian withdrawal, leaving scorched earth and destruction behind. Uneasily, I wondered if the final act would be to burn the building to the ground. There were all sorts of reasons why they might think that a good idea.

It suddenly seemed a bad idea for me to be there. I began to retreat, back towards the big oak door. Voices made me stop. I heard Martha's voice raised in query. A man replied. Then, through a gap in the doorway in front of me, I saw them both emerge from a stairwell I hadn't noticed.

They paused and held a hurried conversation, in Russian. Martha clapped the man on the shoulder and turned away. It looked like she had given him instructions. She walked briskly away along a corridor. He started to descend the stairs.

Something was going on down there, and that old curiosity drew me forward again. I moved quickly through the doorway to the head of the stairwell. For a moment I paused, listening. Then I headed down the stone steps, gun in hand. Something significant seemed to be down here. I needed to know what it was.

Following the spiralling stone staircase, I descended cautiously, gun in hand, until the curve ended and I could see very plainly where I was. The view I had now left no time for contemplation. I had to act now, or not at all.

There was a large open space down there in the basement. There was also a small room off it, with a door. In the open doorway, the man I had followed had taken out a gun and was about to shoot a trussed figure lying on the floor. As his gun came up to the firing position, I fired twice.

He was hit, and spun away. His gun sought me. I fired again. This time he went down hard. I hurried over and checked for a pulse. There wasn't one.

My ears were ringing from the explosions, which were bound to have been heard elsewhere in the house. In case anybody came to check why there had been three shots fired, I had to move fast.

The bound figure on the floor was wrapped in plastic sheeting that was fastened with tough duct tape. Even my Swiss Army knife struggled to cut through it. If I hadn't seen the man I had killed raising his gun, I would have assumed the wrapped-up figure on the floor was a corpse, and I wouldn't have bothered with it.

But the figure moved as I wrestled with the wrappings. Definitely alive. I worked faster, concentrating on the head. Oxygen would be in short supply. I tore back the plastic from the face, and recoiled with shock. It was no innocent child I had uncovered.

Chapter Forty-Seven

WHAT THE HELL! My heart jumped and I stared for a moment, scarcely able to believe it.

Lenka? Surely not! But it was.

Her eyes were shut and she didn't seem to be breathing. I gritted my teeth and started searching for a pulse at the same time as I pulled frantically at the wrappings encasing her body.

There was nothing in her neck or her wrist. I could feel nothing at all. Damn, damn, damn! If only I had arrived sooner.

She was still warm, though. And she had moved. Surely it

wasn't too late? I reached under her jacket but could feel nothing. Warm skin but no pulse.

It was too soon to give up. I delved deeper, down into her groin, forcing open her trousers and pants. That was very much the last resort. If there was nothing there, often the very last place for a pulse to survive, there would be no hope at all.

Nothing. I could feel nothing, no movement. Nothing at all. I kept going, searching, pressing, desperate for some sign that life still lurked in that small lifeless body.

Then I got something. My finger tips felt a small tremor. It was enough. I ripped her clothing away and got down on my knees to try CPR, my own pulse racing now as a surge of hope tore through me.

I could have done with some help, a partner to share the load, but I was all there was. I clung on and pumped like mad, and was rewarded after a minute or two by signs of stirring. I turned her on her side and pulled away to get some air into my own lungs. Suddenly Lenka's mouth opened and a dribble of vomit, blood and saliva oozed out of it.

Simultaneously I heard less welcome signs. Someone was coming down the steps. I grabbed the Glock from the floor and straightened up fast.

A female voice – Martha's – called out querulously. I assumed she wanted to know what was going on, where the man was.

Martha came into view, as did a man behind her. She saw me, and she saw the gun. She froze.

'Come on down, Martha,' I said grimly.

'Don't be stupid, Frank!'

She was recovering fast.

'Now!' I snapped.

But she dived sideways. The man behind her opened fire with an automatic weapon. I fired back as they both withdrew, but I had no idea whether either of them was hit.

From the foot of the steps, I fired again, futilely it seemed. They had got back to the top, and I was still down here, trapped now.

There was a pause, a quiet minute or two. I guessed one of them had gone for reinforcements. Rushing up the steps before they arrived was an option, but one I dismissed very quickly. I wasn't in suicide mode. Not yet.

'Come on up, Frank!' Martha called. 'There's no reason for you both to die down there. No reason for that at all. Let's talk sense.'

'Fuck you, Martha!'

I fired another round up the stairwell, but only the one. Once these bullets were gone, I had no others.

'Last chance, Frank! Are you coming?'

Somehow I avoided roaring abuse at her, and telling her what a lying, treacherous, scheming bitch she was. That might have made her believe she had won. I didn't want that. So I kept quiet, but it wasn't easy.

There was no more dialogue between us. A few seconds later there was a very loud clang and I realized the entrance to the stairwell leading down to the cellar had probably been sealed with a heavy trapdoor, and no doubt bolted as well. The relief that there would be no more bullets coming my way soon gave way to the realization that the situation was not much better. The cellar had only that one entrance.

A rustling behind me brought me spinning round. In the minute or two of desperation and chaos, I had almost forgotten Lenka. But she was still there. And she was moving.

Not moving very much, I have to say. But an arm had flopped sideways, she was wriggling a bit and an eye had opened. It wasn't much, but it was very welcome.

I crossed over to her and got down to strip the rest of the plastic sheeting away from her.

'Welcome back!' I said, doing my best to give her a cheery smile. 'You had me worried for a minute or two.'

'Frank? Frank, where am I?' she croaked.

She was speaking, and speaking in English. So she had recognized me. Her brain was working again. It hadn't been damaged

'It's a long story,' I said as cheerfully as I could manage, 'and I don't know all of it myself. Let me help you sit up.'

I got her in a sitting position, her back against the wall. Then I went hunting around the cellar. I found a tap and brought her some water in an old jam jar I rinsed out first. She was able to take hold of the jar after she had taken a few sips. So I left her with it and went searching again, this time for a way out of the cellar.

I didn't find one. What I did discover was that the cellar was every bit as secure and impregnable seeming as I had feared. My spirits sank as I grasped there really were no easy options. The place was built of big, solid stone blocks that provided the foundations for the house. Walls, floor and the vaulted ceiling were all the same. It was also below ground. There wasn't even a tiny window.

I grimaced and made my way back to the stairwell. I didn't have any hopes about that, either, but I had to make sure. The top of the steps was closed off now by a big, solid trapdoor, as I had thought. It was made of timber, but it might just as well have been cast iron or steel. My knuckles didn't get a sound out of it when I rapped hard. Nor could I raise it even a millimetre.

I went back down the steps and took another look at Lenka. 'How are you feeling?'

She nodded. 'Fine,' she said with determination, but her attempted grin just looked sickly. 'Give me another minute.'

I didn't ask what the hell had happened to her. The priority was getting out of here, and soon. My fear, and expectation, was that when Martha and the rest of the gang abandoned the house, they would set it alight to conceal any evidence they might inadvertently leave behind. Fingerprints and DNA do not survive fire. So if we didn't get out soon, we might not get out at all.

There wasn't much in the cellar to give me hope. It was devoid of tools and equipment, as well as of alternative exits. In fact, it was pretty well bare, a stone box without ornament or redeeming features. The only exceptional thing in it was a big drainpipe that ran from ceiling to floor in one corner. It looked like the main drain for the building. The only other good thing was that we were not in darkness. They had forgotten, or hadn't bothered, to switch off the light.

I studied the drainpipe. It was cast iron and about a foot in diameter. My guess was that although it was corroded, it was a lot younger than the house. When houses like this were built, they wouldn't have had any inside drainage at all, any more than they would have had running water.

There were implications from that. One was that at some point in the house's long life, a hole must have been cut in the vaulted ceiling to allow the pipe to be inserted. I doubted if a hole had been drilled and cut all the way through a solid stone block. More likely was that a block had been removed, the pipe inserted and then the surrounding space filled with something or other. Possibly bits of stone in some sort of primitive cement. With growing interest, I wondered if there might be a weakness I could exploit.

'What did you do to me, Frank?'

I turned around, and saw Lenka struggling to pull her clothing back into position.

'Saved your life,' I snapped, impatient with the insinuation.

'Thank you,' she said then, looking up at me with a tired smile.

I shook my head. 'Jesus, Lenka!'

I didn't want to tell her how I had found her. She could work that out for herself. 'Feeling better?' I asked instead.

She nodded. Then she began to get to her feet, sliding herself up the wall.

'How did you get here anyway?' I asked, reaching out a hand to steady her.

'Leon sent me. I followed them.'

'Leon sent you? He said nothing to me.'

'I was your back-up, in case you lost them.'

I just stared at her for a moment, thinking it would have been nice if somebody had said something about all this to me before now.

'It is how we work,' she said softly. 'Always. I told you that once before, in Montenegro.'

'Trust nobody?'

After a brief pause, she nodded.

'You Podolskys!' I muttered, exasperated.

Lenka grinned and said, 'What now, Frank? Do you have any idea how to get us out of here?'

Chapter Forty-Eight

WITH LENKA WATCHING CLOSELY, I tested the drainpipe, pulling it first one way and then the other. Nothing happened. I could feel no give at all. Corroded it might be, but that pipe was made of strong stuff, and seemed good for a lot of years yet.

Even so, I worked away at it. After a few minutes Lenka joined me, lending her weight and whatever power she could summon to the task. It made no difference. Lenka gave up and retreated. I didn't blame her. She was lucky still to be breathing, never mind working, the ordeal she had undergone.

I stuck at it. Possibly the pipe moved fractionally, infinitesimally. Possibly. But probably not. I kept going. In my desperation, I fancied I could smell smoke.

Then Lenka returned, bringing with her a wooden pole she had found somewhere. I stood back as she inserted it behind the pipe and invited me to use it as a lever against the wall. This time the pipe did move. Not by much, but I could feel it tremble. I could hear it creak, too.

Lenka added her weight, and with both of us pulling together, the pipe really moved. We heaved once more. The pipe groaned and leant away from the wall a little.

'Again!' I yelled, confidence growing.

This time the pipe suddenly gave way. It came away from the wall altogether and a section of it fell into the cellar, showering us with white dust. I wiped my eyes and coughed. When I looked up, the dust had cleared and I could see a hole. Above the hole there was a dancing, flickering light. Smoke began to pour through the gap we had created, and we fell back, coughing.

There wasn't much time to spare or to waste. I stood back and started ramming the edges of the gap with the wooden pole we had been using as a lever. I made the hole slightly larger, but not a lot. I could see now that rather than removing the block of stone, the pipe fitters had drilled and chiselled a hole through it to accommodate the pipe. I felt like screaming with frustration and rage.

I despaired. My head might go through the gap, but not much else. The hole was far too small for an escape route, no matter how hard I jabbed at the surrounding stone.

Lenka tugged at my jacket, trying to pull me out of the way. 'Let me try, Frank.'

I shook my head. 'It's no good, Lenka.'

'Come on, Frank!' she said impatiently, the fire back in her voice. 'Lift me!'

I studied the hole for a moment. Then I leant down, got her on my shoulders and stood up, thrusting her towards the ceiling. It looked pretty futile to me, but we had to try.

Lenka contorted her body. She thrust one arm through the hole first. Then she ducked her head and wriggled upwards, her other arm dangling. But it was no good. I felt her weight on my shoulders as she came back down.

I set her back on the ground, and she immediately began to work her way out of her jacket. Off it came, followed by her shirt and trousers. She stripped down to her underwear, glanced up at me with a grin and said, 'You already know what I am like underneath, Frank. Don't look so shocked, please.'

I smiled sheepishly. 'You think there's a chance?'

'Let's see,' she said, the bounce and confidence, and the strength, returning. 'Lift me again, please.'

She actually felt lighter without her clothes. Ridiculous, I know, but she really did. I began to feel a stirring of hope as her bare legs wrapped themselves around my head and neck and she pressed herself higher.

It was a terrible struggle. I lost hope again, but Lenka

persevered long after it was reasonable. She contorted her body and squeezed one bit after another of herself through that ridiculously tiny gap in the stonework. This time she worked both arms through first, and then her head. But it was only as her legs left my shoulders, that I realized she was finally through. She had done it!

I stepped back, coughing from the smoke pouring through the gap now Lenka was no longer blocking it. I wiped my eyes and face, and waited. I expected to hear her call something to me, but that didn't happen. I began to worry. Had she passed out in the smoke? Had she collapsed?

Then I heard noise from the stairwell, a scraping and creaking, followed by a loud clang as the trapdoor was raised and dropped against the wall.

'Please bring my clothes, Frank!' Lenka called. 'We must hurry!'

I scooped up her clothing and scrambled for the steps.

Upstairs there was smoke and dancing light, and the roar of the flames as they devoured the house. Everything was well ablaze. Fortunately, the top of the stairwell was close to the rear entrance to the house. Coughing badly, shielding our faces, we dashed for the back door, with me half-carrying the near naked and exhausted Lenka.

We emerged into wonderfully cool air and kept going. We didn't stop – not even for Lenka to dress – until we were a hundred yards away from the house. Then I relented and halted our mad race. Lenka was pretty well done by then, out on her feet, and I wasn't much better myself.

I held on to her for a few moments while she gasped and shivered. Then I helped her get dressed, all the while wondering at the strength and durability of that tiny body. I marvelled even more at Lenka's mental strength and resilience.

Chapter Forty-Nine

WE HEADED BACK TO the car as quickly as we could, not troubling about anything else very much but simply getting there. Lenka was doing her best, and had recovered slightly, but she was a pale shadow of the street fighter I knew her to be. Her ordeal had sapped her physical strength and taken a lot out of her mentally as well. It was a wonder she had managed to do what she had back in the cellar. Without her brave struggle, neither of us would have survived. Smoke inhalation would have done for us pretty quickly.

When I asked her how on earth she had managed to squeeze through that tiny gap, she just said she had done some caving, pot holing, and had used some of the technique she had learned doing that.

'For getting through small spaces?'

'Of course. Sometimes small spaces that last a long time.'

'Like a tunnel, you mean?'

'Exactly, yes. Maybe for a kilometre or more. And sometimes,' she added with a bit of a twinkle in her eye, 'sometimes under water, too.'

Dear God, I was thinking. What else can this woman do? She would be a handful if she wasn't on your side. That reminded me to ask her how Martha's gang had caught her.

She shrugged. 'I don't know. They guessed, I suppose. And laid an ambush.'

'Maybe they expected me to walk into it?'

'Maybe. I don't know. They hit my car and it turned over. I must have banged my head. When I came round, I was tied up.'

Then it got worse for her. I decided to halt the questioning. It couldn't be doing her any good.

'Not far to the car now,' I told her cheerfully.

She nodded but didn't say anything more.

The car was where I had left it. So was the driver, but he was

210

dead. Someone had shot him in the head.

'Another one gone,' I said, shaking my head. 'When will it end?'

'Only when Bobrik is dead,' Lenka said flatly. 'It is the only way.'

I thought she was probably right. It was hard to see how else the killing would ever stop. Even I could see that now.

We put the driver's body in the boot and set off to drive back to Prague. There was still business there to conduct. Most of all, and more than ever, I ached to settle with Bobrik. He had a lot to answer for.

Lenka used my phone to call her brother and quickly update him. I left her to do it. Driving was difficult enough in those conditions, especially after the last few hours, and I needed to concentrate on that.

'Leon will make arrangements,' Lenka said when her conversation was over. 'But he wants to continue with the meeting with Bobrik.'

What kind of arrangements, I wondered? What did that mean? Lost in translation, I thought.

'So the negotiations with Bobrik will continue?'

'For now, yes.'

'What does he want us to do?'

'For you to join the meeting, the discussions, but to say nothing about these events here. I will do something else. I must go to the airport. So I will take the car when we reach the Presidium.'

I wondered if she was capable of driving, but didn't ask. So far as I was concerned, Lenka was free to do whatever she wanted and felt herself capable of doing. I'd never met anyone like her.

The airport, though? What was that about? Again, I didn't ask. I suppose I was getting used to how the Podolsky family operated. They would tell me only what they wanted me to know.

In the Presidium car park, I surrendered the car to Lenka and then made my way inside. After cleaning myself up as best I could in one of the toilets, I headed upstairs for the meeting. Guards checked me out and borrowed the Glock before permitting me to enter the conference room, where people were milling about and being served drinks by a couple of waiters.

Leon came across to join me. He looked at me questioningly.

I nodded. 'OK, thanks, Leon. We made it.'

'Good.'

I glanced around and added, 'It looks as though the meeting is over. Am I too late to participate further in the negotiations?'

'Yes, I'm afraid so, Frank. But all is well, I think.'

'The mine?'

'We have reached agreement, and now our lawyers are dealing with the legal documents.'

'You got a good deal?'

'I believe so, Frank.'

'It looks as if Bobrik thinks he did, too.'

Leon just nodded. I hoped like hell that he hadn't given away the family silver.

Leon must have guessed what I was thinking because he said quietly, 'Keep the faith, Frank. Keep the faith.'

What I could see right then was that Blatko and Vorodin were happily chatting away with Bobrik, who seemed happy as Larry. He was laughing at our hosts' jokes and agreeing with everything they had to say to him.

My mind jumped back to the house his people had just evacuated and torched, and to the trail of bodies lying behind him. I needed to get out of here before I exploded. I couldn't see any reason for Leon to be content with the outcome of the negotiations, none at all. It looked to me as if Bobrik might have got his money back, as well as the Svoboda gold mine. I felt sicker than ever.

One of the waiters was offering me a glass of something or other, and I accepted it. Whatever it was, it just tasted bitter to me. I sipped anyway, easing the burning pain in my throat from the smoke I'd had to breathe.

The waiter looked vaguely familiar, but it wasn't until he turned away that I recognized him. It was Charles, the man who had helped me escape from Leon's hotel when it was being shot to pieces by more of Bobrik's apes. What was he doing here?

I glanced at Leon with the question on my lips. Leon smiled and gently shook his head just once. Something was going on, I realized then. My interest piqued, I straightened up and became more attentive. Perhaps there was a script behind this scene that I didn't know about. I hoped so. I hoped so like hell.

Somehow, like many of the others, Leon and I had drifted out onto the terrace with its wonderful view of Prague at night. I wasn't sorry. The room had been insufferably hot. No wonder Charles and a colleague had opened the big patio doors.

A couple of pigeons from the river perched on the low wall at the edge of the terrace for a moment. When they saw we were drinking rather than eating, they took off again, disappointed. I moved over to the edge of the terrace and watched them disappear down into the darkness of the riverside, where a million of their kind roosted safely on the wooden pilings in the river that protected the ancient bridge from boat traffic and flood-borne debris. It was a long, long way down, but I watched their progress all the way. Then, with an involuntary shiver, I turned around.

Blatko and Vorodin came out onto the terrace. More people followed, including Bobrik. I stood next to Leon. Bobrik was at the far end, where Charles was still serving from a tray of drinks. It looked as though Vorodin was preparing to make another of his little speeches.

He was. He began, his social smile soon converting to a more serious expression. Leon translated in an undertone for my benefit.

'It is with great satisfaction,' Vorodin said, 'that we are able to bring the recent hostilities amongst the Russian community in this wonderful little country to an end. Nothing could make us happier.'

Amen to that, I thought, if only it were true.

'My colleague, and friend, Mr Blatko,' Vorodin continued, 'holds the legal documents that have been negotiated and approved here today. The negotiation was not without difficulty, as you all know, but now it is over.'

He turned to Blatko and took from him the several documents

that the lawyers had presumably prepared, and that Leon and Bobrik had presumably signed.

'Unfortunately,' Vorodin continued, 'one party to the negotiation did not come here openly and honestly, in good faith. One party decided to ignore our conditions, as hosts, and to continue to engage in unacceptable activities.'

Now, with a dramatic gesture, he suddenly ripped up the legal documents and hurled the pieces to the floor, stunning me and almost everyone else on the terrace. 'The agreement is null and void,' he announced, 'and now the penalty will be paid.'

He was looking directly at Bobrik as he spoke, and his head seemed to move in a small nod. I turned my head to look at Bobrik, too, and was only just in time to see what happened.

What I saw was the waiter, Charles, suddenly dip low, wrap his arms around Bobrik's thighs and heave him upwards. With a yelp – perhaps surprise, perhaps protest – Bobrik flew over the wall at the edge of the terrace. With a scream, he hurtled down to join the pigeons along the riverside.

'Come, Frank,' Leon said quietly a moment later. 'Our business is done here. It is time to go.'

Without a further word with anyone, we made our way out of the room and took the elevator down through the atrium, to leave the Presidium for the last time.

Chapter Fifty

BACK AT THE VILLA, Olga joined us. Two Podolskys. Only Lenka missing. I told Leon and Olga what had happened to me, and to Lenka.

'So the tracker worked?' Leon mused.

'It was the phone that worked,' Olga said. 'Martha soon got rid of the tracker.'

'I thought she switched her phone off, or handed it over?' I pointed out.

'Yes, she did. One or the other. But I had put something inside the phone that she didn't know about. It continued to transmit.'

'Why did you do that?'

Olga shrugged. 'Martha,' she said, as if that was explanation enough. Perhaps it was.

I nodded. Clever Olga. Clever bloody family, in fact! Even if between them they had nearly got me killed.

'Leon, it's a pity you didn't work Martha out, but you did know what was going to happen at the Presidium, didn't you?'

Leon nodded. 'Not everything, but something. Yes. I knew Blatko and Vorodin had found out what Bobrik was doing, and wouldn't stand for it. They were offended. The rules of engagement we had agreed beforehand were breached, and it was known from the beginning that there would be penalties if that happened.'

'But not, exactly, what those penalties would be?'

Leon shook his head. 'Not exactly, no.'

'What about Charles? How did he come into it?'

'He was borrowed for the evening from my hotel.'

'And instructed to do what he did?'

Leon raised his hands in a gesture of helplessness. 'Let us say that because I was the innocent party, I was given the opportunity to seek redress. Redress? Is that the correct word?'

'You bloodthirsty bastard,' I said with a reluctant grin. 'Fuck whether it's the right word or not!'

These people!

'There is something else you should know, Frank,' Leon continued. 'You have been such a good friend and comrade that I must tell you, although the matter is still a little delicate.'

'Go on. I could stand a bit of something delicate.'

'Blatko and Vorodin are very well connected in Moscow.'

'So you said once before.'

Leon nodded. 'There have been consultations, and I understand they were told to advise me that it is possible that our differences can be reconciled.'

I wondered what the hell that meant. 'Go on,' I urged.

'The Kremlin became dissatisfied with Bobrik, and....'

'And now he's dead, bless his soul.'

'Indeed. They want us to know that they will stop pursuing the Podolskys, and our business interests, with one condition.'

'And what is that?'

'If I accept the position of governor of a region in Siberia or the Far East, perhaps the one where our gold mine is situated, we will be allowed to pursue our interests in peace. We will be able to move freely in and out of Russia once again. It is an offer I have accepted.'

That was quick work, I was thinking.

'Even the online news agency?'

'Yes,' Olga contributed happily. 'My baby!'

'It is true,' Leon admitted. 'Surprisingly.'

I was struggling to get my head around all this. 'And you will live in Siberia, or wherever, as Governor of Something-or-other?'

Leon shook his head. 'It is not necessary. I will visit, of course, and formally I will have this role, but mostly I will be required to help develop infrastructure in the region.'

'Organization – and investment, you mean?'

'Exactly. It is a price we, as a family, are prepared to pay.'

I nodded thoughtfully. How the world turns, I couldn't help thinking. It was just one damn thing after another!

Just then the door opened and Lenka appeared. She looked even more tired but there was also a glow about her. She looked uplifted, excited even. She smiled at us all, hugged us one at a time, received our greetings, and then said something to Olga. Olga got up, crossed to a big TV screen and turned on the power.

By then, I had ceased my wondering. Something was afoot, and I guessed I was about to learn what it was. I didn't bother asking. I can do patient when needs be.

Olga had chosen the CNN channel, perhaps in deference to my language capabilities. A rolling news programme was showing. We all watched, and waited in silence. Then the item we awaited – me unwittingly – appeared.

A private plane flying from Prague to Minsk, and on to

Moscow, had crashed, apparently, in some remote mountains of which I had never heard. The crew and up to ten passengers were all believed dead. It was believed that engine failure may have been responsible for the accident.

I was stunned. My mind went blank for a moment, but only for a moment.

'Not a bomb, then?' I asked of no-one in particular. 'Engine failure. An accident. Presumably that was Martha's flight?'

Leon nodded, and briefly looked sad. Olga appeared mildly interested. But Lenka was positively triumphant. Remembering the ordeal she had experienced, and remembering how resourceful and relentless she was, I could neither blame her nor feel much surprise.

'It is over,' Leon said with finality.

Not quite. Not for me, at least. There were several questions I wanted answering. Leon and his sisters did their best.

'Why did she do it?' Leon repeated with a shrug. 'Ambition, greed, power? Who really knows? What I can tell you is that it wasn't for love of Bobrik!

'We believe it was Svoboda that turned her head. She discovered we still owned it, even though we were no longer aware of that, and approached Bobrik. In return for helping him in his campaign against me, she would get Svoboda.'

Ownership of a gold mine? It seemed a bit unlikely to me. But how wonderful if you could get it.

'Olga has been able to find traces of email and phone conversations between them that Martha thought she had eliminated,' Leon added, sensing my disbelief. 'It is true. Bobrik would allow her to have the mine, if that meant he could finish with me.'

'But Martha backed the wrong horse,' Olga said softly. 'She believed that Bobrik, with the Kremlin behind him, would win. The Podolskys were a lost cause so far as she was concerned.'

'And, knowing Martha, she was determined to be on the winning side?'

'Exactly,' Olga confirmed.

217

'To help her case with both Bobrik and me,' Leon added, 'Martha deliberately falsified the value of the mine, and made it seem less attractive than it was, and is.'

I nodded slowly. I could see it now. What a performer Martha had been!

Something else that puzzled me was why Martha had told Olga about The Chesters. How had that helped?

'She told me,' Olga said ruefully, 'because she knows what a silly romantic I am. She knew that as soon as I heard about this poor old house I would want to help it – and she was right! Martha is – or was – very cunning.'

'Also, remember,' Lenka contributed, 'we knew that sooner or later we would need a new base if we were to continue with our work. I never liked the old house, but that didn't matter. Olga would deal with it.'

I smiled and shook my head ruefully. All that sounded about right to me.

'But the attack on The Chesters scared Martha,' I pointed out. 'She didn't know about that in advance, I'm certain.'

'That was Bobrik playing his usual games,' Leon said. 'He didn't tell her because he wanted to remind her who was boss – and it wasn't her!'

'And there was nothing she could do about that,' I suggested, 'because by then she had burned her boats with you. There was no going back. She had to put up with whatever Bobrik did. Is that right, do you think?'

Leon nodded. 'I believe it is, yes.'

I turned to Lenka. 'You warned me about her, didn't you? Foolishly, I ignored you. But what was it that made you distrust her?'

For once, Lenka smiled. 'I knew she understood our language,' she said with a shrug. 'Martha denied it, but I knew. I could tell. Intuition, do you call it?

I smiled ruefully and nodded. 'I should have trusted my own instincts. I knew that, too.'

'So I didn't trust her, and she knew it,' Lenka added.

I just nodded.

So there we were. All, or most, questions answered. But I had still to come to terms with how I felt about Martha, or should I say the two Marthas?

There was the evil version that had been responsible for the terrible things done to Lenka, as well as the cold-blooded decision to consign us both to the flames in that horrendous basement. But there was also the Martha who had seemed so close to me in a different way, a loving way, and of whom for a time I had been very fond.

Is it possible for there to be two different versions of the same person? Of course it is. Psychiatrists call that state psychosis. That's what I call it, too.

Chapter Fifty-One

WE DROVE THROUGH THE village, bypassing The Black Bull, and on up the valley. Now it was spring, everywhere looked different, familiar still but not quite the same. The grass beside the road, and in the fields, was a bright green now. The patches of gorse were a vivid yellow. The hawthorn was in leaf, and even in blossom, in sheltered, sunny places. Groups of lambs chased each other across the green sward.

'It looks different,' Lenka said suspiciously, as if she distrusted her eyesight, or perhaps her surroundings.

I nodded. 'Very.'

'But it is still very beautiful,' Olga pointed out. 'Even more so, I think. Don't you agree, Frank?'

I did. Olga was right. Lonely, bare, desolate even, the valley might be, but it was also strangely, quietly beautiful.

It wasn't only the countryside that looked different, of course. The Chesters looked different, too. None of us had been back to see the old house since it had become a true ruin. Now, as it came into sight, I slowed slightly and there was a collective intake of breath and a leaning forward to peer at the view.

I had been almost dreading the moment, and indeed it was a shocking revelation. Instead of a house badly in need of repair, there were gaunt, smoke-blackened walls reaching for the sky. No roof, of course. That was entirely gone now. Windows and their frames had disappeared entirely, as well. Where there had been a front door and an entrance porch, there was now a gaping black hole.

I parked outside the gateway and we climbed out of the car and assembled quietly, ready to walk past the signs informing us of Danger, Falling Masonry, No Trespassing, Keep Out – and the rest – that officialdom had sensibly installed.

None of us said anything for a moment. We were too intent on absorbing our first impressions. Lenka stared at the ruined walls of the house she had never liked almost with satisfaction. Poor Olga, whose project this had been, seemed to be looking everywhere but at the ruined house. I couldn't blame either of them.

As for me, I just wanted to get it over with, and get the hell out. It hadn't been my idea to come here with them. Leon had asked me if I would. If he hadn't been visiting his new fiefdom in Siberia, I might have told him to bring them himself.

'Do you want a closer look?' I asked eventually.

'Of course,' Olga said.

Lenka sighed and nodded agreement.

'Come on, then!'

I set off up the gravelled drive, which was about the only thing that hadn't really changed much at all. We trudged around the outside of the building and then risked a peek inside, through what had once been French windows opening onto the lawn. There were a few bits of floors and ceilings improbably still hanging by a thread, but mostly the interior was a cavity, an open space. I didn't have to caution my companions about the danger of going any further inside.

We moved on. Looking through gaps that had once contained windows, we could see that although most internal walls had simply disappeared, there was an arched stone passage, a tunnel, running from the main back door that seemed sound enough still. We ventured along it, and found that it led to the empty space that had once been the great hall in the centre of the building. From the foot of what had been the main staircase, it was eerily possible to look up and see a big blue sky.

'Seen enough?' I asked, touching Olga's arm.

She nodded.

'Come on, then. We'd better get outside. There'll still be masonry and half-burned timbers falling for a while yet, I would think.'

'Bound to be,' Lenka said with grim satisfaction.

I felt dispirited, but I could see Olga was sick at heart, and perhaps in a state of shock too. After all, she hadn't seen the fire raging, as I had. Being told was one thing; seeing was quite another. This was her first visit since the restoration project had begun, and had so quickly ended.

Back outside, I ushered the two women away from the building. We walked through the rubble scattered across the derelict lawn and sat together on a wrought-iron seat beneath a big, old sycamore tree that was already in leaf, undaunted by the cataclysm that had devastated the house. The rooks in the nearby pinewood, too, seemed unconcerned as they went about the business of raising their young. We sat and contemplated the once great building. It was hard to come to terms with the damage that had been done.

I stood up. The others looked at me expectantly. 'I'm just going to have a quick look around the other side,' I told them.

'I'll wait here with Olga,' Lenka said. 'I don't want to see any more. Be quick, Frank.'

I set off to circumnavigate the house. It was a sad prospect but I was curious and wanted to see how close the walls were to collapse. Once that happened, only the trees would still be here, the sycamore and the nearby pinewood. And an even bigger pile of rubble.

Yet, oddly enough, from the corner of my eye as I walked, the house was still a powerful presence. Changed, totally ruined, but it was still here.

'Wait, Frank!'

I turned and allowed Olga and Lenka to catch me up. Then we walked on together. I was looking for major cracks in the walls, signs of impending collapse. There were none, none that I could see. That gave me a bit of a buzz. They built big, tough walls a thousand years ago, walls made to last. Look at this place! It was a ruin, but a standing ruin.

'Is it going to fall down, Frank?' Olga asked.

I shook my head. 'I don't think so. Not soon, anyway.' I turned around to gaze back at the towering walls. 'It has survived the winter, and I think it will be OK until we get some really strong winds.'

Then I noticed a bright eagerness about Olga that had not been there a few moments earlier. 'What?' I prompted.

'Could the house be rebuilt?' she asked.

I hesitated. 'It could, I suppose, but it would take an awful lot of money.'

'But it could be done?' she pressed.

I nodded. 'Probably. Anything can be done, if you throw enough money at it.'

'We have the money, Frank. Putting some of it to such good use would be a fine thing, wouldn't it?'

'You could build a new house for a lot less.'

'I don't want a new house! I want to put this one back together again.'

I stood and turned it over in my mind, my pulse quickening as I thought about it. 'Well, if that's what you want to do, Olga,' I said slowly.

She turned to her sister, who was nodding for once with what looked like enthusiasm. 'We've still got the plans, Lenka, haven't we? We haven't got Andrei, unfortunately, but perhaps we can find someone to take his place.'

'Let's do it,' Lenka said crisply.

Then it was my turn. They looked at me expectantly.

'What?' I said defensively.

'Will you stay and help us?' Olga asked.

'Me? What could I do?'

'Please, Frank!' Lenka said, taking my arm.

I attempted to weight it up sensibly, but how could I say no?

'For a time, perhaps,' I said with a sigh, trying hard not to smile.

'Leon will be pleased,' Olga said.

All three of us turned then to watch a helicopter coming over the nearby hills. It seemed to be heading straight for us. I stared at it, and shook my head. With another sigh, and another smile, I wondered if I would ever be free of the Podolsky family.